Y0-CBJ-651

# Scandal

ALSO BY PAMELA BRITTON

*Seduced*
*Tempted*

# Scandal

## PAMELA BRITTON

NEW YORK    BOSTON

Warner Forever is a registered trademark of Warner Books, Inc.

*Cover art by Franco Accornero*
*Hand lettering by David Gatti*
*Book design by Giorgetta Bell McRee*

ISBN 0-7394-4473-5

Warner Books

Time Warner Book Group
1271 Avenue of the Americas
New York, NY 10020


Printed in the United States of America

For Codi Juanita Rose Baer
Because you're so patient when Mommy's busy.
Because that day I found you in my chair,
industriously typing away, made me laugh.
Because I love it when you tell people,
"Mommy colors books for a living."
And though I know it will be years before you're
able to read this, I want you to know that each time
I lock myself away in my office, I miss you,
pumpkin. May you always be my little friend.

# Acknowledgments

My heartfelt thanks go to:

Barnes and Noble in Redding, California, for being so nice to me whenever I'm there to write. Shaan, you manage a fabulous store. Carol and Pam, your smiles always make *me* smile. Thank you!

Thanks also go to Piney, Janelle and Linda of the Elegant Bean for all the coffee, muffins, more coffee and more muffins and . . . coffee.

For helping me with research, I must thank Maldwin Drummond, Honorable Historian, Royal Yacht Squadron, for verifying my research and shedding light on British yachts.

Lastly, thanks go to my many writer friends here in Redding: Kathy Coatney, Patti Berg, Libby Hall (aka: Laurie Paige), Diana Robertson, Cindy McCormick Martinusen, Terry McLaughlin, Jean Darby for the gift of her book, *Dearly Beloved, I Still Love You,* and Lois Bauer. Your support is what keeps me going. Bless you all.

# Scandal

# Prologue

It all began over a dog. Silly as it may seem, the day Charles Reinleigh Drummond Montgomery, sixth earl of Sherborne, flattened the duke of Wroxly's terrier was a dark day indeed.

Never mind that the dog had often been likened to a canine cannibal. And that it had bitten no less than ten and five children. And that in recent months a bounty had been placed upon its head: ten shillings (the result of a collection Wroxly Park's staff had gathered) to whoever disposed of the carnivorous pooch. None of that mattered, for the dog was loved by the duke, so much so that Rein, who had no preference either way, felt very bad indeed when the thump turned out to be . . . well, not just a thump.

"What have you done?" the duke asked as Rein laid the precious Pookey before him.

Rein, who was to think later that he'd never seen a man turn so instantly pale, said, "He ran in front of my phaeton, Uncle." Actually, Rein was reasonably certain the dog's proximity to his carriage had been *no* coincidence, but he kept such theories to himself.

"You ran him over?"

"Actually, it was more of a glancing blow. Very quick, I assure—"

"You ran *over* him," the duke raged, his eyes turning as red as that little speck one saw in the corner of a bovine's eye.

"I'm sorry, Uncle." And Rein truly was, for he was not without compassion. Truth be told, he had rather a fondness for animals, even those that enjoyed the taste of human flesh, like Pookey.

But the duke was pointing to the door now, his finger stabbing the air with so much force, his whole arm vibrated. "Get out."

"Now, Uncle—"

"I refuse to tolerate your presence for a second more," he said with a veritable waterfall of saliva. "You charge from one scandal to another. Indeed, look at you now, a bruise around your eye—"

"It was an accident."

"Long have I considered *you* an accident."

"I say, *that's* rather harsh."

"You are a blight on our family tree. Placing an ad offering Windsor Castle for lease," the duke raged.

"You heard about that?" asked Rein, wiping at his cheek.

"Suspending a carriage from Windsor Bridge," his uncle went on, ignoring him.

An engineering marvel, not that Rein had done the mathematical calculations.

"Creating fake stones and tossing them upon your professor as he walked into Eton's schoolyard, thereby giving him a fit of apoplexy—"

"I never meant to actually *harm* the man—"

"And then getting not only yourself, but my *Willy* thrown out of Eton, and that after being expelled from Oxford because of that incident with the barmaid—"

"Yes, but that was *years* ago—"

"And then to come here and do"—his uncle's eyes caught on the dog, his expression turning to one of grief—"this to my precious Pookey."

Which made Rein feel as vile as the wet bottom of a bag filled with rotted apples. "Uncle, I truly am sor—"

"No," the duke shot back. "No. I will not listen to another word of your excuses. For eighteen years I have tolerated your presence, but no more. From here on you shall never set foot at Wroxly Park again."

"But I—"

"Out," the duke roared like a Shakespearean actor. "Out, I say,"

*Damned spot,* Rein silently added. But he didn't chastise the old man for stealing the great playwright's lines. No. Instead he bowed and exited the scene.

And there it might have ended, but for one thing: Ten years later Rein became the duke's heir.

About the same time Rein was banished forevermore from Wroxly Park, eleven-year-old Anna Brooks was trying very hard to understand where she fit into the world. Born to a captain in the King's Navy and a gently bred but impoverished seamstress, she was not exactly poor, not exactly orphaned (her mother and father were alive, but often sailed together), but rather the girl in the village whom everyone knew would become a governess, or a missionary, or *something* that involved Anna supporting herself in some humdrum way.

This was a source of constant irritation for Anna, who'd been taught by her mother that a woman's life could be far from humdrum. Why, she could even captain a ship (which her mother did upon occasion, when her father's superiors weren't looking). So when she overheard Lavinia Herbert say to Elliot Spencer, a boy whom Anna had developed a *tendre* for, that Anna would do well to enter a convent so that she could begin her life's work early, Anna was outraged. Work in a convent, indeed. She was destined for a far greater purpose in life than tending the gardens at Our Lady of the Fountain's Convent. Unlike Lavinia, Anna had a brain.

And so she came up with a plan, and a rather good one at that, she thought. Working day and night, she began to construct her greatest creation, something that would prove her brilliance: a ship (though it was more the size of a rowboat), for Anna was something of an inventor. But this ship would be lighter, faster and more maneuverable than other ships.

Alas, it didn't turn out quite that way.

Oh, she built the ship. It just looked rather, well, odd. First, it was shaped rather queer: like a fish caught in the throes of a death arch. And the mainmast tipped to port. And her sail . . . well, Anna was quite convinced window coverings were not meant for sails, even if they did look unique, what with the pattern of roses imprinted upon them.

Still, on the day of the race, as Anna optimistically stood by her "ship," she was proud. The thing did, indeed, float, even if it was in the way that flotsam often clotted together on a stagnant lake.

The people of Porthollow, bless their hearts, were not cruel enough to laugh when they saw her creation reclining on the sand. Indeed, they called out good luck to each other and smooth sailing as the racers stood by in preparation for launch on that sunny and clear day. Elliot, that youthful object of her secret fantasies, however, suffered no such compassion, Elliot being a boy, and everyone knew how unfeeling a male child could be.

"You'll sink within ten seconds," he predicted from his position next to her.

"I will not," Anna said, fussing with her cloak nervously.

"You will."

But Anna had taken her boat out last evening and so she knew she was relatively safe. Thus, she decided not to argue the point. Instead she flicked her cloak off her shoulders in the manner of a great naval captain, gave Elliot an arch look and shoved off.

Things didn't work out quite the way she'd planned.

One, the boat she'd spent so many hours crafting had gotten wet (as boats were supposed to do), the result being that the poor quality wood was now water-saturated, thus making it more heavy and the boat—much to Anna's dismay—no longer buoyant.

Two, the pegs she had pounded in to secure the timbers had swelled and worked loose during the night, the result being that the moment she shoved off, she heard a rather startling couple of pops followed by an ominous twang.

"Hell's bells," she used her father's favorite curse.

She glanced up at Elliot, who had launched his sleek little sloop next to her.

He smirked from his hunched position beneath the mainsail.

She closed her eyes.

He started counting.

She was up to her knees at five.

Eight saw her to her waist.

Nine put her up to her shoulders.

And ten? Well, ten was garbled by the water in her ears.

Anna decided she would allow herself to drown.

Alas, Elliot would not let her.

He dove in, coming to her rescue like Titan protecting his ladylove. Anna's keen intellect suddenly reasoned that this was a much better way of gaining his attention, so she held her breath, feeling strong, manly arms swoop her up and pull her to the surface.

"Anna Brooks," he gasped as they surfaced, "you are the silliest fool I've ever seen."

Anna didn't care. Oh, she just didn't care. The feel of Elliot's arms around her. The touch of his body against hers. The scent of his salt-laden coat . . . it made her head swim. As Elliot carried her toward the shore, her "ship," his sloop and the concerned cries of the crowd forgotten, she decided she would remember the moment for as long as she lived.

And, indeed, a half hour later as she made her way home, wet, embarrassed, bemused and yet never defeated, Anna did relive the moment. Again and again and again. Elliot had rescued her. He had held her close and . . . well . . . while he hadn't kissed her, he might have if she'd played her part a bit better. Things couldn't have gone better.

Hmm. She frowned as she walked up the middle of the lane. Perhaps they could have gone better. She'd like to have been able to sail her boat. Too bad she hadn't taken into account the weight of the wood once wet, a lapse on her part. And those pegs. She should have compensated for the swelling. For half a heartbeat her mind spun with a mathematical calculation, one that compensated for the weight of the wood and the amount of swelling and the pressure such swelling would cause. Elliot was momentarily forgotten. After a short moment, a voice penetrated her musings.

"Oh, miss," Anna heard someone say.

Anna hated being interrupted when she was in the middle of a calculation. It was the same feeling she got when she was interrupted reading a book. *Pop.* Out of the story. She looked up, surprised to see Sarah, the maid of all work her parents employed, standing off to the right of the road.

"Been waiting for you, I have."

"Sarah, why are you not in town for the May Day celebrations?"

For a moment the pretty little maid couldn't speak, she was so overcome with emotion.

And Anna knew. She just knew in the way that people know when someone is coming up behind you. The way a person knows bad news is on the horizon by the way a body shivers with cold. The way one senses something ominous has happened, though not exactly how, or what, only that it has happened.

"It is my parents, is it not?"

The maid nodded, her eyes filling with fresh tears.

"I'm so sorry, miss. So sorry. Their ship went down two weeks ago."

Two weeks ago?

Anna closed her eyes, a pressure building behind them. She tried not to cry. Lord, wasn't that silly? She tried not to cry so Sarah would not feel bad. But she couldn't stop the tears. A grief filled her such as she'd never known before, and would likely never feel again. One so instant and so all-encompassing she could only find the strength to utter one word, "No," in a small voice.

Mama.

Papa.

*Gone.*

Though Anna was only eleven, though she'd yet to experience life and all its pains and sorrows, she was bright enough and astute enough to realize the blow she'd just been dealt was one that would change her life forever. That nothing, absolutely nothing, would ever be the same again.

And, indeed, it never was.

Ten years after a heartbroken little girl went off to live in London, the poor duke of Wroxly was told that Rein Montgomery was now his heir.

"My heir?" the duke roared.

"Yes, Your Grace." The man swallowed, watching as the duke's face reddened past his gray hairline.

"Impossible," and his green eyes all but snapped the word at his solicitor.

"I'm afraid not."

"I will not allow it."

"You have no choice."

"We could kill him," the duke affirmed, his jowls quivering like a chicken's wattle as he bobbed his head. "Kill him as he killed my Willy." He nodded for emphasis, the ducal hair, which had never been very prevalent, shaken into streamers that stuck out in the manner of porcupine quills.

"Your Grace," the solicitor felt the need to point out, "your son died in a duel—"

"He would never have involved himself with that woman if his cousin Rein had not expressed interest in her himself."

"Yes, but the fact remains that your son involved himself with a married woman, one whose husband felt understandably cuckolded when your son—"

"My son would never have done something so dishonorable if not for Rein Montgomery," the duke said, his voice rising in volume until he doubled over in a fit of coughing, a cough that had gotten worse since his son's death. When he regained himself, he straightened, saying in a low voice, "I will not have that—" The duke swallowed. "I will not have that wastrel, that instigator, that *killer* inherit my lands, not while my poor Willy lies in the ground."

At that moment, the solicitor felt almost sorry for the duke. Only the glimmer of madness he saw in His Grace's eyes caused that pity to turn to concern.

"Something must be done," the duke said.

And, indeed, something was done.

\*    \*    \*

Two years after Wroxly heard Rein was now his heir, the poor duke died too. Tragic, Rein thought, as he studied his nails (and admitted he needed a new manicure). Probate had gone quickly. But as Rein sat listening to the reading of the will, he admitted he could barely contain himself as he waited for the solicitor to get to the good part, the part where his uncle left him everything.

"'As to my heir, Charles Reinleigh Drummond Montgomery . . .'"

At last. Rein perked up.

"'. . . I leave nothing.'"

Rein blinked. Blinked again. Then said in a low voice, "I beg your pardon?"

"'I can, of course,'" the solicitor read on, "'do nothing about those lands that are entailed. However, the rest of my estate—those investments that produce the Wroxly wealth—those I leave in trust . . .'"

*In trust?*

"'. . . until such a day as a new heir is born, or the title passes on. Those incomes will then revert to the rightful heir, unless . . .'"

And Rein knew he wouldn't like what came next. His hands clutched the arms of the red chair he sat in, his cheek twitching in a spasm.

"'. . . the current duke of Wroxly can prove his worth . . .'"

What the blazes did *that* mean?

"'. . . by living on his own for four weeks' time without aid from friends or family, and without telling a single soul of his plight, and by leaving to do so immediately so as not to alert those friends and family, and so that he is unable to stash certain funds to help him through the process.' "

Stash funds? What the *blazes* was the solicitor talking about?

" 'If, and only if,' " the solicitor read on, " 'the new duke of Wroxly succeeds in this endeavor, will he be allowed to inherit the properties mentioned above.' "

"What the blazes *is* this?" Rein could contain himself no more.

The solicitor looked up, lowering the paper he'd been reading from to a position right above his well-polished cherry desk, the reflection of his nearly bald head a mirror image on the desk's surface.

"This," the solicitor explained, the glass in his spectacles turning almost white with a glare, "is what the duke came up with to test you."

"Test me?"

The solicitor nodded. "You, Your Grace, shall live on your own for one month's time without aid from friends or family or servants, and without using a penny of your own wealth, nor telling anyone who you are. You must live by your wits and your wits alone, and if you do not"—the little man tapped the edges of the will on his desk—"you won't get a farthing of the money generated by ducal investments. In short, Your Grace, if you fail in this challenge, you will be destroyed both financially and personally."

And all Rein did was stare, his hands clenching tighter and tighter until the fabric caught under his nails.

"Bastard," he hissed.

# Part One

*Once upon a time a fair maiden met a prince,
though at the time, she had no notion
he was a prince. . . .*

# Chapter One

In March of 1819, at exactly eleven-thirty in the morning, during an overcast spring day that blew blustery and cold, Anna Rose Brooks rendered the duke of Wroxly senseless.

Of course, at the time, she had no idea he was a duke. Indeed, seconds before the accident, she'd been atop the roof of her tenement—the two- and three-story buildings in St. Giles so packed together they formed a sort of field—cursing at her kite because the daft thing was about to sink onto the busy street below.

"No," she told the triangular shape that hung in the air above her head, darting and ducking this way and that with a crackle of the canvas material. "You shall not do this," she added, tugging on the string.

Blast it, she'd spent hours crafting this particular design, but the bloody thing kept insisting on zigging and zagging against the gray backdrop like a ball between two buildings, lowering, and then lowering some more, and then not lowering—diving.

"Ballocks," she cursed, letting go of the string. She ran to the edge of the roof, her heart beating a disastrous thump as she watched her precious invention fall toward the carriage-jingling, pedestrian-clogged street below. A man had just stepped out of a carriage, his hat and walking stick firmly in hand. He must have caught a glimpse of her kite as he stepped out, for Anna saw him glance up.

What happened next Anna would swear wasn't possible. Indeed, she would later tell her best friend Molly that it appeared as if the hand of God himself pressed down on her kite. Suddenly it took on the speed of a battering ram, and even from her perch way up on high, she could see what was about to happen. So, too, could the man, at least judging by the way his eyes widened.

And widened.

And then widened even more.

The kite whacked him on the forehead like a tree branch bent back by a mischievous child.

*Thwack.*

Anna covered her mouth. The man fell to the street, arms splayed like Jesus on the cross—without the cross. She stared, waiting for him to move. He didn't. A passerby paused for a second, looked down, then stepped over him as if a prone man were nothing unusual in St. Giles, which, she realized, it wasn't. The pedestrian walked on.

Others had begun to notice, too. Someone from across the street dodged traffic to kneel by the man's side. Another person ran forward. When the first man looked up and crossed himself, Anna darted back from the edge.

And then the magnitude of what had just happened hit her. She straightened in horror.

*What if he's gone to kingdom come?*

She lurched up, the cloak she wore getting tangled up

in her feet, which made her step back, which then pulled her neckline taut, causing her to strangulate for a full three seconds before she sorted her feet, the garment and her wits out (though the last was questionable).

*What if I've dicked him in the knob?*

For a few breathless—no, panicked—moments she contemplated dashing off in the other direction. Hiding on the next roof over, perhaps, or maybe even pretending she hadn't noticed her kite—a kite that was really an experimental sail—was responsible for the man lying in the street. But what with the myriad of carriages thumping and clanging about as they passed, pickpockets and goodness knew what else on the loose, she couldn't just leave him there.

"Never seen anything like it," old Ben the coconut trader was saying when she reached the street below—out of breath, marginally less panicked, but cringing when she saw where her victim lay: atop a stream of rotted vegetables, gnawed bones and bilge water otherwise known as the gutter.

"Knocked him clean off his feet," he added. "Like a rider what got smacked in the head by a wood beam. Back went his head, up went his feet, *splat,* down he went."

"Is 'e dead?" asked one of the market maids, the wilted purple flower in her bedraggled black hat bobbing as she glanced down.

*Aye, is he?* Anna silently asked, approaching more slowly now.

"'E's had 'is bell rung," a chimney sweep answered as he knelt to check for a pulse, his ash-covered finger leaving a mark on the man's neck. "But he's not ready for a bone box yet," he announced with a look up, his eyes two slashes of white in a sooty face, tall black hat matching his bedraggled jacket. "Pity. Like to get me hands on those clothes o' his. Bang up to the mark. Must be a gent. Look at them shiny boots."

Anna almost collapsed in relief. He would live. She hoped.

Old Ben looked up just then, his wrinkled face frowning, and Anna knew he'd spotted her. Worse, she knew *he* knew who'd been flying the kite, well, sail. And why wouldn't he know? On the back of her invention, marked as plain as eyeballs, were the words, "If found, return to Anna Brooks, No. 7, St. Giles High Street." But even without that, everyone in the rookery knew of her fierce determination to win the contest sponsored by the Navy. And that she'd been flying her sails whenever she took a break from selling her wares at Covent Garden. They had all encouraged her. But now that she'd bashed someone in the knowledge box, they might not be so supportive.

"You've done it now, Anna, lass," Ben said, confirming her fears.

A glance down at the gentleman who lay there with his arms splayed out like that statue of Jesus at St. Paul's Cathedral made Anna realize she had, indeed, "done it."

"Look at the size of the knot on his knob," the chimney sweep said, coming to his feet, which—as sad as it may seem—didn't make him much taller than when he'd been squatting down. Anna followed his gaze, wincing at the red circle imprinted on the gentleman's head and that very oddly resembled a sundial. An inch and a half in diameter, blazing hot in color, it was exactly the same circumference as the wooden dowels she used as a frame for her sails. Hell's fires.

"Will he live?" she asked, coming to Ben's side.

"Unfortunately, yes."

All of them jumped back, Anna almost into the path of an approaching carriage before old Ben pulled her forward, the jarvis yelling at her as he rolled on by with a spray of mud and stinky water.

Green eyes opened, blinked, then closed again. "Tell me I am not lying atop what feels and smells like a rubbish heap," he said, his aristocratic face flinching, his nose twitching like a rabbit's. Or maybe it was the tiny flecks of mud that made him look like he had whiskers.

No one said a word.

"I take it from that stunned silence that I am, indeed, lying upon said rubbish heap."

More silence.

"I was afraid of that."

Anna inched forward, watching as her victim opened his eyes again, glanced around, his gaze alighting upon each of them like a dragonfly darting from lily to lily. She held her breath for a second when it alighted on her, but like that winged creature it didn't linger, instead coming to a stop on Ben.

"What the blazes hit me?"

Ben, the traitor, looked at Anna.

The chimney sweep looked at Anna.

The market maid looked at her, too. Hell's fires, had everyone put it together that she had done it?

Apparently so.

"My kite," she said rather reluctantly.

"A kite," the man groaned, his hand clutching at his

head, his words barely audible over the disorderly noise of the street. "Rendered low by a child's toy. Bloody hell."

And then he laughed, though to be certain Anna didn't realize at first it was laughter she heard. There was so much noise and confusion in the road—street hawkers crying out their rhymes, a dog barking as it darted between moving carriages, more than one driver yelling at the cur as it passed, their voices echoing off the tall gray buildings that surround them—that when the low rumbling penetrated her eardrums it didn't register at first. But then the rumble became an audible guffaw, one that was abruptly choked off with a wince of pain.

"Well," Ben said, "seems as if he's recovered."

"That 'e 'as," the sweep said, melting into the crowd on the street.

And then the market maid turned and left, which meant Anna had nothing but noise to keep her company, that and wry green eyes that stared up at her, not to mention a knot of guilt as big as her ball of twine heavy in her stomach.

"Would you be wanting some help getting up?" she asked, because it seemed as if she should offer to do *something*.

"A lovely idea," he said, after which he moved onto an elbow, the muck beneath him emitting a horrible sucking sound that brought to mind body functions and leaky bellows.

"Good lord," he said, pausing for a second. "Tell me that didn't come from me."

"'Twas the mud," said Anna, squatting down near him.

Their eyes met, and suddenly Anna felt like . . . well, off balance. As if she stood upon a shore as a wave drew into the sea . . . as if the whole world moved at a blistering pace around her, but she stood still, alone, yet not alone. And then his eyes moved away and Anna came back to earth, or rather St. Giles, though she found herself blinking a bit and wondering what the blazes had just happened.

" 'Tis me who smells, isn't it?" he said with a glance at his surroundings, his hand lifting to his head, eyes widening a bit as they felt the bump.

She nodded. "Aye."

He closed his eyes, tilting his head back, Anna watching and trying to glean just who he was, this colorful dragonfly that had landed in the mud and muck of one of London's seediest sides of town.

"Good lord, this day just couldn't get worse, could it?" He opened his eyes, looked heavenward. "You're up there laughing Yourself into hysterics, are You not? Or perhaps You're down there." At which he glanced down, saying, "Bastard." But when his gaze caught her own, his expression grew wry again. "I smell like a sewer."

Who had he been talking to?

Oh, lord. She really *had* damaged his brain box. The ball of twine grew bigger.

"There's an inn not far. Mayhap the bluffer will let you change there?"

"Bluffer?" he asked, brows lifting. He had extraordinary eyes. Green as the patina that colored an old piece of brass. Green like glass bottles when stacked six deep. Green like—

*Lord love you, Anna, you've gone as crackers as your grandfather.*

"Innkeeper," she said, realizing that he was still staring at her in confusion. *Well, of course he's struck all amort, Anna, love. He doesn't speak like you.* For despite the mud on his clothes, it was as plain as pikestaffs that he was a gentleman. She'd never seen fabric so fine as his dark blue jacket, the collar covered in fancy velvet that looked so soft Anna longed to drag her finger across it to see if the nap would reverse. And though she hadn't heard a person speak with the distinctive flat syllables and well-enunciated vowels of the hoity-toity in ages, she recognized it now, marveling that her own words had once sounded so pure and untainted. A long time ago.

"A lodging house. Capital idea," he said.

"Here." She stood, offering a hand, though she felt the usual pang of embarrassment she always felt at her work-worn fingers. She shoved the embarrassment aside, the smell of the busy street somewhat less cloying when inhaled from a distance of five feet three inches. He accepted her assistance, his fingers slipping into her own as naturally as a glove, his hand warm and soft and so large it completely enveloped her own from fingertip to palm. And as he stood she found herself wondering just who the blazes he was. He was so tall, and—she swallowed crookedly—handsome.

That was the reason why she'd reacted so strangely earlier. And it wasn't merely a handsomeness of his dial plate, what with his arrogant cheekbones and aristocratic nose. Rather, it was something in the way he surveyed the world, in the way he looked around him as if he knew whatever he wanted was his for the taking. Power. That was what he exuded, like a bird of prey in the lofty way it hung suspended in the air over the world. And like that bird of prey, there was also a rapine air that made Anna shiver in . . . what? Fear? No, not fear. Something else.

"Who *are* you?" she found herself asking.

"I—" He looked down at her, green eyes narrowing for a second. His mouth opened again, then closed. "I'm afraid I can't say," he said at last.

Panic hit her square in the heart then, the organ slapping her chest with enough force to make it hard to breathe for a moment.

"Where am I?" he asked, looking around them.

Oh, lord. Oh, saints above. She really *had* damaged his idea pot.

"St. Giles High Street," she managed to say, though it felt rather like her mums had gone numb.

"St. Giles?" he exclaimed, the well modulated words as foreign a sound as a Turkish accent, and then he winced. "Good lord."

"Steady, now," she said as he swayed on his feet, and she counterbalanced him with her own weight. It was then that she realized his walking stick and hat had been pilfered. Blast it—though she supposed she should be grateful that he hadn't been picked clean like a piece of carrion.

"It seems as if I've been hit harder than I thought."

*Ach,* she thought, *it would seem so.* "Here," she said. "Lean on me a bit."

"My walking stick."

"Gone," she said.

He looked around. "So it is."

"And your hat," she added, in case he looked for that, too.

"Good lord. Who would take a hat?"

"You might be surprised," she muttered, then gently pushed on his back. "C'mon, gov, I'm going to take you to me ken."

"Your ken?"

She translated for him, "The tenement I share with my grandfather."

"Would it be closer than the lodging house, by chance?" he said, looking suddenly pale.

"Aye."

"Then I would be most obliged."


"You don't, by chance, live on the moon?" Rein asked a few moments later when they headed up yet another flight of spectacularly dirty stairs, the third set, to be exact.

He glanced down at the woman who'd added a crowning glory to his splendiferous day. Young, and obviously of the lower orders if they were in St. Giles. Lord, he still couldn't believe he'd been dropped in such a place, and that his hat and walking stick had been stolen. But the woman before him seemed to be confirmation of the low place he had landed. She wore the uniform of the poor: gray cloak and battered half boots. Fifteen, perhaps sixteen years old. Too young to suit his taste, though in another lifetime when he'd been fond of lithe young things, perhaps not.

"Some days it feels that way," he heard her murmur,

clutching that silly child's toy of hers like it was her only treasure. And perhaps it was.

Rein looked away, the anger chipping at his cheek again. Damn them. He'd been dropped in St. Giles, of all places. Why not the docks? Or Whitechapel? Gracious, if his uncle wanted him dead, there were easier ways to do it. And for half a moment he thought about going back to the solicitor and telling him exactly how he felt. Outraged. Angered. Furious. Surely the probate court had noted the ludicrous nature of the will. He should contest it immediately.

Only the idea of giving up so quickly stung. No, it rankled. His uncle had obviously thought such a challenge beyond Rein. Rein would be damned before he proved his uncle right.

The sound of a child's cry rang out from the landing below, a plaintive wail that brought to mind hunger. Other sounds could be heard, too. Coughing, yelling, a cacophony of noise that filled Rein's ears and made his head ache like the very devil. The wooden stairs they climbed were scuffed with marks, as if a thousand heavy feet had scaled them with soles as hard as stone. The stairs creaked with every step, the sound echoing off the narrow walls that had been plastered at one time or another, but had long since lost that plaster to clenched fists or age.

"I'm afraid my grandfather is away for the moment," said the small sprite next to him as they came to what must have been her landing, her kite balanced on a finger before her. "I should warn you," she added, "our rooms are a bit . . ." He glanced down, but she wasn't looking at him; rather, she looked at the door and frowned, the cloak she wore so battered and worn he knew it'd been years since it was new. "Rather at sixes and sevens," she finished.

Rein didn't move, just waited for her to open the door. She seemed to have to force herself to do so, reaching out to give the door a turn and a tug.

Sixes and sevens, Rein decided a second later, did not begin to describe it.

Strange contraptions covered every available surface of the small, small room. Odd things like a table with a ladder affixed to the side of it, and a giant wheel with stirrups attached to a huge fireplace bellows pointed directly at them. Shelves covered every available wall, odd bottles and devices on surfaces not taken up by books.

But beneath it all lay a poverty no amount of machinery could disguise: a bare wooden floor, each board as nicked and scarred as an old coin. Three dirty windows stretched across the front, one threadbare and dingy armchair sitting near a hearth crouched low in one corner.

"My grandfather is an inventor," she said in a solemn little voice.

"What does he invent?"

"Things," she said. "Or he used to, before he became ill."

"I see," he said.

She peered up at him, then back into the room again, perhaps seeing it from his perspective for the first time, for she frowned, her teeth—very healthy teeth, he noticed—nibbling her bottom lip.

And well she should look askance, not that he'd be rude enough to point that out to her. "It is—"

"Don't say it," she said. "I know. I do me best to keep

it clean, but it never seems to work. Grandfather comes fumbling in and messes it all up. Here. Sit down." She guided him toward the armchair. "But first let's see about getting you cleaned up." She undid her cloak, removing it as she turned away from him so she could hang it by the door, and when she turned back to him, Rein received his second shock of the day.

"You're not a child, are you?"

# Chapter Two

Rein watched as her hand froze. The arm she held toward him had stilled. "Child?"

Rein's head suddenly ached even more. "You're not. Good lord," he huffed. "I had no idea."

Perhaps it was the way the light came from behind him to illuminate her plain brown dress with its V-shaped lace collar, the apron around her waist accentuating her trim figure. Perhaps he merely started to think straight. Whatever the reason, for the first time Rein looked beneath the cloak of poverty she wore.

She had unusual and rather pretty amber eyes. Intelligence sparked from within those eyes. A startling amount of intelligence.

And as he leaned back and observed the whole, he admitted she was rather like a rose, one he might pass by because it looked dull and colorless, but which upon closer inspection revealed petals not dull at all, but rather a striking combination of colors rarely seen. Such was she, her hair not red, not blond, but rather a combination of the two, like a mist near a waterfall that turned gold and red in sunlight. She had delicate features, too, small nose and chin, and yet those eyes. Her eyes dominated her small face, the only thing seeming to counterbalance it a set of full lips that looked plump as summer strawberries.

She was staring at him in confusion that quickly turned to concern. "No idea 'bout what?"

He shook his head, winced, then said, "But I suppose it matters not."

"Matters not?"

She didn't understand. Not at all. And then he reminded himself that this was not a Mayfair drawing room he sat in. Alas, they were far from that. Obviously, she had no notion of the social protocol that disallowed a man and woman to be in the same room together . . . alone. And why would she?

"Please ignore my ramblings," he said. "I find I am rather scrambled."

Not surprising, given all that had just happened. Lord, he still couldn't believe the predicament he found himself in.

"If you are scrambled it is because of me," she said, holding out her hands again—rather worn hands, he noticed. Work-worn. "Please, give me the coat, Mr. . . ."

He looked up. A name. She wanted a name. "Hemple," he said quickly. Gads. Hemple? "Wilt," he added, which wasn't much of an improvement.

"Mr. Hemplewilt?" she said, looking oddly relieved. "You remembered your name is Mr. Hemplewilt? Lawks, that's a relief. I feared I might have ruined your jobbernole forevermore."

Jobbernole? She must mean *head.*

"And do you now remember being dropped off in St. Giles?"

St. Giles? Why the devil would she ask such a question? Of course he remembered—

And then it hit him.

Good lord. She believed him concussed.

And in the next second something else hit him, an idea, one that made his eyes narrow, though it tugged at his injury as he did so.

*Why not?* he asked himself. Why not let her go on thinking he was ill? He had no place else to go, having been stripped of coin, valuables and, good lord, even his signet ring. If he let her go on thinking . . .

"I'm afraid I don't remember being dropped in St. Giles," he said, studying her reaction to see if it was as he expected.

And, indeed, she looked so horror-stricken he almost took pity on her. But he had far too much at stake to let such a silly emotion as pity take a hold of him.

"In fact, I wonder if I might stay here a bit," he added. "Until I recover."

"Stay here?"

"Indeed."

"But—"

"I assure you, 'twill only be until I recover myself from the injury your toy inflicted."

That sent a look of guilt into her eyes—exactly his intent.

"Of course," he added, "if you'd rather I leave, I shall certainly understand. I do hope, however, that I can find my way home."

"Oh, ah . . ." Her teeth worked those plump lips of hers. "I'm not—"

"Just for an hour or two."

"Yes, but I've got to return to selling my wares at Covent Market. If I leave you here, you would be alone, since my grandfather is away. When he returns—"

"I'll introduce myself," Rein finished.

"No, 'tis not that." Those teeth went to work again. "He's rather odd, you see."

"Really?" he asked, and if she'd been a member of the *ton,* she would have recognized the politely curious look he gave her.

"Yes, well, if you think his inventions are odd, you should meet the man himself."

"Rumpled clothes," he theorized. "Messy gray hair, vacant look in his eyes?"

"Exactly," she said with a smile.

Rein became motionless as he observed the effect the smile drew on her face. What was before merely pretty became simply stunning. Good lord, what was such a rare gem doing in St. Giles? Someone ought to have plucked her for his mistress long before now.

Her smile faded, and then she stilled suddenly, too, almost as if she'd sensed the direction his thoughts had taken. And indeed, for half a moment he found himself wondering if he might seduce her, found himself thinking that to do so might be an interesting diversion. Alas, he admitted with a sigh, he had no time for diversions, at least not yet.

She must have misinterpreted his sigh, for she said, "Here, now. Do not fret."

Fret? Not in a great many years.

"I suppose it'll do little harm to have you rest here a bit. But you mustn't touch a thing. Grandfather is very particular about his inventions."

"I shall not stir from this chair."

She gazed down at him a bit longer, almost as if she stared at a rare bird that had somehow found its way into her room. He supposed he was that rare bird, one she'd likely not see again in her lifetime—a duke. Far, far above her plebeian world.

"Well, then I suppose this is goodbye."

No, not for a bit. His eyes swept her up and down. Not for a long bit. "I suppose it is."

"It was a pleasure meeting you, Mr. Hemplewilt."

"And you, too, Miss . . ."

"Anna Rose Brooks," she said with a nod.

Now it was his turn to smile, though the urge to do so took him by surprise. "Rose is your middle name?"

"It is."

"I breed roses."

"You breed roses?"

"Indeed."

"That means you must have land."

He pretended to have to think on that answer, and, indeed, he was wondering how much to tell her, or rather, how much he was *allowed* to tell her. "A great deal of it," he told her truthfully.

"So you're a gentleman?"

"I am." Which was true, too, he thought, though he refrained from telling her who he was. Perfect.

"Landed gentry," she seemed to murmur to herself. "I'm not at all surprised."

"You would be a *Rosa damascena*," he found himself

saying. Odd, because he hadn't meant to speak, nor say something so ridiculously florid. Usually, he merely crooked a finger to get a woman's attention. "Or a damask rose. Delicate, beautiful, yet hardy enough to survive in any environment."

She lifted a brow, and to his surprise went through a transformation, one that gently rebuked him even as she placed her hands on her hips. "And how many times have you said *that* to a woman?"

"I am not at all sure," he answered honestly, having to press his lips together to keep from laughing. Lord, laughing. An hour ago, he would have sworn such a thing would be impossible.

"That I can believe."

"But never have I meant it more." Which was also true.

"I'm certain you haven't," she said with a scoff-filled shake of her head, but then her eyes narrowed in on his bruise and all rebuke fled. "There's a wash pump two buildings over. You could cleanse your wound and your jacket there, then hang it before a fire to dry, though you'll need to stoke the coals. Do not, however, attempt to use the bellows attached to the wheel," she warned.

And then she backed away.

"Adieu," he said with a nod.

"Good morn," she said, snatching her cloak and turning toward the door.

His gaze dropped to her sumptuous derriere. He couldn't help it. It was a fetish of his, a woman's bottom. She had a rather delectable one, he noted. Nice and round, with just enough flesh around the hips to offer a good grip.

"Goodbye, Anna," he said softly, and for his ears alone, testing the name on his tongue, rolling it, savoring it like he would a small candy. And he did like it . . . her name. He was quite fascinated by it, and her.

And if Anna had seen the look that came over Rein's face, if she'd seen the rakish, hell-raising, rooster of a smile that lifted the corner of his lips, she might have felt a great deal less complacent about leaving a stranger in her home.

A great deal less complacent, indeed.

# Chapter Three

Four hours later, as an exhausted Anna climbed the stairs to her grandfather's apartment, the straw hat she wore to market dangling from her grasp by its ribbons, she still thought of him.

Mr. Hemplewilt.

Tired as she was, her heart pumped in reaction to the silent recalling of his name. Lord, it was a good thing he wouldn't be there when she returned, she admitted as she lifted a leg that felt as heavy as a ham hock and climbed another step. She hadn't liked the way staring at that fancy gentleman made her feel. Excited. Curious. And, yes, dreamy as a girl of sixteen. As if she had time for silly dreams!

She paused on a step, though it took her a moment to realize that the reason she'd paused was to cock her head.

And there it was again: the asthmatic *poof-poof-poooof* she'd come to dread. Her grandfather's favorite invention.

*Blast it,* she thought, taking the next four steps two at a time, her cloak entangling in her legs for the second time that day and nearly causing her to tumble. Just what she needed. He shouldn't be playing with that bloody machine again, not after what had happened last time. Lord, they'd been nearly run out of the building by the landlord and her fellow tenants.

She tossed her hat onto the landing, then reached for the door, taking the time to gain her strength before opening the thing. She'd need all the energy she could muster, for she could feel the hem of her cloak rustle from the gusts of air that reached like a hand beneath the door and jerked on the hem of her cloak.

"Heaven help me," she said, placing her fingers on the handle as she mentally counted.

One.

Two.

Three.

She braced herself as she turned the knob, and a good thing, too, for as soon as the catch gave, wind gusts from the other side of the door nearly knocked her off her feet. Papers flew, as did dust and a lone insect that no doubt wondered what sort of nasty business it'd stumbled into as it flew by at hurricane speed. She had to squint to see into the room.

"And . . . the faster . . . you pedal . . ." her grandfather huffed as his feet pushed on the leather straps of his Colossal Air Current Creator, his stark white hair plastered against his head as the pressure escaped the room, "the faster . . . the bellows . . . pump."

And through the papers and the dust and the debris, she saw him.

Mr. Hemplewilt sat upright in the armchair, an expression of horror, fear and fascination on his face as he clutched the armrests and watched her grandfather pedal nowhere fast. His eyes met hers.

Anna felt the wave hit her again, or perhaps it was her grandfather's invention. The giant bellows happened to be pointed in her direction, the result being that she got the worst of it. She put an arm up to shield her eyes and she screamed at Mr. Hemplewilt, "Get out."

"Get out?" he mouthed back, as if he hadn't quite heard her, and perhaps he hadn't, for the machine was terribly loud.

"Get out," she called again.

Mr. Hemplewilt got up slowly, his eyes moving back to her grandfather almost as if he were about to witness a carriage accident and he was held rooted to the spot by morbid curiosity.

"Mr. Hemplewilt," she called more sternly.

He crossed carefully past her grandfather, his steps gradually growing faster. Perhaps he sensed that things were coming to a crisis, or perhaps he became propelled by the wind gusts flying through the room. Either way, he ended up moving quite quickly.

"What of your grandfather?" he asked as he darted past her.

"He won't stop pedaling," she said. "It's an addiction of sorts. He goes and goes until the final cataclysm."

"Cataclysm?"

"You'll see."

Anna stepped back, using the tips of her fingers to pull the door toward her. Mr. Hemplewilt helped, and together they got the thing closed—just in time, as it turned out, for the bladder that had been slowly filling with air to the right of the machine suddenly burst with a pop that snapped at Anna's ears. Her grandfather's mad cackle of glee rang out.

The silence afterward was nearly deafening. Well, silence but for the moan of wind that escaped from beneath the door with a high-pitched whistle until paper and debris clogged it.

"What the blazes *was* that?" Mr. Hemplewilt asked.

"The Colossal Air Current Creator."

"Colossal *what*?"

"Air Current Creator."

And there it was again . . . that rumble she'd first heard down on the street below, only this time it turned quickly into deep, masculine laughter.

Anna stared. She blinked, too, but only a few times. Lord, he was a sight now that he no longer had mud covering his face. He had ivory skin so soft it spoke of a valet's care and a lifetime of leisure. Neatly trimmed black hair stopped just above his shoulders. And that scar. Aye, he had a scar across his chin, one that caught the meager amount of light that oozed out of a small window above them.

"Amazing," he huffed. "I have never, not ever, seen such a thing in my life. Your grandfather should be knighted just for daring to ride such an instrument."

Anna blinked some more.

"What is its purpose?"

She pulled her gaze away, felt the oddest sensation in her mouth, rather like the time she'd bitten into that persimmon and gotten the moisture sucked out of her tongue for her troubles. "It's ah . . ." She had to work her mouth a bit. "It's supposed to be used to chill buildings."

"Is it really?"

"It is."

To which he looked utterly delighted. "I might like such a thing myself."

He stopped himself so quickly Anna had a feeling he'd been about to say more. And then she noticed something else. "What the blazes happened to your clothes?" she asked as her eyes darted over his threadbare brown coat and buff breeches with leather patches on the knee so old and worn they looked as scarred as the surface of the moon.

"I sold them," he said quickly.

"You *sold* them?"

"Indeed. For a half crown and a shilling plus what I'm wearing."

Half crown one shilling? He'd gotten a touch over a half a crown for that fine jacket with the collar that made Anna long to rest her face against it? And for his boots, too? She opened her mouth, about to tell him he'd been cheated—and royally—but something in his expression stopped her, something that made her think he knew he'd been taken, but that he'd been willing to take the coin because he was desperate for it.

"Who *are* you?" she suddenly found herself asking again, for she had a feeling he was much more than a landed gentleman. Then once she asked that, she couldn't stop the rush of words. "What are you doing in St. Giles? And most importantly, why are you still here?"

"Who am I?" he repeated, his eyes looking suddenly dark. Her hands pressed against the door as she became aware of the smallness of the landing they shared. Lawks, it was almost as if he meant to discombobulate her.

"I am a man who finds himself before you through

wretched fate and circumstance." Those eyes of his burned into hers. "One who needs your help, Miss Anna Rose Brooks."

She swallowed, the gulp feeling like a ton of bricks as it went down. "Yes, but why?" she found the intelligence to ask. "Why are you here? Do you remember now?"

He drew back, and Anna realized then that he'd sidled next to her without her even noticing it.

"As to that, I lost a wager."

"A wager?"

"Indeed," he said. "For it came to me quite suddenly. My memory, that is. Indeed, I lost a wager to a chum of mine, thereby forcing me to live on the streets for one month's time."

To live where? Lud, she could hardly concentrate. Oh, yes . . . live on the streets. She straightened, almost knocking him in the chin as she did so. He was that close. "Live on the streets?"

"Aye, for one month's time."

"Here, in the rookery?"

"Indeed," he said, the mint-scented word almost making her forget her next words. Almost.

"Have you damaged your knowledge box?"

"Not since this morning," he said with a wry grin.

"Do you know what it's like to live here in the rookery?" she asked. "'Tis dangerous, it is—too dangerous for the likes of you. Men will cut your throat for the buttons on your jacket. Well, mayhap not now, but still, murderers and convicts roam freely while those silly watchmen call out the weather . . . as if anyone cares a rabbit's whisker that fog is overhead. And if a cutthroat doesn't get you, then likely a sickness will. The sewers alone will make you ill."

She shook her head, placing her hands against the flat of the door. "Do yourself a favor, Mr. Hemplewilt. Forget about your wager and go back to your home, wherever that may be."

He'd begun to stare at her strangely. Oh, he still peered down at her intently, those lovely eyes of his unblinking as they held her own. But his gaze had narrowed, flicking around her face until finally settling upon her lips.

"You sound rather impassioned."

She lifted her chin, though that brought their two heads closer. "I should be, for this wasn't always my life."

"No?"

"No, indeed." She forced herself to hold her ground, though she wanted to dart around him and gain some distance. Still, she didn't move, just held his gaze as she said, "I was raised in Porthollow, on the coast, in as pretty a house as you've ever seen, but then my parents died and I had to come here. I still remember the shock, the horror, the fear. It's not a place for a fancy mort like yourself."

"Ah, but you see . . ." He reached up and touched her cheek. She shivered. She coiled. She couldn't breathe. He touched her. He shouldn't. She let him. "I shan't be here alone. *I* shall be living with *you*."

What had he said? Lord, she couldn't think again. That touch of his hand made her buntlings twist like a pair of wringing hands. Again she seemed to feel a wave of air, a great big rolling one that all but pulled her feet out from under her. Or perhaps that was her grandfather's invention as it slowly died down, air from beneath the door trying its best to reach her cloak. Whoosh, whoosh, whoosh, from the other side. Or perhaps that was her heart?

"I . . ." She swallowed. *"What?"*

His hand stroked the line of her jaw, the look on his face filled with curiosity as he gently touched her, almost impassively, like a great master might touch his favorite work of art.

"Your grandfather," he said softly. "He invited me to stay, in exchange for the half crown I earned selling my clothes."

Stay? What was he—

She stiffened, their bodies brushed and she finally darted around him, her back to the stairs as she said, "What?"

His eyes looked into her own, the corner of his mouth lifting up as he said, "And I find myself quite looking forward to it."

# Chapter Four

*Stay?*

Was he daft? Had she misheard him? Was his brain more mashed than she thought? What did he mean, *stay?*

But the look in his eyes told her. He meant stay. With them. Share their rooms. Eat with them. Lord, *sleep* with them.

Suddenly Anna felt like a mouse with a cat's paw stuffed into its home, a giant black cat with green eyes.

"You can't," she said.

"I cannot?" he echoed back, one of his brows rising.

"No. He's not right in the head—my grandfather, that is. Gracious, *you're* not right in the head. You, none of you—men that is—are right in the head. What do you mean, *stay* with us? We don't even know you."

He leaned toward her. Gracious, she could all but feel a charge of energy as he drew near.

"You *could* know me," he said in a low voice. And now in addition to a paw in the hole, there was an eye looking at her. Two handsome green eyes that made her feel pinned down by that paw. "If you wanted to," he added.

"I don't want to," she wheezed.

He took a step toward her. Anna resisted the urge to re-treat down a step. "No?" he asked. "Pity, for I don't be-lieve you have a choice."

A gust of air darted again from the room, stirring the hairs on her head and bringing with it the smell of him. She caught the scent of his breath—a minty scent that made her think of the hard candies she used to eat as a child.

"I've a choice," she said. "I run the household now that my grandfather's too befogged to take care of him-self. And you can't stay," she said again.

"Ah," he said with a foxlike smile. "But I'm about to make you an offer you cannot refuse," he said. "Let me stay for a night. If I'm too much trouble, I shall take my leave on the morrow. If, however, I prove to be an exem-plary guest, you shall keep the half crown I gave your grandfather *and* let me stay for the duration of my time in St. Giles, for which I shall pay you generously, *after* I have won my wager."

Stay for the duration? Was he mad?

Was she mad for feeling a stab of excitement at such a notion?

For she was honest enough to admit that she didn't fear *him*; rather, she feared this . . . this *feeling* she got whenever he was near. He was like that shiny new coin she'd found in the gutter one day. She'd wanted to keep it. But at almost the exact moment she'd found the thing, Lizzie had walked by, her poor gaunt face lifting into a smile, though she'd had nothing to smile about since her husband had died, leaving her alone with four young bairns to raise. Before Anna'd known what she was doing, she'd handed the coin to her friend . . . and had occasion to remember that generosity every time her stomach growled for the next three days.

But if he stayed, his blunt would pay for food. And since she'd missed half of her usual market time this morning in order to test her sail she'd paid the price for it. His half crown would more than make up the difference.

She met his gaze, looked into the eyes of a man whose ilk she would likely never see again. Gentry. Perhaps even noble, for as she looked down, she caught a band of white around his pinkie finger, as if he'd worn a ring there until recently—a signet ring, perhaps?

She looked back up at him sharply. Aye, he had the look of quality—what with his angular cheekbones and the lofty look in his green eyes—and the airs, though he was a bloody sight more handsome than that nobleman she'd once caught a glimpse of as he'd exited his club.

Her gaze sharpened, too, as they stared at one another, and though something inside Anna screamed that she was mad, she found herself asking, "How much blunt?"

"Twenty pounds."

*Twenty pounds?*

"Of course, you shall not receive the coin until after my wager is won, but you have my word that you shall, indeed, receive such a reward."

*Twenty pounds!*

"One night," he said in a low voice, like a serpent come to Eve to tempt her with an apple. "Half a crown for your troubles, and another *twenty pounds* if that one night should turn into a month."

"One night," she found herself repeating back, though she hardly believed she might agree to such a thing.

"One night."

*Half a crown for her troubles.*

She needed that bloody half-crown. "One night only," she agreed, thinking she could be rid of him on the morrow. Surely nothing would happen in that short amount of time.

"Excellent," he said, and there came that feeling again. Gracious, she wished he wouldn't look at her like that. She knew the ways between a man and a woman, had prided herself on keeping free of entanglements. The last thing she needed was a bairn. But this man . . . she knew intuitively that this man might pose a threat to her.

"You shall not regret it," he added.

But Anna feared very much that she might.


Anna's misgivings only increased when she walked inside and spied the damage her grandfather's invention had done.

Blimey.

Like a riverbank clotted with debris after flood waters had receded, her grandfather's inventions dotted the carpet like uprooted shrubs. A few were either tipped back or covered with papers: the drawings her grandfather sketched in the middle of the night, the thick blots of ink—testament to his mad hurry to get the images down—strewn everywhere. Most of those sheets lay on the floor, or pressed against the sides of walls. Soot from the grate coated every surface, some of the smoke still hanging in the air, the light from the windows trying valiantly to punch its way through the dim gray fog.

Lord, it would take her days to clean up the mess.

She turned to tell Mr. Hemplewilt to tread carefully . . . and caught him staring at her backside. But instead of looking abashed at being caught doing such a thing, he gave her a slow, sexy smile that made Anna feel as if the white apron around her middle were suddenly jerked tight. Cad.

Her eyes narrowed as she turned away, spying her grandfather near a window. Dealing with Mr. Hemplewilt would have to wait.

"Where did he go?" her grandfather asked, his face and hair nearly as black as that chimney sweep who'd crouched over Mr. Hemplewilt earlier in the day, thanks to the ash from the grate. His white cravat had been powdered by the stuff, too, though his black jacket looked none the worse for wear.

"He was just here."

"Who, Grandfather?" But, of course, Anna knew exactly who'd gone missing. What was more, her grandfather didn't seem to notice he stood right behind her. Bother it all.

"That man," he said, looking as befuddled as a bird knocked from the sky. "I was demonstrating the Colossal Air Current Creator, only once the cataclysm hit, he disappeared. Poof. Gone." He stiffened, well, as much as he could with somewhat stooped shoulders. "Good lord, you don't think he's been blown out the door, do you?"

And his look of horror, quickly trailed by excited curiosity, had Anna saying, "He's right here," lest her grandfather begin a mad search of London's streets for one airborne gentleman. He'd gone that batty in recent years, Lord love him.

"Where?" he asked.

Anna turned to Mr. Hemplewilt, who stepped forward in the secondhand clothes that didn't quite conceal the gentleman beneath. "Here, sir," he said as he straightened. "Your granddaughter wanted a private moment with me."

Which made Elijah Brooks look between the two of them blankly. "You know Anna?" he asked.

"Yes, Grandfather, he does. Fact is, Mr. Hemplewilt here is going to take you down to the pumps to get you cleaned up."

"I am?" she heard a deep baritone ask.

"You are," she said, placing her hands on her hips, all but daring him with her eyes to contradict her. If he did, she would use it as an excuse to . . .

What?

God help her, she really could use the money he would bring them.

But that didn't mean she'd have to like it. And that was when she got her first inkling of what it would be like to live with a man who made her feel like butterflies kissed her skin. Who made waves rise within her, and naughty thoughts enter her head. She would be living with him for a night—she would allow him no more—but she had a feeling that was all a man of his ilk would need to charm the skirt off of her.

Her heart began to flutter like those butterflies were rushing at her ribs in panic.

So when he said, "As you wish," with an inclination of

his head that looked almost regal, she used it as an excuse
to turn away, remove her cloak as she did so and not look
up as she began to pick up the debris from the floor.
Under normal circumstances the state of the room would
fill her with exhaustion. So much to do. Always. Work,
work, work. But today she was so self-aware, so angry at
this latest turn of events, that she hardly paid attention.

"Come, Mr. Brooks," she heard Mr. Hemplewilt say.

"Come?" her grandfather said. "Do not tell me to
come, sir. I am no dog."

But with a soft, soothing voice—gentle, even—he
convinced her grandfather to follow him from the room.
And though she told herself not to look up, though she
told herself to concentrate on her task, Anna still
turned—still met Mr. Hemplewilt's gaze as he led her
grandfather out. Their eyes met, and for some silly reason
she blushed. He smiled. She blushed even more—*her,* a
woman who'd had her bubbies squeezed by passing ruf-
fians, who'd put up with every type of sordid comment
that came along with selling items at Covent Market, who
prided herself on the fact that she could mince bawdy
words with the best of them and never think twice. She
looked away, and when she reached for the next item on
the floor, she noticed her hands shook.

When Rein returned a half hour later, he felt as driven
to the edge of madness as Mr. Brooks apparently was.

Lord help him, the man was as crackers as old King
George.

"Why are you following me?" the daft fool asked,
turning back to him.

Rein thought about explaining to him—yet again—

that Anna had sent him along to help, but a half hour of having his hands batted away, his ears blasted and his legitimacy questioned at every turn had given him a headache, and so he said nothing as the man turned back to their front door, opened it and stepped inside.

He went right to a draped-off corner of the room, shoved aside the edges of the curtain, turned and jerked it closed.

"Don't just stand there, close the door."

Anna Brooks stood by the hearth, cooking, the smell of stew filling the air. Rein's stomach grumbled.

As if hearing the rumble—and perhaps she did—she narrowed her eyes. "Don't expect meals to go along with your lodging. I've enough to do around here as it is."

He would bet she did, he thought, studying her. And yet even with exhaustion pouring from her eyes, she still looked lovely. Her hair hung loose and down her back, the mermaid strands of flaxen hair curling around her head. And those eyes. Would he ever get used to her eyes? Those amber gems sparkled at him, flashing in anger and exasperation.

"Well, are you coming in?"

He stepped inside, saying, "Thank you, I believe I shall."

"Close the door," she ordered.

He stopped. Oh, yes, of course. "I'm—" He caught himself just in time. *Used to others closing doors for me.* "Grateful to you for letting me stay," he finished, turning back to her.

"Yes, well, I still might change my mind," she said, waving that spoon of hers like she was tempted to bash him over the head. He lifted a hand to the spot on his forehead, wincing. Not again.

She pursed her lips before going back to cooking. Rein looked around. Debris still littered the floor—not as much of it as before, she must have picked up a bit, but enough that it still looked like the aftereffects of a storm.

"Your grandfather should work for the government. The war department would pay good money to unleash his invention on the French."

"You might have a point," he thought he heard her mutter. When she glanced back at him, she looked rather waiflike all of a sudden. So solemn and despondent. She had the sadness of a thousand lost souls in her eyes and the wisdom of one twice her age if he didn't miss his guess. "I suppose we ought not to look a gift horse in the mouth."

He assumed *he* was said gift horse.

"But you'll have to sleep on the floor," she said after a sudden frown was shaken off her face. Well, it didn't disappear entirely. Like an ink spot, it clung to her cheeks and the brackets around her mouth.

And then what she'd said sank in.

"*Sleep on the floor?*" he repeated, aghast. Why, it looked like the bottom of an ash bin. Come to think of it, the whole place looked like an ash bin.

"You have a better idea?"

Well, yes, come to think of it, he did, but he didn't think she'd appreciate his idea of sleeping with her.

"Sleep in the chair if you don't wish to be on the floor."

A chair? He likely hadn't slept in a chair since his wet nurse had held her in his arms. What could she be thinking?

He was a duke. He almost opened his mouth to tell her so, but stopped himself just in time. Lord, that deplorable will. *Ballocks, ballocks, ballocks.*

"The chair, if I must."

"You must," she said, turning back to her stew. Rein's gaze fell to her rear, those sleeping arrangements he'd thought of a moment ago charging back to his mind like a herd of cavalrymen, swords drawn and flags waving, except the sword in this instance was between his legs.

"Here," she said, then walked over to a chest snuggled against one of the few walls left uncluttered by shelves and opened it. When she turned, she seemed to give him a wide berth, going around that odd table with the ladder attached to its side before turning toward the uncomfortable armchair he'd been seated in earlier. "Let me show you how it works."

It took a few blinks to get his eyes unstuck. "Work the chair?"

"'Tis tricky."

Lord, was she communicating with the spirit of his deceased father? He wasn't that slow. "I believe even I can operate a chair."

With the practiced motion of one who'd done a lot of cleaning, she flicked what looked to be a rag—an old shirt, in this instance—over the chair. A cloud of dust rose around her. Coughing a bit, she bent down and fiddled with something on the side of the chair. Rein wished for a moment that the dress she wore was low-cut—alas, it was not. Her lovely hair shifted over one shoulder rather fetchingly.

Clank.

The back of the chair reclined.

His startled eyes moved to the chair as next she pulled something out from beneath the seat. It was a cleverly concealed board that lengthened to serve as a leg rest.

Why, she'd converted it into a bed of sorts. "How utterly clever."

"It is, rather," she said, straightening. "One of my grandfather's better inventions. Go ahead. Try it."

Rein moved forward, utterly enchanted. It was a sign of his delight that he didn't even notice the filth—well, not much, anyway. And then he was sighing as the previously uncomfortable armchair, the one with a seat as hard as his cousin Alex's head, turned into a plush and unbelievably comfortable bed.

"There's just one problem," she said as he leaned back.

*Blam.*

That was the sound the chair made as it fell backward, Rein suddenly given a rather unexpected and close-up view of the wall behind the chair. "Devil take it," he exclaimed, his hand lifting to his head, which suddenly ached again due, no doubt, to the sudden loss of altitude.

"It has a tendency to do that."

Just then the leg board slid back, and Rein's legs bent horizontally as it did so.

"And that," she said.

And as Rein looked up at her from his position as the human Z, he realized she'd known he would end up in such a position. What's more, she relished seeing him thus. He could see it in the way her lips stretched and flexed as they tried not to smile. Her eyes twitched and twinkled and very obviously tried not to scream the word, *Ha.*

Why, that little minx.

"I think I damaged my head again."

"That I sincerely doubt. However, there's a pickled brain in brine water over there. You're welcome to have it, since I fear you need it more than the jar."

And that was when he found himself on the verge of laughing, and filled with a sincere admiration for her cleverness in getting even with him for hoodwinking her grandfather into allowing him to stay. But most of all, that was when Rein decided he would have Miss Anna Brooks one day soon. One day *very* soon.

# Chapter Five

Anna decided to avoid him. Only that was impossible to do when the man one tries to avoid is up the next morning looking as fresh-faced and handsome as the portraits of noblemen she'd seen in an artist's shop down on Bond Street.

"I have decided to help you at market this day."

He'd decided to do what?

She looked past him, out the windows behind the brown chair he'd slept in last night. The sun had yet to rise, and Anna had supposed he'd be asleep. Alas, he must have heard her getting dressed, for he even had his brown jacket on, the worn and battered boots he'd traded for those shiny black beauties he'd been wearing yesterday looking too big for him.

"What do you mean, help?"

"Well. Since you seem to be rather busy, I thought I might help you sell your wares, whatever those might be."

Sell her wares? "Are you daft?"

"At times, yes, but I believe today's idea falls under the wanting-to-earn-my-keep category."

She lifted a brow. He wanted to earn his keep, did he, now? Well, he'd have to work hard to do that. Truth be told, she'd promised herself that she'd give him the boot this morning.

*Twenty pounds.*

Yes, well, twenty pounds didn't change the fact that he made her feel things she knew she ought not to feel for a man who was all but a stranger.

*And if you do not win the competition . . .*

She *would* win the naval competition.

*And today is the day you retrieve the material for your sails.*

Oh, bugger it. This was exactly the reason she should tell him to go. He made her normally logical brain think illogical thoughts.

"You'll only get in the way."

"Not if you tell me what to do."

"I'll tell you what you should do. Leave."

"Leave?" He looked aghast.

"Aye. For in thinking on it, I've no notion if you're even worth twenty pounds."

He straightened. "I assure you, I am."

Was he? If his clothes were any indication, he was. She shook her head. "No. I want you gone by the time I return."

He looked thunderstruck. "You are passing up the opportunity to earn twenty pounds?"

"I am passing on the opportunity to have a strange man, one whom I know nothing about, live with us." And with that, she turned, hoping he would leave her be and simply do as she asked.

He didn't. Indeed, what he did was follow her. Anna felt her ire increase. She felt something else, too. His nearness made her aware of how much bigger he was than her, the masculine smell of him drifting down to fill her nose and making her aware that she was all but alone with him, her grandfather asleep on the other side of the curtained-off wall.

"I beg you, Miss Brooks. Do not turn me out on the streets. Alone, penniless, with no place to go."

And something about that voice, about the utter desperation she heard in it, made her turn, made her glance up at him.

"I am not at all accustomed to begging for charity, but I shall do whatever it takes to gain yours. My head still aches, my memory is still faulty, I have no notion of where to go or what to do. You are all I have, Miss Brooks. Do not turn me out."

Green eyes, as green as the fields she could see from her rooftop when the skies were clear, stared down at her with such an intensity she heard herself swallow.

"Please," he added.

*Handsome* didn't begin to describe him. All night long she'd thought about him, thought about the way just looking at him made her feel—edgy, uncomfortable, curious. What worried her most was she didn't have time to be curious about a man.

"If you do not want the twenty pounds then at least let me stay until I've regained my health. I shall pay you the rest of the coin I have."

No. She shouldn't.

"Please," he said again.

And something within Anna stirred. A memory, one of coming to this place and feeling just as afraid, just as alone.

*Don't do it, Anna. Don't give in.*

"One more night," she said, silently cursing herself for being so soft.

He looked so relieved, so thankful, Anna took a step back for fear he might kiss her.

Her heart began to somersault in her chest at the thought.

If a man like him kissed her . . .

*You'd what, Anna?*

She didn't know, and she didn't want to find out. And therein lay the crux of the problem. By inviting him to stay for one more night, she opened herself up to more silly fantasies of being carted off to a new life by a man with princely good looks. They were fantasies she hadn't had since she was a girl.

"One night," she repeated, as she turned away and opened the door at the same time she grabbed her cloak.

"One night," he said back.

She didn't turn, just kept her hand on the door, flicking her cloak around her when she was on the other side. Lord, why had she done it? Why hadn't she just held firm and told him to leave?

*Because you've never, not once, had a man ask you for something.* Because he hadn't demanded, nor threatened, nor gotten angry. Because he appeared to be in genuine need, and Anna Brooks understood all too well what that felt like.

All too well, indeed.

*　　*　　*

But if she thought she'd escaped him, she should have known otherwise. As she exited the alley that ran between her building and the next—her barrow pushed out in front of her—she was startled nearly out from under her straw hat when a tall form materialized by her side.

He'd followed her down.

"Goodness," she cried, dropping the handles of her barrow, the utensils she sold at market tinking as she dropped her end. "You scared ten years off my life."

"Beg your pardon," he said, the early morning light casting a gray pall over everything, including her.

She took deep breaths, feeling more out of sorts than she ought for being merely startled. "What do you want?"

For a moment his eyes heated, and Anna thought he meant to say something other than what he said.

"I told you abovestairs. I intend to help you sell your wares today." He glanced into her barrow. "Whatever those wares might be."

She felt a rush of air leave her as she huffed in disbelief. "Help me? Don't be daft."

The look in his eyes faded. He lifted a brow, a habit of his she'd begun to notice. "I didn't realize that a cloud of uselessness hung over me."

That made her feel instantly contrite. Gads, she'd turned into a shrew. "'Tis not that I don't think you'd be useful," she said, scrambling for a way to soften her words. "'Tis that you're, you're . . ."

*Aristocratic. Handsome. Out of place.*

"You don't look like a market maid," she said.

*Silly, silly, silly thing to say.*

His brows lowered, and yes, that was a smile that came to his lips. "Ah. I see. I don't believe I've ever had any complaints that I'm the wrong sex before."

She crossed her arms in front of her, feeling mortified by her own ridiculous words and suddenly uncomfortable at the way he looked at her.

Was that a flirtatious glimmer in his eyes? She could swear it was.

She shook her head, turned away. "I don't have time to waste," she said, picking up the handles of her barrow and pushing off, the metal tools protesting her rough handling by jangling loudly. "Follow me if you want, just stay out of my way."

He didn't reply, and Anna had to glance out of the corner of her eye to discover he had, indeed, followed her.

Blimey.

She navigated the piles of refuse that sprouted up at odd intervals along the walkway, her nose wrinkling as she passed beneath windowed buildings that housed family after family, sometimes two or three to a room.

"I believe my boots are too big," she heard him murmur, and when she darted another glace at him, it was to see him looking down woefully. "I am getting a blister on the back of my heel."

"Welcome to life as one of the lower orders."

He looked over at her, then around, seeming to limp a bit. "Where is everyone going?"

He must be from wealth, indeed, if he didn't know that. "To work, gov, some returning from a late night, others out to find employment."

She saw his eyes settle on a woman with two babes at her feet, their bedraggled appearance revealing their poverty, saw the look in his face turn to one of dismay as he turned away, his gaze falling on the dismal facade of the two- and three-story buildings they passed.

"I never realized."

She knew what he meant. "No?" she said as a cart with a huge draft horse jangled by. "Then you're a lucky cull. This is the good part of the rookery."

He glanced over at her then, his green eyes staring at her in a way he'd never looked before. It was as if he'd rubbed at a piece of glass with his sleeve, his expression turning to one of puzzled curiosity as he looked through it.

"You weren't born here, were you?"

"I told you yesterday that I wasn't."

"Yes, but I suppose I didn't really believe . . ."

Believe what? That she could be reduced to such straits?

She took a firmer grip on her barrow and sped up a bit. "Mr. Hemplewilt, I'd like to get myself to market. I'm late and conversation slows me down."

With that, she sped up even more, expertly weaving her way through pedestrians and carts that choked up like mud through the neck of a bottle the closer they got to Covent Garden. And as the number of people increased, so, too, did the number and quality of the buildings and shops they passed. With each step they took, they cast off the dirt and grime of the rookery and took on the mantle of London's premium market. When they neared the wide-open square of Covent Garden, she slowed at last.

"Mornin', Anna," the rose trader said.

"Roses," she heard Mr. Hemplewilt say, the clomping steps of his too-large boots on the stone covered ground slowing.

Anna kept on going. Maybe she'd lose him among the barrows and stalls—some permanent, others not so permanent stalls that made the market resemble a busy anthill, people already milling about as they shopped for their wealthy masters, or sometimes themselves.

She was looking for Molly, her best chum. The two of them normally walked to market together and then sold their wares side by side. But her friend had had to leave early this morning to purchase her oranges, so when Anna went to her usual spot, Molly was already there.

"You're late," Molly said, a large wicker basket of oranges at her feet, her pretty face and wide blue eyes shielded by a straw hat that matched Anna's, except hers had a blue ribbon that tied beneath her chin.

"I have reason," Anna said, looking back in the direction she'd come, the smell of flowers and citrus and vegetables mixing into a familiar smell both pungent and sweet. Sure enough, Mr. Hemplewilt made his way toward them, though he was a good twenty paces behind.

"Is that him?" Molly asked, looking at Mr. Hemplewilt as if he were the Holy Grail. "The man what you clouted with your sail yesterday?"

"It's him," Anna said, positioning her barrow next to Molly's.

Molly looked delighted. "I thought you said he was only staying the day,"

"He stayed the night."

"Did he, now?" Molly said suggestively, her brown brows wiggling.

"It's not what you think," Anna said, feeling her cheeks color yet again. Blast it all.

"Are you certain?"

"I'm certain."

"And who is this pretty lady?" Mr. Hemplewilt asked as he stopped before Anna and Molly.

"This is my friend Molly Washburn," Anna said.

Rein stopped before her, taking her hand and lifting it to his lips.

Anna bristled.

"Charmed," he said in a silky voice.

Every market maid in the square looked at them, from the flowermongers across from her barrow, to the coster-mongers behind and to the right side of her. Anna felt the urge to turn away. So she did, pulling out her knives and peelers and mashers and other items she sold. She had the end space down a long aisle just so she could hang the things off the narrow walls of her barrow.

"Ah," she heard a masculine voice say. "They're uten-sils."

"What did you think they were?" she asked without looking at him, feeling . . . very well, she could admit it, she felt piqued that he'd kissed Molly's hand.

Gads, she was dicked in the knob for certain.

"I thought they were weapons."

She turned to him.

"Weapons?"

He smiled. Her heart stopped. Lord help her, with the sun just breaking the plains of the buildings, his eyes looked even more breathtaking, especially with a twinkle in them, one enhanced by the rays of light that turned the gray buildings and square around them a yellow-gold.

"Indeed. Something to toss at the poor blokes over-come by your beauty."

*Her beauty.*

She looked away, telling herself to stop being so silly. Men had been calling her pretty since her first days at market. The trick was not to let it affect her.

But it felt different when Mr. Hemplewilt thought her beautiful. He wasn't like the dirty, unkempt blokes what usually tried to get under her skirts and squeeze her bubbies, that was for sure.

"I sell the tools that help people prepare the vegetables they buy here at the market," she explained without looking at him, her hands shaking for some reason.

"Do you?" he asked.

She nodded.

"Well, then, I shall help you peddle them."

Anna turned, her eyes narrowing. Molly stood behind Mr. Hemplewilt. Her friend had grabbed two of her oranges, and now held them at the apex of her thighs with a suggestive look.

*Molly,* Anna silently admonished. A further glance around revealed several of the other women in the market laughing. Lord, they'd never let her forget this day.

"Mr. Hemplewilt, if you want to help me, you'll do so by staying out of my way."

The oranges had moved up to her friend's breast, Molly wiggling her brows.

"I'm afraid I can't do that," Mr. Hemplewilt said.

The oranges moved up to her eyes, her friend moving her head up and down as if eyeing him or, more specifically, his bum.

"Molly, you have a customer," Anna said, her friend whirling about. She did, indeed, have a customer, a male, one who held out his hands with a wide smile and said, "I'll take those."

# Chapter Six

"I say, my good man," Rein said, turning to Molly's customer. He reached into her barrow and pulled out . . . something. "Would you like to purchase a . . ." Rein glanced at the tool. "A thing to go with those oranges?"

"Mr. Hemplewilt," he heard Anna hiss.

"No thanks, gov, I just want me some oranges." The man looked over at Molly and leered.

Rein frowned, lowering whatever it was he held. But when the man turned to Anna after paying for the oranges and leered, too, Rein straightened. "Well, then, since your transaction appears to be complete, I'll thank you to stop looking at Miss Washburn like that," said the king of flirtatious smiles and suggestive looks.

But that didn't count.

The man looked up at him—yes, up, Rein having the advantage of a good foot and years of experience in staring down at a foe.

"She started it," the man said.

Rein took a step forward. "Away," he ordered, pointing. He heard a sigh—several of them, actually—and turned. Three flower girls across the aisle were huddled together, the fresh faces smiling at him as if he'd just stormed a castle and offered them the keys.

He pulled his shoulders back. Well, now, that was more like it.

"Lord help me," he heard Anna murmur. "By day's end they'll all be clamoring for his name."

Rein turned, feeling a pleased smile come over his face. "There is only one lady whom I should like to know my name."

Was that a blush he saw? He couldn't tell, for she tipped that hat of hers down, fumbling with her utensils as she did so.

A glance at her friend Molly revealed an encouraging nod, her brows wiggling in silent approval.

Rein decided then and there that he rather liked Anna's friend.

But Anna looked up right then, saw the look they exchanged and narrowed her eyes. "Mr. Hemplewilt, if you'd like to help Molly sell her wares, by all means then help her. Leave me be."

"Anna—" her friend said.

"I don't need your help selling mine."

And hearing those words, coming as they did on the heels of what could only be described as a jealous look, made Rein feel even better. Excellent. She was starting to like him, only she didn't want to admit it.

"Ah," he said, his eyes heating as they observed how pretty she looked, yes, even in that worn out and bedraggled straw hat. "I could be of service. If you'd let me."

She narrowed her eyes again. "No."

And that was the problem with Anna Brooks: His normal mode of seduction did not appear to work. Ballocks. He removed the teasing smile and said, "Not even if you have something to gain by allowing me to do so?"

Her expression didn't change. "I shall leave," he said, nodding to go along with his words, liking his spur-of-the-moment idea. "On one condition."

No change in her expression. Stubborn chit.

"You allow me to help sell your wares for one hour's time, after which we shall take a tally. The person who has sold the most things"—he waved toward her barrow—"wins."

"Done," she said, so obviously convinced of his failure that she didn't even appear to consider that he might give her some competition. Lord, it amazed him how much that stung.

This time it was his turn to narrow his eyes. Picking up the first utensil he felt in her barrow, a sort of bowl-shaped thing with holes in it, he turned and faced the crowd. That number of people had grown in the few minutes they'd been in the square. Rein was surprised to see so many people out and about at such an early hour. Did none of them attend parties? As he eyed the men and women who could only be termed the serving class, he supposed not.

"Peeler for your vegetables," Anna cried out, startling Rein, who turned and looked at her askance. Within ten seconds she had a buyer, a man whom Rein was convinced was more interested in peering down her dress than the utensil she sold.

"A . . . thing for your . . . things," Rein called out.

He heard Molly snort, turned to her with a lift of his brow. He'd get no help from Anna.

"It's a sieve," she explained.

"Molly," Anna accused. "Do not help him."

"Can't help it. My sense of fair play," she said, turning to peddle her own wares.

Thus ensued a battle of the voice, Rein and Anna crying out to attract potential customers, but it quickly became apparent that Anna had the advantage. And why wouldn't she? Rein thought. She'd years of experience over him, her savvy eyes picking out the most obvious customer—usually men—her tone and voice and manners suggesting that her inventions would do a lot more than help a person to cook.

Rein seethed.

Seethed until the moment he was struck by an idea. Excusing himself from Anna, who didn't even deign to look up as he left, he used the coin he promised to Anna to buy a potato, going back to Anna's barrow and selecting one of her vegetable peelers, something that seemed to sell well. He would find another way to pay her, perhaps by performing at that theater he'd seen advertised for playactors.

She lifted a brow, pausing from her song for a moment to watch as he lifted the vegetable. Rein ignored her, searching the crowd to find the most likely target in the growing throng. When he'd done so, selecting a portly man with chubby cheeks and smile lines near his eyes, Rein lifted the peeler, took aim, and let fly.

A sliver of skin landed on the cheek of his target.

"What the devil?" the man said, turning toward Rein.

He heard Molly laugh. Rein stepped forward to say, "And that, my good man, is only a glimpse of what this device can do." He closed the distance between him and his subject, slicing at the potato like a beaver did a log.

"A bargain at four pence," he said with a smile, doubling Anna's price, for there was one thing Rein knew how to do—a thing that every member of the *ton* could do—size up a man's worth by the cut and quality of his clothes. He judged this man to be an upper servant of some sort, perhaps even a butler. "Only think of how much time your cooks will save."

The man eyed Rein askance. But then his gaze caught on the slivers on the ground. He looked back up. "Four pence?" he said.

Rein felt hope, nodded.

"Done," the man said, digging into his black jacket.

Rein's smile could no doubt be seen across the square.

"You lying cheat," Anna said as the man walked away.

"Yes," Rein said with a smile. "Isn't it lovely?"

Her lips pressed together, her eyes narrowing until they were nearly shut beneath the brim of her hat.

He used his profit to buy a head of lettuce next. Anna eyed him once more when he stopped by the permanent stall of an apple merchant and asked to borrow three of the man's crates. The long-whiskered man agreed, and Rein took the crates to his spot near Anna. Next he took a wicked-looking knife off one the pegs on the Anna's cart, retrieved the head of lettuce and placed it on the top of crate.

He waited.

Anna waited, too. He could tell that she was sneaking glances at him, her cries to the crowd rising and falling as she turned, walked a few paces and then turned back.

Rein lifted the knife.

Anna snuck another glance at him, brows scrunching together in a frown.

When a sufficiently large group of people walked by, Rein brought the knife down with enough force to shower lettuce pieces through the air.

"Bloody hell," Anna cried.

Rein smiled at the startled crowd. "If you think that is amazing, just envision what it would do to a side of beef."

Everyone but a woman looked away. Rein came around the side of his crates, going over to her holding out the knife. "See, not a nick in the edge. Truly an amazing device," he said with a smile normally used for the women of his social set, the ones he wanted to bed.

"How much is it?" the woman asked, thrusting her gaze down.

"For you," he said, "a special price."

The woman giggled, and without asking what that price was, opened up her reticule.

Rein wanted to throw back his head and laugh. He was doing it. Not only that, but he was bloody good at it, and earning more money than Anna. When he glanced at Anna, it was to see her staring at him with her hands on her hips. He had to give her credit, for she didn't give up. No, indeed, what she did surprised him, for she went and bought her own head of lettuce, only she chose to behead hers in midair, one of the two halves landing at the feet of a bloke whom she smiled at winsomely. She sold the knife for more than Rein had sold his.

Thus began a competition the likes of which Covent Garden Market had never seen. Many a good head of lettuce went to the guillotine that day, the area around

Anna's barrow looking like a produce cart caught in an accident. But Rein had an advantage that Anna did not. Most patrons were women and Rein had no compunction about using the skills he'd acquired in ballrooms to charm the coins out of a lady's purse.

Thus, at the end of the hour, Rein had won, not only that but he had sufficient profit to pay off Anna. Anna knew it, Rein could tell, for she shot him a glare when a nearby clock tower chimed the hour.

"Cheat," she said, standing among lettuce entrails as if it were a park and not the remnants of their war.

"Mimic," he answered back.

"You left me with no choice."

"You were afeared of losing," he offered as the true explanation.

But rather than deny it, rather than look away, Anna said, "I was." And then she did something else that surprised him. To Rein's utter delight, he gave him a brief smile, just a small one, but one filled with grudging admiration.

"You can stay," she said.

And he did. The whole day. And at the end of it, Anna had to admit that she liked Rein Hemplewilt. She truly liked him. Perhaps it was the way he'd come to Molly's defense. Maybe it was the way he'd been so determined to help. But whatever the reason, as she prepared herself for bed that eve, she admitted he was quite a bonny man.

That worried her. That worried her a great deal.

With a sigh, she sat down on her bed, tilting her head back and stretching her spine. She had so much work to do, and the last thing she needed was a man to complicate matters. In the corner of her room lay her life's work—well, what would become her life's work. Material for her sails. A pile of fabric she'd scrimped and saved to buy, having spent every last farthing on the extravagant purchase. She needed to convert that material into the triangular design she'd invented. And she needed to do so in time to test the real sails on a ship—for the smaller version sail—her "kite"—needed to be enlarged in order to see if it would work.

But she refused to think of that. Or Mr. Hemplewilt. She stood up. Well, stood up as much as she could in her little attic room, removing her white cotton apron as she did so. The ceiling sloped down on either side of her. But the room was warm and hospitable, the bones of the walls exposed without any boards to cover them. She'd made it her own in recent years, covering the tiny little windows with scraps of material she'd bought from the rag man. Her "drapes" were colorful; like an artist's palette tipped on its side so that the colors ran together. She'd done the same for a bedcover, painstakingly sewing together pieces of red and blue and yellow fabric until she had a quilt of sorts, one tiny square that she prized above all others made of velvet. She grabbed that quilt now and headed out the tiny door nestled beneath the V of the rafters.

Tiny droplets of moisture did battle with warmer air currents from the attic as she slid beneath a dusk sky, fog having rolled in early that afternoon, as so often happened in London. The exit to the attic wasn't really a door, but more of a hatch that dropped down. She had to slide her legs through first, then her body. For a second she dangled her brown skirts before she dropped with a thud and a crunch of dried leaves beneath her bare feet. It always amazed her how leaves got all the way up to the third story roof.

She'd discovered her hidden world when she was twelve, though at first she'd hoped the hatch would lead to a storybook kingdom, a land that might take her away from the drudgery of her life. Unfortunately, it hadn't. Fortunately, she'd found a private haven. On the right day, a body could see clear to the green edges of London. On an evening like tonight, however, fog pressed down and kept sound from escaping. It would be dark before its time, the sun descending behind the rookery with a last gasp of color. Down below, a coal porter sang his song, carts and carriages sloshing and clanking through the mud and muck; like a well-made timepiece, London never stopped.

She settled herself on the bench she'd made out of scraps of wood as one of the many chimney plumes that sprouted up like mushroom caps from the tar and gravel roof spilled a murky black smoke that didn't have the energy to climb. She sat near enough to the edge of the roof that if she craned her neck just right, she could watch all that smoke fall, swirling and spiraling on its way to pollute the street below. But she didn't. Instead she lifted her feet onto the bench, throwing the cover around her shoulders and resting her elbows on her knees as she tried to summon the energy to get started on her sails, and to forget about Mr. Hemplewilt.

"Miss Brooks."

Anna screamed. And for a moment silence reigned over St. Giles. Or so it seemed.

"I beg your pardon. I did not mean to startle you."

She turned on her bench. "What the blazes are you doin' up here?" The blanket she clutched around her neck slipped a bit. Anna jerked it back up.

"I came to ask of supper."

"There's a pot of stew on the hearth just like there is every night."

"Is there?" he asked, and the look in his eyes, the way they seemed to turn darker—though how that could be when nothing but a dismal evening sky shone down on them, Anna didn't know—made her wonder if perhaps he felt the same sort of pull, the same current of energy that she'd felt for him all afternoon.

"There is," she said.

*Leave, leave, leave.*

But he didn't, just continued to stare down at her in a way that made her heart beat harder with each passing second.

"I had a splendid time at market today."

"Oh, aye, it's a jolly parcel of fun to stand on your feet day in, day out."

He frowned. She realized she was being too contrary. He'd helped her double her profits this day. She should be polite.

"Is that your room I just came through?" he asked.

"It is," she answered, suddenly as jumpy as a flea on the alley cat she'd befriended down below.

Silence, Anna mentally asking him to leave, her hands clutching her coverlet so tight, she felt the fabric digging into her palms.

"My, that's a long way down," he said, very obvious attempt at conversation.

"Mr. Hemplewilt—"

"One moment, please, Anna. I am observing the view."

Anna.

He'd called her Anna.

She opened her mouth to rebuke him, but he'd moved forward, and as he stood there at the edge of the roof, looking over all of London, Anna was reminded of a feudal lord of old, one that perused his kingdom as he clasped his hands behind his back. Arrogant. Powerful. Lordly.

And masculine.

That was part of what drew her, she admitted. She liked the authority he resonated, and that he seemed to want to use that authority on her.

"If you don't mind, I'd like some privacy," she forced herself to say.

*Go, go, go,* she silently begged. He made her think of things, made her recall a life long past, fantasies long suppressed, of knights in shining armor and handsome princes come to carry her off.

He turned away, his silhouette framed by a gray sky.

"I am not going until you tell me what that mound of fabric is that lounges in the corner of your room."

She toyed with getting up and leaving herself, only she felt somehow safer sitting upon the bench, the blanket wrapped around her.

*A hand reaching out to stop her, one that spun her around so he could kiss her.*

The image tossed itself so quickly into her mind she found herself saying, "It's for my sails," just to cover the way her body throbbed in reaction to the fantasy of his lips moving down to cover her own.

"Sails?"

"Aye," she admitted, having to swallow once before her voice box would work.

"Sails for a ship?"

"Yes," she said impatiently, though it was an impatience for herself, not him. She looked away. The sun had fallen down low enough so that it slipped its scarlet rays into the layer of fog and smoke that covered London, turning it fuchsia. She inhaled deeply and pulled the blanket tighter, almost as if it could shield her from him.

"And are sails something else that you sell at the market upon occasion?"

"Mr. Hemplewilt, I would like some privacy," she said again.

"Not until you answer my question."

And there it was again. That autocratic tone. Her name on his lips, as if he often said and did what he wanted.

*Anna.*

Her name sounded so different than the way the culls in the rookery said it. Soft, like the notes of one of those fine instruments she'd heard when she'd been lost years ago and found herself in a toff's neighborhood far, far away.

"Please don't call me that."

"Call you what?"

"Anna," she said, and as Rein stared at her, she shifted that worn and ragged bedspread around her so that it drooped a bit over her shoulders, her knees drawn up so that her work-worn half boots rested on the bench. Lord, when he'd first seen her sitting on her bench, her hair loose and down her back, wide eyes gazing out at London's landscape, he'd had to stop for a moment

Stunning.

Beautiful.

*Perfect.*

There had been a moment then when he'd found himself wishing she wasn't a market maid. When he'd wished, instead, that she had a different vocation, one that would allow him to simply take her work-worn hand, lead her to bed, and take her.

God, how he suddenly wanted to take her.

Instead he found himself acting polite, for if he did not, he might ruin his chance at residing with her and her grandfather for the next few weeks, thereby forcing him onto the streets.

And so he said, "Very well, Miss Brooks, but you still haven't answered my question."

She looked like she wouldn't answer. He even saw her sneak a glance at the trapdoor he'd squeezed through earlier.

"There is a competition being held in three weeks' time, one sponsored by the Navy. I plan to enter my sails."

"A competition? Sails?"

"Aye," she said with a nod, her hair rustling over that ridiculous cover of hers. "The Navy is trying to improve the speed of their ships. They've announced a one-hundred-pound reward for the person who can do that."

He stiffened, for the sudden memory returned, of stepping out of the carriage, looking up and seeing a triangular shape fall toward him like a comet from the sky. "Good lord. The kite."

She nodded. "Aye. It's a smaller scale version of my design."

He'd wondered why she'd been flying such a childish toy. Now he knew.

*Egads, not just beautiful. Brilliant.*

And for a moment, envy filled him, but he quickly covered it up by saying, "I am most impressed."

"Thank you," she said, standing suddenly. "I have work to do," she said, looking away and stepping past him.

He caught her elbow as she went by, his hand sliding down her arm until it reached her fingers.

She gasped, staring at their connection for a moment before looking up to say, "Unhand me."

Rein immediately let her go, though not because of the steel he saw in her eyes, but because as he'd touched her, he'd suddenly realized that he shouldn't have done so, for to touch her felt . . . dangerous.

*Dangerous?*

"Beg your pardon," he said.

"Don't come up here again," she said. "I have few pleasures in my life and my privacy is one of them."

And with that she jerked her head up and turned, leaving the roof without a backward glance. Rein watched her go, motionless, thinking he must be afraid to touch her for fear she might order him to leave her home, and then what would he do? That must be what concerned him, for it certainly couldn't be her.

Could it?

# Chapter Seven

*He'd touched her hand.*

It was the first thought on Anna's mind when she awoke the next morning.

He'd touched her. Her worn and battered hands . . . and he'd not flinched at their coarseness.

*Ach, you'll not be thinkin' of that again.*

And she wouldn't, she vowed. She wouldn't think about how his hand had felt so soft against her own flesh. Or how embarrassed she was about her dry, red—and, yes, blistered—fingers. About how she'd wished for a second, as his handsome, noble face had stared down at her so enigmatically, that she'd taken the time to rub fish oil on her palms.

*Silly, silly, silly,* she thought as she pulled on the white apron that covered the skirts of her brown dress. *Fish oil won't erase what you are. A woman what uses her hands for a living.*

She tied her white apron around her waist and then shoved a battered and worn straw hat atop her head. The ribbon beneath her chin looked frayed, Anna suddenly noticing the disrepair the lace around her dress's collar was in, too. Bloody hell, what a sorry state she'd been reduced to.

So far away from a world of balls and castles.

"I often wondered," her best mate Molly said from behind her as they headed for the market that morning, the two of them taking turns trailing each other through the busy streets like ducks on a pond, "what type of man it'd take to get your attention."

"Molly, if you don't stop badgering me I'll clout you with a masher."

"Mornin', ladies," Bertie the tobacco seller said as they passed by his shop, the gray-haired old gent giving them a tobacco-stained smile. This part of town was filled with storefronts, and Anna and Molly sometimes entertained themselves by staring into the windows of them. Fine hats, premade dresses and shoes were sold. The lovely, soft shoes Anna swore one day she'd have made for herself. But today it was too cold to do much more than hurry toward Covent Garden Market, Anna certain it would rain before the sun fell behind the ocean.

"Evenin'," they called back over the sound of the dustman's cries. But the minute they passed him, Molly hurried alongside Anna. Molly didn't have a cart, Anna listened to the whiz of her barrow's wheel as it passed over sucking muck, she rather envied her friend.

"Charlotte said she saw 'im the first day he arrived," she said with a twinkle in her green eyes. "Told me he'd had a jacket as fine as spun silk. Is that true?"

The jacket *had* been made of silk, Anna thought as they passed between the three- and four-story buildings, not that Molly would know. Molly was what Anna would call local—London bred and born, something Anna envied. It was easier not to covet luxuries if you'd never had them before.

"'E's as handsome as he is arrogant, and the only reason why he's in St. Giles is to win a wager. To my way of thinking that makes him a sapskull, and you know how I feel about sapskulls."

"He *is* handsome," Molly said in a matter-of-fact, this-is-bloody-fabulous tone of voice, brown ringlets bobbing as she tipped her head back and smiled. "Did you kiss him after you got home from market?"

Anna took a firmer grip on the work-worn handles of her barrow, ostensibly to push her way through the thick mud, but in reality to get ahead of her friend.

"Does he make your crinkum-crankum heat like a—"

"Molly," Anna hissed, tipping her head so that her hat would shield her cheeks so that Molly wouldn't see them color.

"He does, doesn't he?"

No answer.

"You're as hot for him as a bed brick, ain't ya?"

Anna refused to speak.

Molly went silent, too, as they worked their way through the crowd, pausing for a moment when a marble shot out in front of them just as they crossed near an alley. A boy of about ten darted out to catch it, fetching the glass ball with a nod of thanks for stopping.

"So it's happened to you at last," she heard Molly plainly over the *zzzzz* of a passing carriage's wheels to her left, a fat drop of rain landing on the brim of her hat.

"Raining," Anna said.

"Don't change the subject."

Anna pressed her lips together in irritation.

"You've finally found you a man what's tempting you to bread and butter."

Anna stopped suddenly. "I just met him, Molls."

"Does that matter?"

"Yes."

*Liar, liar, liar.*

Molly smiled like a cat that just finished eating a bowl of fish. "If you weren't burnin' for him, you wouldn't 'ave skulked out of your rooms this morn to avoid waking him."

"Not true."

"It is. You didn't want him with you today for fear of the heat he'd stir in you."

"You make me sound like a fireplace grate."

"Then why you denying everythin' I say?"

"Because I'm in a hurry and talking slows me down."

"Liar," Molly repeated.

And she was. She knew it. She just didn't know what to do about it.

He didn't show up at the market, even though she'd looked for him all day.

*Fool.*

She'd looked and he hadn't come and that should have filled her with relief, not annoyance. And yet, she couldn't deny the way she felt.

Which was why when she opened the door later that evening she told herself she would not react to his presence . . . if he was still there. Not only that, but she would ask him to leave the moment she saw him.

"Bloody hell," she cursed, observing the mess that

greeted her. After all her hard work cleaning up last time, her grandfather must have activated the Colossal again. Lord, she wished she could come home just once and not work more hours. Just once.

"Anna."

She turned. Mr. Hemplewilt stood by the wall to her left. Her heart took off in another direction now, slowing for a beat as she stared across at him.

*Go on, Anna. Ask him to leave.*

But something about him, something about the look in his eyes, made her stiffen.

"What is it? My grandfather?" She turned toward the room he occupied—well, if one wanted to call tattered cotton sheets that served as walls a room.

"'Tis not your grandfather," he said, stopping her with a hand on her arm.

Anna froze. He'd touched her again. She stared down at his hand, wondering how she could feel his warmth through the material of her cloak.

"Then what is it?" she asked again.

"Anna," he said, the look on his face seeming to turn to one of sorrow. "Someone came into your rooms today."

It was so opposite of what she thought he'd say, so completely a shock, that it took her a moment to form a reply, and even then it wasn't much of one. "I—" she frowned. "Our rooms?"

He nodded, looking around at the mess.

And suddenly Anna understood.

"I caught the person as I returned from washing this morning. He nearly knocked me down the steps. When I realized it wasn't your grandfather, I opened the door and found this." He indicated the debris around him. "When I went upstairs, I discovered worse."

And the grim look in his face, the way he wouldn't meet her eyes for a moment, the way he shook his head, made her race for the ladder.

"Anna—" he said, trying to stop her. But she had to see, had to see if they'd stolen her one and only irreplaceable possession, the thing she had wagered her entire future upon, the item she'd spent all her saved blunt on.

He couldn't have stopped her if he'd tried, but he didn't try. And so she fumbled with the ladder, nearly fell as her feet tangled in her cloak and brown dress. In the end it might have been better if the man who had done it had simply stolen from her. But no, he had done far worse than that. He had ripped it, no, shredded the mound of precious material, rendered the canvas useless in an act of malicious violence that made Anna fall to her knees.

She stared. Her brain simply couldn't absorb it. She knelt on the floor, her cloak falling around her like spilled gray paint.

"Why?" she asked, her voice a monotone. "Why would someone do this?"

"There was a note," she heard Mr. Hemplewilt say. "It was addressed to me."

"You?" she said numbly, still staring at the ruined material, as if by doing so it might magically piece itself back together again.

"Yes, me." He lapsed into silence. Anna stared up at him. All the money she'd saved, all the years she'd put it aside, only to spend it all on this one purchase . . . She'd been terrified to do it. It'd been such a gamble, one she'd hoped would pay off.

It wouldn't.

It would never have the *chance* to pay off. She bowed her head, the blow hitting her so hard, she could barely stomach it. She was going to retch. She could feel it gathering in her throat.

"The letter was a threat, Anna, toward me. It advised me that I give up. My . . . wager, that is. That I go home. I have spent the better part of this day doing my best to deal with the situation. I'm afraid I've not met with much success."

Home. He had a home. Someplace grand, she would imagine, while she had . . . nothing.

But his words had her jerking her head up in reaction. "Are you telling me someone did this to me because of your bloody wager?"

He didn't say a word.

She lurched to her feet. Where there was once despair, now there hung only rolling, red anger.

"Are you telling me one of your chums did this to me because he wanted to win a *wager*?"

"No. Yes," he said, in his green eyes a look she'd never seen before. Regret. Sorrow. Pity. "Someone did do this because of me—obviously. But I don't know who. The, ah, chum I've wagered against told me he had nothing to do with this. And I believe he would never do something so malicious. It makes no sense."

"No sense? Obviously your chum wants to win his wager."

"No." He dropped his head, inhaled with an audible

sound through his nose. "Yes. No, though I suppose discovering who did it will not repair the damage."

"It will when you go and see this man and tell him to replace my canvas."

"I cannot."

"You cannot?" she asked with a flick of her head to dislodge the blond ringlet that obscured her right eye. "Do not tell me you cannot."

"Part of the wager is that I not contact anyone during my stay here. I took a chance today and visited my chum anyway, but I was warned not to do so again."

Speechless. For a moment she couldn't form a thought. And then they all tumbled about her head until one erupted past her lips. "And so you would see all my hard work destroyed because you refuse to confront the man who did this to me?"

"No. I will replace your canvas."

Relief. Her shoulders bowed in the aftermath.

"But you shall have to wait until after the wager is won."

"*What?*"

He must have realized he'd spoken the wrong words. And, indeed, Anna felt the urge to go to him, to shake him, to rattle the teeth of the very man who'd occupied almost every waking thought she'd had since meeting him.

"Anna, there is a great deal at stake here."

"Do not speak to me of what is at stake." Anna took a step toward him, her cloak swirling around her legs like an angry cat. "My competition is in three weeks. I have three weeks to finish my sails, three weeks to sew six staysails. I don't have *time* to wait for you to win a silly wager."

"I'll make it up to you. I'll buy you whatever you wish when my time here is done."

"What I *wish* is to win this competition."

He didn't say a word, and in that moment Anna wondered what it was she ever saw in him. Fancy cull with his fancy airs and his fancy way of treating people. She'd forgotten how selfish and self-absorbed men with money could be.

" 'Ave you any idea how much work I've put into my design?" And listen to her dropping her *h*'s and speaking like a street girl. But she didn't care. Her world—the one she'd looked forward to after winning the competition, because she was certain she'd win it—was being ripped apart, literally. "I've spent weeks—nay, months—ever since the competition was announced. But it's not just the competition, it's more than that. My parents' ship went down because they couldn't outrun a storm. They *died* because British ships are so slow. For years I've toyed with ideas to make them go faster." She spun on her heel, went to her bed and pulled out from beneath it her drawings, flinging them at his feet, the ink outlines of hulls and prows skidding to a checkerboard stop at his boots. "But I don't have the funds to build a ship. It wasn't until this competition that I realized I was aiming too high. I could concentrate on the sails first, then move into ship-building later, if I can find a builder who'll trust a woman's mind. But I need to win that competition first. Win it and the prize money and prove that a woman can be twice as clever as a man. Only now I—" her gaze caught on the canvas.

The anger left her.

Like a bellows with a hole popped into the side, the fury drained away from her, leaving behind a sharp anguish that was as painful as a blow to the stomach.

"Why do I try and explain?" she said, her gaze still on the sails. "You've no notion of what work I speak of, the time, the energy I've invested. One need only look at your hands to see that. What do you know of hard work?"

Rein couldn't answer her question. Indeed, as he stared at the dejected form of Anna Brooks, he felt a sense of impotence he hadn't felt since he was a lad. It had been a shock to learn today that he was not allowed to visit his uncle's solicitor. The man had been most incensed to see him. But Rein's argument that he was not asking for help, but rather trying to discover who had done such a horrible thing to Anna had been met with deaf ears. He'd been banished. Again. Told not to return, though it'd taken half a day to find his way to the man's office.

"Leave," she said. "I don't have the time for your nonsense."

He almost did as she asked, almost turned away and skulked out, but as he looked at her, as he watched her kneel down by the fabric and then begin to examine it as if seeking a way to piece it back together again, he found himself saying, "No. I shan't."

She looked up, her eyes shimmering with a glassy sheen he instantly recognized as tears.

"I shall fix this, Anna Brooks, that I promise. I don't know how, I don't know when, but I *shall* fix it."

It was the skepticism he saw in her eyes that shook

Rein free of self-doubt. By god, he *would* fix it, even though at present he had no idea how.

"Give me twenty-four hours, Anna. I promise to resolve this."

She held still for a moment, then she blinked, swallowed and looked down again, her hands beginning to scoop up the fabric.

"Twenty-four hours, gov. That's all you got."

Rein nodded, reminding himself of who he was. A lord, if she but knew. Surely he could find a way to resolve this.

And then he would discover who the bloody blazes had done such a thing, and wrap his hands around the person's throat.

# Part Two

*"I come here seeking my destiny,"*
*said the prince to the maiden.*

# Chapter Eight

Molly knew something was wrong when Anna didn't show up the next morning. Granted, it was a miserable day outside—the kind of day that made a body sorry it had to work out-of-doors, it blew so wet and cold. Fat droplets of rain mixed with smaller ones to form a sort of mist that made it hard to tell where the clouds began and the ground ended. Everything was a slippery mess, Molly's skirts drenched up to her knees, the bottoms of her feet slapping the insides of her half boots, they were so filled with water. Ballocks.

"C'mon, Anna," she said as she tried to huddle beneath her cloak, her arms tucked beneath her armpits for warmth.

Never before had Anna made Molly wait. Her friend knew the dangers of loitering alone. Thankfully, this was their neighborhood, but still . . .

"Mornin' to you, Henry," she said, not wanting to pull out her hand to wave.

"Morning, Molly," the street sweep said, his big broom dragging behind him.

"Bother this," Molly muttered after he'd passed, the

noise of the street and the other passing carts swallowing up her words. She had to dodge a stream of water that poured from a hole in the roof as she stowed her basket alongside the building. Lord willing, no one would steal from it.

By the time Molly made it up the last set of stairs, she was cursing her friend in rhythm to her steps. Had she diddled the fancy gent last evening to the point that she'd slept through the dawn? Didn't she realize that a night of pleasure didn't mean a body could skip selling wares on the morrow? Oh, she had a fine amount of knowledge to share with her friend.

"Anna Brooks," she called as she knocked on the door. "You'd best have a good excuse for leaving me out in the cold."

No answer.

"Anna?" she called again.

The door opened.

Molly stepped back. She couldn't help it. It was as if the man who answered had bent down and said, *Boo,* so unexpected was his presence. Lord above. It was Anna's Mr. Hemplewilt.

"Where is she?" Molly asked. "She hasn't come down yet and it's long past time to leave for market." He had a spot smack in the middle of his head, a little red spot Molly knew was the place where Anna's sail had clouted him.

"She's still abed," he said, his beautiful green eyes sweeping over her face—yes, they were as pretty as a pair of marble orbs Molly had seen in a glass shop window one day. But rather than narrow with interest as most men's eyes did, he seemed rather disinterested as he said, "She had a bit of a late night last eve."

"Did she, now?" Molly couldn't help asking with a suggestive lift of her brow.

His brows swept up though he didn't smile. "I fear you have the wrong idea, Miss Washburn."

Well, then, there was something wrong with Anna.

"But I shall tell her you came by."

Molly stared at him. He stared right back.

"My thanks," she said at last.

He backed away, the door slowly closing. Molly wondered what the blazes might have happened.

So engrossed was she in her thoughts that she hardly paid heed as she rounded the bend of the first landing. "Lord above," she cried out as she ran smack into a chest.

"Beg your pardon," a masculine voice said, setting her back from him. "I heard you coming down. I should have called out."

Words died with the speed of a gnat hitting a wall as she peered up at him. What a looker. And not just because of his broad shoulders. No. It was his eyes that captured her attention. Blue, as blue as the sky if tipped upside down and captured in a small bottle. As blue as the buttons on that fancy toff's jacket she'd seen yesterday. As blue as the feathers of a blackbird when struck by the summer's sun. They seemed to swallow her whole, those eyes, making her freeze as she gawked at him.

"No," she said with lips that refused to work for a moment. "'Tis my fault."

They stared at each other for a moment before the man looked up the stairs she'd just descended, his brows lifting before he looked back at her again. "I wonder, did you just come from the rooms upstairs?"

"I have," she said bemusedly.

"Excellent. I have it down as belonging to my friend Mr. Montgomery, but I'm not so certain I have the right of it."

He wore a hat. Odd, how she hadn't noticed it before. Then she spied the red hair. She felt a stab of disappointment. Red hair. She'd always hated the color. Then she looked into the man's eyes again and decided she could tolerate their children having red hair.

"No. 'Tis only one set of rooms upstairs. Me friend Anna Brooks lives there with her grandfather."

The man looked disappointed. "Are you certain? There's no other person living with them?"

"Well, they haves themselves a visitor, but his name's Hemplewilt."

The man's obvious disappointment made Molly say, "But I'll help you find your friend," with a wide, flirtatious smile.

She thought for a moment that he might refuse, but then he looked her up and down, a slow smile crossing his face as he said, "My thanks . . ."

"Molly," she said with another flutter. "Me name's Molly."

"Freddie Stills," he said with a smile of his own. "Bow Street Runner."

Rein paced the length of the little room exactly five times—ten steps each way, if one avoided the massive machine in the middle of the room—before he decided he'd best go up and check on Anna. He'd heard her up there rattling about last night, had wondered if he should go up and check on her, but he knew she would not welcome him and so he'd remained belowstairs, pacing, wondering . . . thinking.

Who knew he was here? And why would that person do such a thing to Anna? He had no cousins—well, he had one, but he would never do such a thing, and he wasn't in line for the title.

And so the best he could come up with was that this was part of his uncle's plan. That his uncle had paid for someone to try and frighten him. That might be why his solicitor had been so rude to him yesterday. And the more he thought about it, the more it made sense. Just as it made sense that his uncle likely had someone watching him. How else was the solicitor to know if he adhered to the test?

But with the solution came no peace, for it didn't solve Anna's problem. Bloody hell, it drove him mad. The Bank of England held thousands of pounds in his name, none of which he could touch to replace Anna's canvas.

"Curse it," he mumbled to himself. He was going up.

"Anna," he said after he pulled on the cord that dangled from the roof and controlled her ladder.

No answer.

"Anna," he called again, more urgently this time. When she didn't reply again, Rein clutched the sides of the ladder. Granted, she might be angered at this breach of privacy, but he refused to take the chance that something might have happened to her. Gray light cast a murky glow as he reached the top, one of the three windows in her attic partly open so that he could hear the noise from the street below. He turned his head.

And there she was, asleep against the far wall. A lone candle had melted into a mountain range of wax near her legs, the thing long since burned out.

Asleep, her hands still resting on the strips of sails she'd obviously been trying to piece back together again when she'd nodded off sometime in the middle of the night.

Something odd filled Rein then. Indeed, he stood there for a moment wondering what it was he felt. Then he cast it aside as he pulled himself into her room. Her canvases lay spread around her, the strips she'd been mending rumpled in her lap. Her hair fell loose over her shoulders, the brown dress she wore all but obscured by the long strands.

Asleep.

On silent feet, he moved forward.

She had smudges beneath her eyes.

And yet, still, her beauty took his breath away.

"Anna," he said softly, testing the waters a bit. She didn't move, not even to flinch at the sound of her name. He frowned.

"Anna," he said more loudly, moving forward to kneel on one knee and touch her shoulder. "Anna, come," he said. "You should take to your bed."

But there was no reaction. And so Rein did something very surprising then—well, for him, at least. Generally speaking, if a woman chose to sleep in a broom closet, he wouldn't care. Yet something wouldn't allow him the same attitude toward Anna.

And so he leaned forward, gently inserting his arms behind and beneath her. Before he could think twice about it, he'd picked her up, her body so light and fragile in his arms he wondered where she found the strength to do all that she did. Her head fell into the crook of his arm.

Rein felt peace then; it was the only way to describe it. As he held Anna Brooks, a sensation rose within him that he'd only ever felt once before—when he was twelve and he'd been given a rabbit as a pet. The rabbit had been killed by bees not long after, but he still remembered the awe, the wonder and the pleasure in knowing that the creature he held in his arms was his.

Did he want Anna to be his?

Certainly he'd wanted to bed her. But now something felt different. Good God, he couldn't believe he felt this way, but he wondered if he should keep his distance from her. Lord, his father must be rolling over in his grave, for his sire had taught him that women were for the taking. He stared down at her flawless face, his gaze catching on her softly parted lips, the urge to kiss her was not so much a desire as a sudden need. He wanted to kiss her because he . . . wanted to kiss her.

Gently, he lay her down on her bed, straightening and staring down at her. Almost he turned away, but at the last moment his gaze caught on the misfit of a bedcover she'd sewn together. He pulled it over her, only it didn't seem warm enough in the chilly room, what with rain pecking at the windows. He spun on his heel and retrieved her battered and torn cloak, then gently placed it over her. She nestled beneath the thing like a babe. Only then did he allow himself to turn away. His gaze caught on the sails again. She'd only sewn a portion of one. One. She'd need to do five more in less than two weeks' time, and that while working at the market. A frown came to his face then, for even he was smart enough to realize there was

no possible way she could accomplish such a feat. Indeed, the material seemed to be in such tatters, he
doubted she could repair enough of it to make one sail.

He glanced back at her, sleeping so peacefully beneath
the white sail, her hair spilling out around her. And then
Rein Montgomery, a duke of the realm, did something
he'd never done before: He set to work.

# Chapter Nine

Later that morning, Anna woke slowly. A feeling such as she'd not felt in ages descended upon her. It was a peaceful feeling, a sort of childish contentment that she'd only ever felt when she was young and happy and safe within the walls of her mother and father's home.

She stretched a bit, eyes still closed, but as she swam in a tide pool of contentment, she couldn't help but think something felt off.

She couldn't recall getting into bed.

And she was still dressed.

The canvases.

She shot up, smacking her head on the low side of the roof that her bed lay under. "Ouch," she muttered. Ballocks. Already the day was off to a rollicking good start.

The canvas.

And as the hopelessness of the situation once again overcame her, she felt the pain in her temple produce a sting in her eyes. It wasn't tears, she told herself. No. She might have lost the canvas. She might have lost every farthing she'd saved up and spent on her investment, including farthings she didn't have—a moneylender having been only too willing to take as collateral the barrow she used at market. But she wouldn't give up. She had no choice. If she didn't have six sails hoisted upon a ship by the time of the competition, she was done for.

Her eyes moved to the corner of the room where her canvas lay, only to jerk at what she saw instead.

Rein Hemplewilt slept across the room.

She pulled up the covers, shocked at the way the back of her neck tingled at just the sight of the bloody man in the same room with her. And after the trouble he'd caused her! She should be wearing garlic and carrying a stake. But there could be no denying her body suddenly thrummed as she took in the sight of him.

He lay propped up against the wall in the exact same place she had been last evening while she sewed her canvas, the material pulled over his legs, white lawn shirt half open. His dark hair was mussed and fell over his brow, his chin even darker than it was yesterday with its stubble of hair.

She slid out of bed then, her toes cringing at the cold, only as she sat up, she got her first glimpse of the sky outside. A rainy sky, yes, but one with light . . . a lot of light.

"Hell's bells," she cried. She'd overslept.

She shot Rein a glare, one that if he'd been awake would have popped the eyes out of his head just by the mental image she shot of him standing there with her hands clasped around his throat. Grabbing her apron, she tied it on quickly. No time to change her dress. She glanced out the window again. Lord, she'd missed the morning crowds.

"Blast it." Why had she overslept? Now was not the time to bungle her one source of income.

"Wake up, you scaly cove."

She hadn't expected him to stir, but he snapped awake so fast, he cracked his head on the post behind him.

"Bloody hell," he said, a hand going to the back of his head.

"Get up and get your things. I want you gone before I return this eve."

"No," he said.

She spun on him. "No?"

He shoved the material in his lap as if preparing to stand, only as he did, his white lawn shirt lifted, too. That appeared to flummox him for a moment, for he stared, his eyes blinking some more. Obviously, he'd sewn the canvas to his shirt. His eyes shot to hers, the look in them one of impatience. He ripped the canvas away, standing abruptly.

"No. You promised me twenty-four hours to rectify things, twenty-four hours that I intend to use."

"I've changed my mind," she said, looking for her cloak. It was atop the bed. How the blazes had it gotten there?

"Pity, for you shall then miss me taking to the stage."

Take to the stage? She turned back to face him.

"Indeed, it came to me just as I nodded off. I saw an advertisement yesterday, one soliciting players. Thus I have decided to help you by embarking on a competition of my own."

"You're going to take to the stage at Piccadilly Theatre?"

"You've heard of it?"

"Of course I've heard of it." Her hands moved to her hips. "But you're mad to be thinkin' of going there, gov."

Though if he won, she realized, the blunt would be enough to pay for new canvas.

No, it was too dangerous. And while she didn't particularly like Mr. Hemplewilt, she wouldn't see him put his life in danger. He'd have enough on his hands when she forced him out onto the streets.

*And don't you be feelin' guilty about that, either.*

"There's a reason why they pay people so much, gov. They have to entice people into performing. Most people end up bloodied for their efforts."

"Indeed," Rein said, still not dissuaded. "That is a risk I shall have to take."

"No," she found herself saying. "It's too risky."

"I do not care. I promised to help you, and so I shall. I am an honorable man, Anna, and for all my faults, I believe in keeping a promise."

She stared at him, hardly daring to believe that he would do this for her. But the look in his eyes, the determination she saw on his face . . .

"What do you plan to perform?" she asked, the perspective shift she suddenly underwent making her feel almost fumble-tongued.

"Poetry."

*"Poetry?* They don't ken to poetry at Piccadilly Theatre."

"Ah, but you see, I don't recite the flowery poetry." He lowered himself a bit—that was the only way Anna could describe it. It wasn't that he moved closer, it wasn't that he stooped down, yet somehow she had a feeling that he'd leaned closer.

"You don't?" she asked, feeling suddenly dry in the mouth.

"Indeed, no," he said with a smile as wide as the London Bridge. "My poetry is—shall we say—bawdy?" His eyes narrowed. "I see that brain of yours working."

It was. She was busy naming a hundred reasons why she shouldn't let his willingness to help her affect her.

"I'm just praying you win the competition," she said. "If not, I'll have to find another way to pay for your funeral."

And so that evening, after Anna returned from market, they set off, though throughout the day she tried to tell herself that she shouldn't be grateful to Mr. Hemplewilt because he was willing to help her. He *owed* her his help.

And yet still . . .

He *could* have left, though she supposed he might be afraid to be out on his own. Still, he might have tried to win the performance for his own benefit. Instead he was going to do it for her.

"Do the crowds never go away?" Mr. Hemplewilt asked as they stood in the doorway of her tenement and looked out over her narrow street. The sun made a temporary appearance, at an angle so low that long shadows stretched into the middle of the street—some thin, some short, depending on the height of the buildings around them.

Anna followed his gaze, seeing her world though his eyes for the first time. It'd stopped raining, but the moisture had caused the roads to turn to muck, sedan chairs tugged along by scruffy-looking men in black hats and blue jackets who worked their way among a myriad of brown or black carriages that spilled their way down the lane like marbles from a bag. A hay cart rolled by with its load ready to spill off the back, and for a moment, just the briefest of seconds, the sweet smell of cut grass filled the moist air, only to be overcome again by the gutter. It was noisy, always noisy, this part of London as active as an anthill no matter what time of day or night.

"No," she said, setting off. It would rain again soon, the sunlight just a brief bit of optimism shot down by a cloudy sky.

"Evenin', gov."

Anna stopped as a tart wedged herself in front of Mr. Hemplewilt.

"Care to sample me wares?" Anna heard her ask with a wiggle of her breasts. The back of the wench's head looked like she'd slept on that mop of blond (or was it gray?) hair, the strands teased into a frizzy mess. She wasn't exactly clean, either. And she smelled like . . . well, she just plain *smelled.* Or was that smell from the big brute of a man who'd just passed by?

Rein looked over at Anna as if to say, *Is she talking to me?* But he must have realized she was, for he straightened, saying, "Thank you, no. I am otherwise presently engaged."

Which made Anna shake her head and roll her eyes. *Otherwise presently engaged,* she silently mimicked. As if this were a fancy drawing room and the woman a well-dressed swell.

"Certain, are you?" said the crone, her hand going to Mr. Hemplewilt's codpiece; at least Anna thought it might be there, for he jumped, shifted, his hand swatting the crone's fingers away.

"Please do not touch me."

Which made Anna reach around him, jerk his arm toward her and say, "He's with me." To which Mr. Hemplewilt obligingly stepped around the tart, his hand going to his head as if about to tip a hat, only to drop back to his side when he realized he didn't have one.

"That woman propositioned me," he said when they were on their way again.

"Aye. Fancy that," she said, walking away. The man couldn't even foist off a decrepit old tart! How the blazes would he survive the evening?

"You look concerned," he said as they passed beneath a lamplighter lighting a wick.

"I am worried for your safety," she said, daring a glance up at him. He looked so handsome. So devilishly handsome this evening. Granted, he wore the same battered jacket he'd traded his own coat for, the same brown breeches and used half boots, but his clothing could not disguise the noble form beneath. Not now. Not ever.

"Are you?" he asked, staring down at her.

"You might get wounded."

"Would that matter?"

She stopped. "Of course it would."

Someone jostled them, the crowded streets bothering Anna for the first time in a long while.

"Would it, Anna?"

And there was her name again, that soft, fluid name that sounded so elegant and pretty coming from his lips.

"It would," she said, looking into his green eyes.

"You mean that, don't you?" he asked softly.

"Course I do."

And was it her imagination, or did his expression turn cynical? "Because in my experience, Anna, people will say and do a great deal to get what they want. You need my help this night, and yet I've a feeling you'd rather I not perform."

"I *would* rather you not perform," she said, meaning it. Oh, goodness, she felt the oddest emotions course through her as she stared up at him. Curiosity. Excitement. Fear.

"Thank you," he said.

"Thank you?" she asked, trying and failing to understand what it was he was thanking her for.

"Thank you for caring about my welfare, Anna. It has been quite some time."

"Quite some time since what?"

He looked away, but not before she saw a joyless look of acceptance quickly concealed behind his eyes. "Anyone cared for me, Anna. Just me, not . . . anything else."

She almost asked him what he meant, but just then he guided her forward, the crowd suddenly worse as they hit a main thoroughfare.

*Cared for me. Just me.*

Was it true? Did he have no one to care for him? And why did such a thought fill Anna with a sorrow?

She shook her head, trying to sort out the emotions she felt as he held her arm, guided her through the streets on their way to Piccadilly Theatre. To perform. For her.

The theater looked smaller on the outside than it did on the inside, Rein thought. Two stories made of gray stone, it had old boards for walls on the interior, a stage with candles across the front at one end.

"Mr. Hemplewilt, please," Anna said as the two of them entered. "Do not do this."

And even though she'd sunk back into the hood of her

cloak—something she did frequently, Rein reasoned, as a way to avoid attention—he could still see the concern in her amber eyes as she glanced up at him. The light glowing from the candles in front was poor, but not that poor.

"Anna, I have no choice."

"My canvas is not worth your life."

Rein felt that odd sense of wonder again, the wonder that came from knowing she cared for him despite not knowing who he truly was.

"I shan't lose my life," he reassured her, asking a passerby for the person in charge of the performances. But she didn't look convinced as he arranged things in the crowded theater, big bodies huddled next to small, thin next to well fed. Indeed, with each act that came off the stage, the crowd grew more and more riled, and Anna looked increasingly ill.

"You'll be on after this bloke," said the little man who managed the stage. "The last to perform, too," he added, "which is likely a good thing. They're getting a bit riled."

And, indeed, someone from the front row yelled, "Ge' him off the stage." One of the fat candles that lined the stage fell when a rotted orange hit it, extinguishing the wick on impact.

Still, Rein wasn't worried.

"Someone shut 'im up," another man yelled just as the poor gent belted a high note—one that was cut off abruptly as a very well-aimed something hit him in the gut.

"Done for," the stage manager said, his fleshy hands clasping the front of his belly as something that sounded like a belch erupted from his throat. Laughter, Rein realized as he watched the man's corpulent little body shake like the whipped cream atop a shaken pie.

Sure as certain, the singer said, "Please. No more. I'm leavin', I am."

To which someone yelled, " 'Bout time," before letting another fruit fly.

"They don't like singers," the stage manager said without moving his gaze away. "Hope for your sake you ain't singing."

Rein shook his head, utterly confident he had nothing to fear. Indeed, he had faced and endured far worse than an unruly audience.

"He's not singing," Anna said. "But that doesn't mean he won't get the same treatment. Or worse."

"They tried to kill me," the singer said as he came off stage.

"Mr. Hemplewilt," Anna pleaded again.

Rein looked down at her, reassuring her with a confident smile. "Have no fear, Anna. I shall emerge the victor. Watch."

She seemed reluctant to let him go as he boldly stepped onto the raised wooden platform that served as a stage, one covered with enough tomatoes and onions to fill Anna's barrow.

Hundreds of faces stared back at him—some from the theater's pit and others from the second floor, their bodies packed together like fish in a barrow.

And it was then, and only then, that Rein began to feel something he hadn't felt since a lad. Fear.

*Get him, Marcus.*

The words were from his childhood, yet he could still hear them as if they'd been spoken yesterday.

He blinked, and when he opened his eyes, a room full of people stared back at him.

"Well?" someone cried, a man with rather a lot of gum and no teeth, but who made up for his lack of ivories in size. Rein should know, for he had a perfect glimpse of his muscular forearms as he hurled a potato at his head. Fortunately, he missed.

Rein opened his mouth, his lips suddenly so numb, it felt like he himself had no teeth.

*Hold his hands behind his back.*

"Ach, 'e's got the fright of the stage, he has," someone else yelled. "Get 'im outta here."

He glanced over at Anna, who waited in the side wings.

*Throw him to the ground.*

He faced forward again, summoning the calm that he'd learned to pull around him in such situations. He opened his mouth. "Friends, Romans, countrymen," he bellowed, "lend me your arse."

"What?" someone cried.

"'E's doing Shakespeare?"

"*Shakespeare?* Don't want no bloody Shakespeare."

"This ain't the Drury," someone else cried.

"*Arse,*" Rein said to that person. "I said *arse,* not *ears.*"

"Get 'im off the stage," another person yelled.

They didn't find that amusing? A second missile whizzed by his ear. Apparently not.

"How about a ditty?"

But the man in the front, the one who'd thrown the potato, let another one fly, only this time it didn't miss. No.

It smacked into Rein's thigh with enough sting to make him cry out, "Bloody hell," and clutch his limb.

An onion came at him then. Rein reacted with an instinct he had thought long forgotten. He ducked to the left and out of harm's way.

It was, perhaps, unfortunate that at that moment more than one person decided to take aim. Indeed, the barrage of vegetables aimed at his head no doubt resembled the cannon at Trafalgar.

"Bloody hell," he cried again, arms raised, which left his midsection vulnerable, something he admitted as a mistake the moment the first onion smacked into him. "Bloody hell," he cried out again.

"Stop it," someone yelled. "Stop it right now."

To Rein's relief, they stopped, though only because Anna had run in front of him, hands outstretched.

"Anna," he hissed. "Go back."

She ignored him, yelling, "The next man what throws something at the bloke will have his tallywags cut off and served to him on a platter."

"At least those tallywags'd belong to a real man and not a sorry bloke what recites Shakespeare," someone answered back.

A few missiles were lobbed at the stage, but only a few, and none of them near Anna.

"Anna," Rein tried again.

But she ignored him, facing the audience boldly now, hands on her hips. She'd slipped out of her cloak, though Rein hadn't seen her do it. The brown dress she wore beneath could hardly be called low, but she dipped forward so that the men had a view of her cleavage.

"Anna," Rein hissed, suddenly impatient.

She didn't straighten because he asked. No, she straightened so she could turn and walk along the front of the stage. "So you think you have bigger tallywags than this bloke 'ere?" She pointed her thumb over her shoulder.

"Come 'ere and I'll show you," someone yelled.

"Ach, gov," she said, "staring at your dried up prunes'll likely turn me stomach."

"Ooo," cried the audience as Anna changed directions. She eyed the crowd. Indeed, she strutted, hands still on her hips, her rear sashaying. "Anyone else think they have bigger tallywags than me friend 'ere?"

What the bloody hell was she doing?

"I've got meself a pair," someone yelled. "And I'll show 'em to you, too, if you like."

Laughter followed the words. Anna proudly stared back, her head held at an aloof angle as she gave the man a look that must have conveyed how unimpressed she was, judging by the chuckles that followed. She was, in that moment, the single most enthralling woman Rein had ever seen. Gone was the Anna who hid herself behind her cloak and beneath that silly straw hat she wore to market. In her place stood a vixen with a spitfire's attitude and a confident lady's allure.

"Very well," she called out, her hands lifting from her hips to silence the audience. "I'll make you a wager."

It amazed Rein how quickly the crowd fell quiet. Lord, it was as if she'd shot a pistol. "We'll have ourselves a contest. Me friend 'ere will go first. If he survives, someone can challenge him. The winner will get himself a kiss."

*Survive?* Pandemonium erupted. Rein hissed, "Anna. No. Do not."

"Who will lend me a knife?" she called out, ignoring him. "I need more than one."

*More than one?* What was she about to do?

The amount of knives passed forward was both frightening and shocking. Everything from long blades to short blades, the men apparently too riled to care that they might not get the things back. He watched as Anna bent forward, giving the audience another view of her breasts.

"Ach, lovey, forget the contest. Run off with me now," said one man.

She looked up and gave the man a wicked smile, at least judging by the audience's reaction. Masterful. That was the word that came to mind. The way she handled the audience was masterful. It made Rein wonder if she'd done whatever "act" she was about to do before.

She selected four knives from the pile, somersaulting them in the air one at a time as she tested their weight and balance.

"These'll do," she said, straightening with the knives in hand, the rest left in a pile near center stage.

"Back yourself against the wall, Rein."

"What?" he hissed at her in a voice meant for her ears only. "Anna, what are you doing?"

She tossed a knife in the air, catching the hilt with a *thiiik* against her palm, and this after it'd tumbled end over end a good two feet in the air.

And he knew.

"Oh, no," he said, straightening. "Absolutely not."

"They'll pull me from the stage and have at me if we

don't give them an act," she hissed, her eyes absolutely and utterly serious.

Rein looked behind her to the audience.

Yes, they would. They wanted a show. They'd be furious if they didn't get one.

"How good are you?" he asked.

She lifted her chin, and he got his first taste of Anna with a saucy smile on her face.

Good lord.

He stared, transfixed, at the way her eyes glowed with amusement. At the way that glow erased the tiredness in her eyes. And if he'd thought her beautiful before, seeing such a flirtatious smile on Anna Brooks's face made him think no woman could ever be as beautiful as her.

"You'll just 'ave to wait and see."

He didn't say anything. He couldn't have said a word if he'd tried. Good lord, she could put the season's incomparable to shame. The past ten seasons' incomparables to shame.

"Go on up against the wall," she said, pointing with her knife, the smile fading. Which made him realize this was no game. Granted, he'd seen the act done before, but only performed by professionals. Not a golden-eyed temptress who kept tossing her knife into the air over and over and over again.

"Go," she ordered once more.

He went—reluctantly, but he went. She took position by the front of the stage, her skirts almost touching the candles that lined the front of it.

"Here we go, then," she called out.

The audience quieted. She tossed the knife in the air one last time before raising her arm and flinging the thing, only as her arm came back, she lost her grip. The audience cried out as the thing sailed above their heads to land with a thunk in the rail around the second floor.

"Hey," someone cried.

Anna turned, looked up and called out, "My apologies," before turning to face him.

"Gonna kill 'im," Rein heard someone else say.

Yes, she was. And for the first time in his life, he remembered the years of suffering through beating after beating, and that came to his aid. Taking a deep breath, Rein stilled. She flung a second knife.

It landed above his head with a thunk and a twang.

Silence, and then a cry of approval. She raised a second knife.

"Anna, one is enough," Rein said.

"Throw it," someone cried.

Anna turned back to the audience. "Should I?" she asked them.

A chorus of "Ayes" filled the room.

"What if I keep my back turned to him?"

Loud cheers.

"Anna—"

She flicked the knife without turning to face him. Rein froze.

The thing landed right next to the first one.

Stunned silence greeted her, then cheers so loud they made Rein's ears ring. She playfully tossed her last knife in the air.

"Do that again," someone cried.

"Do what again?" she called, flinging the last knife over her shoulder once more.

It, too, landed above his head.

*Bloody hell.*

She turned, giving him a wink before she faced forward again and took a bow, but as she did so her hand reached into the pile of knives, grabbing one and turning to face Rein with a quickness that took everyone aback, including Rein. With an expert flick, she let the thing fly. And then the others in quick succession. They sank, one by one by one around his body, outlining it.

Anna looked as close to laughter as he'd ever seen her. Chaos erupted. Rein slowly straightened. His eyes narrowed as his gaze met Anna's.

She lifted a brow.

He lifted an answering brow and then slowly, ever so slowly, smiled, too.

# Chapter Ten

They won the prize.

Anna almost did a little dance down the narrow alley that led to the front of the theater.

"Proud of yourself, are you?" Rein asked from alongside of her.

"I am," Anna said.

"You should be," he answered.

She preened. That was the only way to describe how she seemed to fluff up. If she'd been a bird she'd have shaken her tail feathers, too.

He smiled down at her again, and maybe it was the leftover thrill of performing in front of such a large audience instead of the small crowd that usually gathered at the market when she did her act, or maybe it was the relief she felt at being able to purchase her canvas and enter the naval competition after all, but suddenly Anna wanted to kiss him. She wanted to yank his head down and plant her lips on his to thank him for coming up with the idea of performing in order to save her sails.

"Where did you learn to throw knives?" he asked with a glance down at her.

"Sometimes I toss knives to attract a crowd." The right side of her mouth tipped up. "But that was before I learned the benefits of shredding lettuce."

The two of them emerged from the alley and onto the street. This part of London had lamps, moths hurling themselves at the glass like insect Don Quixotes at windmills. Anna heard their soft little bodies hitting the glass with a *tink-tink-tink.*

"Tell me, Anna, have you always been clever?"

"Yes. Always."

When she met his eyes they both smiled. Such a small thing, a smile, but this was one of the first Anna and Rein had shared and it hit them both like the boom of a Dover wave. They held their breaths; they stared into each other's eyes, each as if seeing the other for the first time. Who knows how long they would have continued to do so but for the fact that a jarvis stopped near them and said, "Need a ride, gov?" from high atop his perch behind the cab, the bedraggled white feather in the horse's bridle hanging limply off one side.

Rein's gaze seemed to hold hers until the last possible moment, and he pulled his eyes away with an effort as he looked up at the driver. "Yes, my good man, we do."

It took a moment for what he said to register, took her a moment to concentrate over the pounding of her heart, the heat cascading down the length of her body, the memory of his green eyes staring at her so intently making her feel special, unique, desired.

"Your carriage, my lady," he said with a small bow as he moved aside to let her precede him into the hack, whose door was suddenly held open by the driver.

"No," she said, shaking her head. "We can't waste the coin."

"*Au contraire,* my dear. For tonight you shall be whisked away by a magical steed." He motioned to the open-faced carriage. "Or hack, as the case may be. And before you say another word, let me remind you that we just won a good deal of coin and that should be enough to ride us home."

*Oh,* she thought.

And the yearning that such a simple thing as a carriage ride raised within her made her think how long it'd been since she'd engaged in just the smallest of luxuries. It made a memory surface of sitting next to her mother and snuggling beneath her comforting warmth.

*Cold, darling?*

*No, Mama.* So many stars above them Anna had sat and marveled almost the whole way home from the fair. She shook her head a bit now, focusing on the hack in front of her.

Dare she? Dare she be alone with him in the confines of a carriage?

Oh, why the bloody hell not? Molly would be proud.

And so Anna took his hand—for once not caring that her fingers felt as raspy as a cat's tongue. His own fingers wrapped around hers—solid, warm, masculine. Feeling like a fairy princess on her way to a ball, she stepped into the carriage, Rein helping her up. She had to force herself to let go of his hand as she took a seat.

"'Ere's a warm cover for you, mum," the jarvis said, placing a wool blanket over her lap. And was it her excitement over going for a ride in a hack that made her stomach flutter, or was it Rein taking a seat next to her?

He smiled at her as the door closed.

"May I?" he asked as he held his hands out toward the blanket.

She nodded.

He lifted it, his fingers brushing her thighs in such a way that it caused her flesh to warm like lantern glass. Suddenly she felt afraid to look at him as he settled the blanket over the both of them, the heat his body radiated beneath the cover nearly as great as the warmth in her belly.

A hackney ride. With a virtual stranger.

She shivered.

The driver flicked his buggy whip with a crack. Anna resisted the urge to clutch at Rein as they set off with a stomach-lurching tug.

"'Tis a bit chill this eve," she said because, lord help her, she couldn't think of another single bloody thing to say.

"It is," he said conversationally.

*You don't know this man. He could be anybody. Get out and walk.*

Instead she peered outside the ring of light the carriage lantern spilled in a wild arc around the interior. The immediate rush of air across her face made Anna want to close her eyes, made her want to tip her head back and inhale.

*Calm down, calm down. 'Tis only a carriage ride.*

"Why do you close your eyes?"

Her eyes snapped open. Had she closed her eyes? "I am thinking," she answered automatically, though she knew immediately what he would ask next.

And he did. "About what, if I might ask?"

*About how frightened I feel all of a sudden. How much I miss my mother. How much I wish I could ask her what this fire in my belly means.*

"'Bout how long it's been since I've taken a hack," she said instead.

"And how long has that been?"

She darted a glance at him, but it was quick, Anna not trusting herself to hold his gaze, not when they were so close. "I can count on one hand how many times I've paid for someone to ride me someplace."

"One hand?" he asked in surprise, his black brows lifting as the lantern light moved over his face, only to swing away again.

"Three fingers, actually."

"Three?"

"Once on my way to London, and . . ." she paused for a moment to quell the pain of the next memory. "Once when I went away and then came back."

"Went away?" he asked. "To where?"

"To where I grew up. A short visit."

He shook his head, his gaze fixing upon her face for a moment before he looked toward a shop front that reflected the glow of the lampposts they passed. Fancy hats sprouted like mushroom caps from a mound of off-white fabric, hats she'd often dreamed of wearing.

He looked back at her all of a sudden, she saw out of the corner of her eye, though she didn't turn to meet his gaze. "Anna, were you always as poor as you are now?"

She stiffened, resisting the urge to glance over at him in surprise. Why did he ask? And why the blazes did the question make her feel as if all the joy had gone out of her evening, her happiness flitting away like air out of a pillow?

"Anna," he said, the sound of her name on his lips gentle, almost earnest, as he said, "Should I not have asked you that?"

She shrugged.

And then he turned her face toward him. The cuff of his brown jacket brushed her shoulder. When she met his eyes, she forgot all about how his touching her made her feel. Lord, there was a look in his eyes, a sort of tenderness.

"Have I upset you?" he asked.

"Yes," she admitted, her voice as uneven as the call of a swallow.

"Bloody hell," she heard him mutter. "My apologies."

"No. Do not apologize," she said quickly, because she felt like she should reassure him. "It wasn't always bad. It only got worse when grandfather's illness kept him from inventing the trinkets and the like that he used to sell to feed us. So I found my own job as a costermonger. Like as not I'd still be selling vegetables if I hadn't discovered my grandfather's face shaver worked better on things that didn't breathe."

But he hadn't even appeared to hear her words.

"Lord," he said, looking back at her, his eyes flitting over her face. "Have you ever begged for food?"

The question actually jolted her. "No. I've never begged for food, not really. When it's gotten bad, I've asked my friends at the market to give us a spoiled apple or two. You'd be surprised how filling slices of apple can be."

"Slices? You've eaten only slices of apples when you've had no food?"

"Sometimes."

He turned away from her, his dark hair mussed and yet so neatly cut. And for just a moment she felt the urge to touch that hair, to run her fingers through it. To see if it felt soft and smooth like it looked. Instead she curled her fingers into her palm.

"You seem angry," she said.

"I should admit that I never . . ."

She waited for him to finish. Waited for him to turn toward her. To say something. "What?" she prompted, her back hitting the seat as they hit a hole in the road.

"Noticed," he finished, finally turning back to her. "I never noticed there were people like you in the world. Oh, I knew they were about—I just never thought about them. I see now how utterly self-absorbed that is."

Never noticed? How could he not have noticed? Unless he came from a world far above her.

Her gaze caught on the white ring around his finger. Signet ring? She opened her mouth to ask, then closed it again. She didn't want to know, because if he turned out to be from a world far, far removed from her own, that would mean . . . what? What did it matter? It was obvious he came from wealth, and that should be more than enough to send her scurrying in the other direction.

"Most people never learn to notice," she said, reaching beneath the blanket to squeeze his hand. Such a forward thing to do, taking a man's hand, yet taking Rein's felt absolutely natural, perfect.

They held each other's gaze a moment before he said, "Tell me about your life *before* London."

No. She pulled her hand away. He grabbed it back, though atop of the cover this time. She wanted to jerk her fingers away, wanted to escape all of a sudden. Tell him about her life? She couldn't do that. One thing she'd learned during her time in St. Giles: Thinking about the past always did more harm than good.

"Anna?" he prompted.

She didn't want to talk about it. She didn't, and yet she found herself saying, "It was wonderful," as her gaze moved up the sky she could see just around the edge of the roof. A rain-drenched moon lit the edges of white clouds so that they looked like torn cotton. In between she could see stars twinkling down.

*What are those, Mama?*

*Those are stars, my love.*

She must have been three, no more than four years old, and yet she remembered sitting in her mother's lap in the comfort of her arms as if she'd asked the question yesterday.

*What are stars?*

*The souls of angels staring down upon us.*

And then, when her mother and father had been buried, her grandfather standing alongside of her at their graveside, she'd looked up, but it'd been day and so she couldn't see the stars. The loneliness and longing she'd felt at the moment was a hurt she'd never forget.

"You grew up on the coast?"

Rein's voice snapped her out of her memories. Had she told him that? She couldn't remember, but she nodded, the back of her throat aching as she fought back unexpected tears. "In a little cottage, one so near the ocean, on the right day you could hear it rolling in from the sea. I used to listen to the roar at night."

*Please don't ask any more questions.* She realized then that she held his hand so tightly she felt surprised he hadn't said anything. She loosened her grip.

"And your father, what did he do?"

Choppy seas. A storm. They'd gone down too fast to save themselves.

"He captained a ship."

He noticed her reaction. "Anna, I'm sorry. I didn't mean—"

"No," she said after a deep breath. She learned that trick years ago. If a body inhales when one is about to cry, it makes the tears go away. "It just reminded me, is all. I miss them."

This time it was his grip that tightened. She looked down at their entwined hands, at the way the skin blanched around where his fingers squeezed her own, at how big his knuckles were compared to hers, how long her nails were compared to his.

"They died at sea together."

"Anna, please, there is no need. I feel horrid for asking—"

"No." She shook her head, feeling the need to talk about it. To him.

*Why?* a voice asked. *He is a stranger.*

She didn't know, just allowed herself to say, "My father was a captain in the Navy. He'd take my mother with him on occasion. She was an avid sailor." Anna forced a smile. "Time and again I heard her say if she'd been born a man she'd a been serving in the King's Navy. My father would let her steer the ship upon occasion—when his crew weren't looking, of course. She used to tell me about it, used to say she did as good a job as my father. One day they went out." She glanced up at him, the story having been told so many times that it came out automatically. "And never came back."

He stared down at her, his green eyes looking almost brown beneath the light of the lantern. "I didn't realize wives were allowed to sail with husbands."

She nodded. "It happens frequent enough that Admiral St. Vincent complained once about the amount of water women use."

"Really?"

"Aye. My mother once told me that when Nelson was injured at Santa Cruz, he asked to be taken to another ship so as not to offend, because of his wounds, the wife of the captain of the ship he was on."

"Indeed?" he said. Then he asked her a mundane question about life at sea, meaning to turn her mind from the pain of her memories. She knew that, and silently thanked him by squeezing his hand.

When they fell silent, she turned the tables on him. "Tell me about *your* life."

He jerked. She could feel it because his hand gave a spasm along with his body, causing him to let go.

"There is not much to tell," he said.

"I suspect there is," she said. "You're gentry through and through. Do you have a title?"

# Chapter Eleven

"A title?" Rein shot out, her words shocking him. "Good lord, what gave you that idea?"

"You've a mark on your pinkie where a ring used to be. Signet ring?"

Why, that clever puss. "Heirloom," he said, the answer not a lie; his signet ring *was* an heirloom. "I removed it so that it would not get stolen during my time in St. Giles."

"So your memory has returned?" she asked.

"It has."

"You never had a problem with your memory, did you?"

Unbelievably clever. And for a moment, Rein felt a sensation he hadn't felt in a great many years: a sensation of being inferior. She was far too clever by half and it made him feel distinctly uncomfortable.

Still, he found himself answering, "I did not," because for some odd reason, he disliked all the lies.

"Are you really in St. Giles because of a wager?"

"Actually, 'tis more of a challenge."

"One you mean to win," she said.

"One I mean to win," he answered with a determination he felt all the way to his soul.

"Are you that desperate for coin?"

"Actually, I am quite wealthy," which was true, for now.

"Then why did you put your life in danger?"

"Perhaps because I am an utter fool."

She blinked. Actually, it was a bit of a flutter. Blink. Blink-blink-blink. He'd begun to realize those flutters were a signal that her puzzled mind pondered a particular problem.

"You are far from a fool," she said.

Which just went to show how little she knew of him. And yet . . . It was her cleverness that attracted him, having struggled to learn things his entire life. She fascinated him with her quick mind. She was clever *and* very beautiful, especially with her hair framing her face beneath that ridiculously tattered cloak she wore.

Beautiful. Intelligent. *His.* Yes, he wanted her.

"A fool sees not the same tree that a wise man sees— or woman, as the case may be."

"Yes, but even a fool, when he holdeth his peace, is counted wise," she shot back.

He almost smiled. He'd given her the one quote he'd ever taken the time to memorize. *Days* to memorize, quite honestly, his mind unable to retain things for longer than a few hours. It was a fundamental flaw of his that he accepted as the way things were.

"You likely know far more quotes than I," he said.

"Why do you say it in that way?"

"What way?"

"As if you truly believe yourself foolish?"

"I am a fool."

"Wherever did you come up with that notion?"

"My father."

"Your father?"

"I was too slow for him, you see. Not bright enough." He stiffened his spine a bit, jutted out his lower jaw and did a tight-lipped imitation of his sire. " 'Work harder, young man. There would be no need for discipline if you tried harder.' " He relaxed then, pasting a small, sarcastic smile on his face. "So I tried to apply myself, only most of the time it didn't work. Not all of us are brilliant, you see."

"Discipline?" she asked, her astute mind catching on the one word Rein most wanted to forget.

"I was . . ." He searched for an appropriate word. "Encouraged to work harder."

"Beaten," she said.

The next smile he gave her was meant to be complimentary, meant to show her that he accepted his faults and his inability to be bright. Only it must not have worked for she said, "I'm so sorry."

He shrugged, then told her something he hadn't told another soul. "I thought things would be better at university, only it was almost ironic how much worse they became. If I thought my father was horrid, it was nothing compared to being pounced upon by three older boys determined to pick on the class dunce."

"What about your professors?"

"They noticed the cuts and bruises, certainly, but I was warned not to tell, and god help me, I feared the repercussions if I did. And so I held my tongue, Anna. One year, two, three. I grew older, wiser, learned to avoid them, most of the time, and when once I chanced to mention to my father that some of the older boys were . . . unkind, he laughed in my face. Said the experience would toughen me up, make me a better man."

"Awful, hateful man."

Her championing him filled him with odd warmth. "In the end I took matters into my own hands. I decided if my father would not allow me to come home, I should get myself sent home." His smile turned wry. "I began to pull pranks. Spectacular pranks, though I dragged my cousin into the whole lot. Still, it worked. Rather well, I might add." He smiled. "So you see, you have before you a man who has struggled his entire life to have half the intelligence you have in your pinkie."

"And yet you, like me, have survived," she said, shaking her head, the starlight seeming to shine from her eyes. "We are survivors, you and I, despite what the world has thrown at us."

He chose that moment to do what he'd been longing to do half the night. Indeed, it was an urge he could no longer ignore. He gently and sweetly kissed her.

"Rein," she gasped as she drew back a bit, her eyes nearly as golden as the flame that flicked inside the lantern.

Slowly, he lifted a hand to her hood, his hands shaking with the motion of the hack, or was it desire? He didn't know, just tipped the fabric back, leaned forward and turned his attention to the second thing he'd wanted to do to her. He kissed the side of her neck, sucking there, lightly, possessively claiming her skin.

"Stop," she groaned.

"I can't," he said between kisses and nips. And then he

did the third thing he'd been longing to do to her. He nipped at the shell of her ear, those little pink ears that always peeked out at him from beneath her hat.

"Rein," she said softly, almost in wonder.

He did a fourth thing then. He pulled back, reached up and cupped her face with both hands, his thumbs exploring the soft, plump fullness of her lips. Her eyes closed as he ran his fingers along the damp opening, her reaction as if he'd touched her far more intimately. He knew then that if he told the coachman to pull off, if he asked the man to leave them be for a bit, he could likely seduce her. But he didn't. Indeed, for some reason he slowly, reluctantly, let her go, her eyes opening as he released her. Those eyes were as dark as the pools of water that lay in puddles on the road.

"Rein, I—" she dropped into silence for a moment. "I liked that," she said with an honesty that made his manhood, already painfully uncomfortable in his breeches, flex into a more throbbing hardness. "I would like to do that again."

He almost smiled, the words so unexpected he wanted to applaud her for her honesty.

The chance for more conversation came to an end when they arrived at her tenement. "Grandfather might not be right in the head, and I don't want him to think—"

"Go," he said, silently urging her to leave before he did something he might later regret.

Such as what?

Taking her. Making love to her in a way that he knew would change her forever. Wanting to brand himself upon her. The urge to do it had his hands clenching the fabric of his breeches. But he didn't move because in that moment, he felt something he hadn't felt in a very long time: honor.

The hackney driver opened her door then. "Out you go, love," Rein said.

She slipped out of his arms as if she didn't trust herself to stay. Rein settled back into the carriage squabs, his whole body wanting to turn in her direction, to go after her, to slake his thirst for her in a way that would ease the pounding in his blood. He watched her look both ways before stepping onto the walkway. Her hood slipped from her head as she all but ran toward her building.

"Go, little Anna," he said, his manhood aching in his breeches as he stared at the spot that she'd been. "Run from the big, bad wolf."

She wanted him. Anna all but ran up the steps of her tenement, the look on Rein's face as she'd left him one she would never forget.

He wanted her.

She took the steps two at a time now, ran as if she'd never see the light of day should she not make it to the top alone, without Rein. Ran and then let herself in, pausing only to rest her back against the door.

"That you, Anna?"

She closed her eyes, her legs burning from her climb, her legs shaking from something else, for no matter how she had struggled to make herself sound sophisticated, experienced, aloof, she felt far from that.

"Yes, Grandfather," Anna said as she removed her cloak and hung it on the peg next to the door.

"Where have you been?" he asked, emerging from his

room wearing only his nightshirt, his hair mussed in the back as if he'd been lying down, his knobby, hairy legs almost as white as his shift.

"I told you earlier, Grandfather. Mr. Hemplewilt and I had an errand to run."

"Hemplewilt?"

She closed her eyes for a moment, praying for strength, as he stood there staring at her blankly. She hated his memory lapses. Hated his mad ramblings. Hated his illness, whatever it was.

"The gentleman what's livin' with us."

"There's no gentleman living with us. I would never allow such a thing. You are young and unattached. Goodness knows what trouble you might get into."

Sometimes she had a feeling her grandfather's mind saw far more than she might think.

"He'll be coming in behind me in a moment, Grandfather," she said, ignoring his denials, for she knew from experience that arguing with him would do no good. "Please do not send him away."

"Who will be coming?" he asked.

She almost closed her eyes, almost leaned her head against the door again. Nights like tonight strained her patience.

"Mr. Hemplewilt will be coming in. I'll be in my room."

She thought he might pound her with more confused questions. Instead, in one of his mercurial mood changes he said, "I'll do as you ask, my dear. Good night."

Suddenly she felt overwhelmed by it all. Her desire for Rein. The task of sewing sails and then testing them with less than a fortnight to go until the contest. Her grandfather. But she forced her legs to work, forced herself to climb the ladder. She paused at the top to take a breath.

Moans.

She stiffened.

Loud moans.

No. Not tonight. Not this night of all nights.

But there could be no mistaking the rhythmic groans of pleasure that drifted across the street and filtered through her window.

She almost covered her ears. Hell's bells, there couldn't be a worse time, not tonight when her lips still felt hot and plump from Rein's lips pressing against her own. Tonight when just the sound of those moans made her body burn as if Rein touched her still. She grew damp just standing there, telling herself to cover her ears, to go back downstairs, do anything but stand there.

But unlike other nights when she'd been able to ignore and sometimes laugh at the sounds, for the first time in her life Anna found herself wanting to listen to them, to get caught up in them, perhaps even turn and look out her window to see if she could spy on the woman who entertained her customers . . .

But no.

She went to the window, a rush of excitement dancing along her thighs as she shamelessly looked across the street.

A man lay atop a woman in a bed that had no covers.

Anna's woman's mound suddenly tightened to the point of pain. Her body erupted into a brush fire of excitement, and her breath caught in her throat as she watched them mate, a single candle by their bedside illuminating their passion-entwined limbs.

They were mating . . . doing what she wanted Rein to do to her. Now. Today. This moment.

She flushed with a heat that made her grow wet, that made her stare unblinkingly as the man tipped his head back and pushed in and out of the woman. She wanted Rein to do the same to her. Rein, who she suspected might be a nobleman, Rein, whom she would never have dealings with under normal circumstances. Rein whom she wanted to kiss, to touch, to—

"Anna."

She cried out, coldness replacing the heat at the shock of her name being softly called from the hole in the floor.

"Anna, I couldn't stay away."

She turned.

He had followed her.

# Chapter Twelve

*Move,* a voice urged Anna as she watched him approach, his whole body in shadow as light from below spilled into the room behind him. But she didn't move. She wanted this man. She wanted him to touch her, to stroke her like she'd seen the man stroking—

"Anna," he said again, only this time the voice was closer, closer. "Will you let me?"

*Move, Anna, move—Grandfather is belowstairs, he might hear you . . .*

But obviously, Grandfather had gone to his bed. He wouldn't hear them, not if she went and closed the trap.

Rein came up to her. And, yes, she could see him now by the light of the moon, could see into the green eyes turned dark with a sensual promise that made Anna grow warm. Behind her, the woman's cries grew louder.

"Will you let me touch you like that?" he asked, his voice so low and yet so guttural it was almost a groan. "Will you let me give you pleasure?"

She pulsed at his words, the ache between her legs growing damp with desire. He was near now, so near that when he reached out and touched her arm, she didn't see him do it. "Will you let me touch you?" he asked, leaning down toward her, and she thought he would kiss her, felt her mouth fill with moisture at the thought, but instead he used his hand to turn her, to make her face the couple on the bed.

"Like that," he said, coming up behind her. He only touched her in two places, the hand he'd used to turn her coming around to caress her breast. Did she groan? She thought she might have. But when she felt the other place he touched her—that spot between her thighs—when she felt his manhood nestle between the cheeks of her backside as he pressed their two bodies together, she groaned. He moved his other hand up to sweep aside her hair, then kissed her as he returned to stroking her breast, and her woman's mound.

"Watch them, Anna, watch them as I do to you what he does to her."

*Move,* a voice urged again. *Move. Grandfather might hear.*

But then he stroked that place, that wet and heated place that craved his touch. She tipped her head back and moaned softly, her head hitting his shoulder.

"Don't close your eyes," he ordered. "Watch them. Watch them mate and learn what pleasure a release can bring to you."

She didn't close her eyes. No, she watched the couple on the bed through slitted eyes. His fingers probed deeper. She muffled a moan again.

*Don't let him touch you. Don't, Anna.*

But it was too late for her. She needed whatever this man could give her with a desperation that made her want to moan yet again, needed to forget her life and the dire financial straits she'd found herself in. Forget the rookery. Forget herself.

"Yes," he said, stroking her, his other hand playing with her nipple. "Let it happen, Anna. Let it come to you."

*Rein,* she silently cried. *Oh, Rein.* God help her, he matched the movement of his hands to the rhythm of the woman's moans. And with each stroke of those fingers, she wanted more from him. She wanted him to touch her deeper, wanted to turn her head and kiss him in a way she'd never kissed a man before, wanted to turn around and give him full access to . . . something.

So she did turn. Heaven help her, she couldn't stop herself from pushing against him, her legs slightly spread as she let him lift her skirts, let him find her again, begged him to kiss her with breathy sighs that echoed the rhythm of his hands.

He bent his head

*Yes,* her mind cried. *Kiss me. Touch me. Tongue me in the same way your hand probes me.*

He must have sensed her need for his tongue entering her mouth in the exact way she'd craved. Their juices blended as he sucked on her in a way that made her want to cry out in pleasure. Behind her lids flashes of light began to spark and sputter. Like the ignited end of a fuse she grew closer and closer to the something which she sought. Time didn't stop, but her world became Rein's, and it was a world governed by the desire to fulfill herself, to let herself float away and be free, to fly . . .

It happened.

She threw her head back, moisture cooling her lips as she cried out, trying to muffle it but unable to do so.

"Yes," she heard him say. "Take it, Anna. Take your pleasure."

And she did, only it wasn't pleasure—it was more than pleasure. This was a soul-searing joy that made everything that had come before pale by comparison.

"Anna," her grandfather called from below. "Anna, is that you?"

No. Not now.

"Anna?" her grandfather called again.

The room came into focus. No, Rein came into focus, his eyes staring down at her with enough intensity to make her still.

"Do not move," he ordered.

But she had to move. Her grandfather might take it into his head to investigate. "He might come up here."

"He won't," Rein contradicted, his hands holding her shoulders. A smell wafted on a heated current of air—a smell both familiar and unfamiliar, a smell that came to her from his fingers. Her smell. Her woman's essence.

"I want you, Anna. Now. This moment. God help me, I want to push you up against this wall and claim you."

"We can't," she said, already pulling back, her legs feeling as weak as a newborn's. "Not with my grandfather—"

"We can," he contradicted.

But, no, for with the passing of her pleasure came an understanding so clear, it was like the pinpoint of a candle's light when seen through a tiny hole. Letting this man have her, acting upon the desires they both shared, might bring her gratification, but it would also bring her a child. What she felt for him, what she wanted of him, could never be slaked in one mating. She'd want it again.

And again and again. A month, maybe less, and she'd be swelling with a bairn.

She stepped sideways, with a part of her feeling surprised and, yes, disappointed when he let her go.

"I . . . can't."

"Damn it, Anna, don't leave me like this."

"I have no choice, Rein. You would see that if you weren't so anxious to have me."

"You do have a choice. I shall ensure that you—"

"Anna?" came her grandfather's voice again, closer this time.

"Stay here," she ordered Rein, "do not follow me down. You may sleep up here tonight. Best to keep you out of sight in any event, for my grandfather has forgotten your existence." And before he could say another word, she turned away, the place between her legs slick with her passion.

"Anna, this is not over."

No, it wasn't. She knew that. This was only a temporary reprieve. Sooner or later they would have to sort out where their passions would take them. Anna just didn't want it to be now.

But if she thought getting to sleep that night would be easy, she should have known better. She had become aware. And so when she got her grandfather resettled into his bed, she didn't immediately crawl onto the mat before the fire. Rein was up there. Waiting for her. Listening to see when her grandfather had gone to sleep. Would he come to her then? Would he push the issue? Did she want him to?

Her breasts still hung swollen with desire, waiting for

his touch. She felt the urge to touch herself, to give herself pleasure, an urge she'd never felt before meeting Rein. Except she wanted Rein to touch her, not her own fingers. Wanted him to come to her now, this moment—to kiss her, to bring her to a throbbing peak.

She removed her dress, her body so sensitized, she drew each brush of the fabric out, letting it caress her slowly, building a desire she warned herself not to slake.

If he came down, would Rein be surprised to find her in nothing but a chemise? Would he like that she'd undressed for him? Should she have stayed dressed in the event he *did* come to her?

She lay down on the mat before the fire, her ears straining, listening, hoping they'd hear the sound of him coming to her.

No, not hoping, dreading. No, hoping.

But he never came. Nor did he stir.

Just a complete and utter silence came from above her. Well, as silent as it could get in a building shared by six families. A mouse squeaked from behind the walls. A child cried out from belowstairs, someone dropped something heavy.

But he never came.

She woke the next morning feeling out of sorts, muddleheaded and, yes, just a touch piqued, and why that should be when she'd told him to keep his distance, she couldn't fathom. But with dawn came the admission, too, that she'd done the right thing. Her body had cooled now, her blood not as thick as it'd swirled last night. So as she grabbed the gray dress she'd washed the evening before and left hanging by the fire, she told herself she should be grateful he'd been honorable enough to have kept his distance.

Only she wasn't grateful, she was . . . disappointed.

"Ach, nice of you to join me this morn," Molly said as Anna stepped from her building a few moments later, warm gruel in her belly, and her cloak pulled well over her face.

"Stow it, Molly. I'm tired and I'll not welcome your skulduggery."

"I'll wager *that* has something to do with a certain Mr. Hemplewilt."

Anna kept quiet.

"Did you diddle him?"

She refused to answer.

"Ach, you did, didn't you?"

Anna stepped around her friend, heading down the alley and to her barrow kept in the basement below. She passed Molly's orange-laden basket as she walked by, the twang of citrus overtaking the smell of the nearby gutter.

"Don't think walking away from me will help. He kissed you, didn't he?"

*. . . his tongue in her mouth, matching the rhythm of his hand . . .*

She opened eyes she hadn't even known she'd shut. She'd stopped before the small door that angled out from the side of the building, the wood water-stained from a leaking drainpipe above, the gray streaks looking as dismal as Anna felt.

"So it's finally happened?" Molly asked. "You've finally gone and given yourself to a man."

"Molly, we didn't lie together," she said as she fiddled with the key she pulled from her pocket.

"No, but he touched you well enough, I can see that."

Anna told herself not to react, but she could be honest with Molly. And truth be told, she wanted to talk about it, no, *needed* to talk about it.

She turned back to her friend. "He touched me."

"Did he bring you pleasure?"

She thought about how to answer, then decided on the truth. "More than I ever thought possible."

"Oh, there'll be more," Molly said with a light in her blue eyes. "Just wait until he gets to the *real* joining."

Anna shook her head, tipping her chin down so Molly couldn't see her beneath the brim of her straw hat. "Molly, I can't let that happen." She met her friend's gaze again. "For too many years I've watched what happens when a woman bears a child. And I'll not be responsible for one more mouth to feed here in St. Giles. Not now, not ever."

"Aye, but Polly the tart what lives below me says there are ways to keep yourself free from the childbed—"

"Polly has three babes of her own."

"Yes, but none since she started having her customers wear pigskin—"

"Molly, please." She held up a hand, because if Molly told her of a way to have Rein and not get with child, she might do it. Indeed, she suddenly admitted that what she feared almost more than a child growing in her belly were the feelings growing inside of her.

And from up on high, Rein stared at the coral-pink colors of a dawn sky, waiting for Anna to reemerge from the alley with her friend next to her.

"Devil take it." One would think a night spent inside a freezing cold room would cool a man's ardor.

Only it hadn't, he admitted as he stood with his hands clasped behind his back. Staying away from her had been hell. He'd thought he could do it, had told himself to do the honorable thing and stay away. Only when had he suddenly turned honorable? It was a badge of honor in his family—well, most of his family—to seduce innocents, and yet suddenly he found himself wanting to live up to the word *noble* in *nobleman.*

And then he saw her, Anna's head bowed as she emerged from the side of the building with her barrow out in front of her and her friend in tow. Rein straightened. The two women merged into the pedestrian traffic like clots of cream through a spout.

Gone. She'd left for the day.

He slumped back, his eyes narrowing as he thought of the feelings she evoked in him, wondering if he could keep himself away from her, wondering what it mattered if he did not.

"It must be hard to keep who you are to yourself."

He turned, too shocked for a moment to do anything more than say, "Who the *devil* are you?" before realizing the man might be a threat.

"Freddie Stills, at your service," said the broad-shouldered man. He tipped his hat, exposing a cap of red hair. He was big, huge even, Rein would guess almost as tall as himself, though Rein had never aspired to have muscles the size of beef legs. Obviously, this gentleman did.

"Mr. Stills?" Rein asked.

"I've been retained by Mr. Lassiter to keep watch on you."

Of course, Rein thought. He'd wondered if his uncle's solicitor might do such a thing.

"You've done well for yourself, *Mr. Hemplewilt.*" He smirked a bit at the assumed name.

"How the blazes did you learn the name I'd given?"

"Your landlady's friend, Molly, is a talkative lass."

"I see," Rein said, surprised to learn that he'd already been checked up on.

Mr. Stills moved to the edge of the roof. "I'll have to admit, I never expected you to last this long." He looked down. Rein knew what he would see: the tops of carriages that rolled by, spotted with dirt and water stains. A rut that lay on the right side of the road, one that carts always seemed to find with a thunk loud enough to be heard on the roof.

"Nice view."

"It's tolerable," Rein admitted. "How the blazes did you get up here?"

"The bloke what you're living with let me in." The man glanced over at him. "A bit crackers, ain't he?"

"A bit," Rein admitted, wondering where this was all going and why a man who was very obviously a Runner judging by his scarlet waistcoat had tipped his hand if he'd been paid to catch him cheating. Truth be told, he'd almost admitted to Anna who he was last night. He'd wanted to convince her that she'd be well taken care of once they became lovers. Only he couldn't tell her that, nor did he truly want to, because the devil of it was, he'd never bedded a woman without her knowing of his wealth and position. Suddenly it became vastly important to him that Anna want to be with him because of *him,* not his title.

"Still, it was a spot of good luck that the lady's toy hit you in the head when you first arrived."

"You saw that?"

"I did. And your trip to the market."

*Egads.*

"I also know that you had a visitor to these rooms the other day."

"How in the blazes did you find out about that?"

"One of your neighbors heard it from the grandfather."

*Good lord.*

"Any idea who it might have been?" Stills asked.

"No. Though now that I think on it, perhaps you."

The man's red brows stretched almost to his hairline. "Me? Why the blazes would you think that?"

"There was a note. It warned me to leave St. Giles. Mayhap Mr. Lassiter thought to frighten me, through you."

"I assure you, sir, he did no such thing. And if he had, I'd have told him no. I'm a Runner, I am. I have honor. You're better off thinking of a family member or two who might have something to gain should you fail."

"Ah, but that is the problem. There is no one behind me to inherit the dukedom. I have a cousin, to be sure, but he is on my mother's side and in no way connected to the Montgomery family."

"Has to be someone else, then."

"Unfortunately, I am unable to investigate at present."

"I can investigate."

Rein felt his brows lift. "You'd do that?"

"I would."

"Why?"

"Because if someone is trying to scare you into leaving St. Giles, it's my business to find out. I'm charged with seeing to your safety—after all, the object isn't to get you killed."

"Then why the blazes was I dropped in St. Giles?"

The man shrugged. Rein found himself studying him, wondering if he might have found a new ally. "My thanks to you, sir."

"Save your thanks for if I turn up something."

Rein nodded. The two of them exchanged glances.

"In the interim, I'll be keeping a closer eye on the place," Mr. Stills said. "If you see anything suspicious, I'll be keeping watch across the street. You can alert me there."

Rein nodded.

"Good luck, gov. I'll be in touch."

"As will I, if I need you."

The man nodded. Rein watched him turn, watched him slip back into Anna's attic, but even when he was out of sight Rein didn't move. Oh, he faced the London landscape again, but that was all. The colors of dawn had changed to a deeper purple near the horizon and a light blue above.

*Could* he have an unknown cousin aware of the will and its provisions, one that hoped Rein would produce no heirs? But if so, why hinder his challenge if the title would pass to the cousin anyway? It made no sense.

Suddenly Rein found himself more muddled than he desired to be. It was all too confusing, Besides, he felt much better now that he knew he had a Bow Street

Runner on his side. Indeed, so much better he found his thoughts returning immediately to Anna.

*Ah, yes, Anna.*

Rein almost smiled. She thought to call a halt to his seduction, did she? Although when, exactly, he'd decided to seduce her he couldn't say. He'd started out last eve with every intention of behaving honorably. Only as he'd lain awake in her little room, smelling her scent, he'd realized there was no reason to deprive them both of pleasure. She wanted him. He wanted her. They would have each other . . . starting the moment she returned from market.

For the first time in days, Rein smiled.

# Chapter Thirteen

Anna stayed out late that evening, with Molly shooting her knowing looks as Anna took a meal with Molly and her family. But she couldn't face Rein. Nor her grandfather. Not anybody. She needed to regroup, to gain the courage to face Rein and tell him he must leave.

He *had* to leave.

But on the way home—Molly's residence was only a few blocks away—her mind churned out so many thoughts and longings and concerns that when she arrived, she was in something of a temper at herself.

Blowing hair out of her face, she turned the knob of her front door. Blackness greeted her, only the glow of the fire stopping it from being that dark, all-encompassing shade of night that signaled evening. Odd, how the thought of stepping inside filled her with trepidation. At least a thousand times she'd entered her rooms, yet this time she was afraid.

Where was he? The fire sent out a puddle of orange light that, unfortunately, didn't reveal the whole room. Her heart began to tap in her chest as she made her way toward her ladder, refusing to look toward Rein's chair.

Indeed, she felt a certain measure of relief when she made it up the first two steps without anyone stirring behind her.

"You're avoiding me, Anna."

Anna's foot came out from under her, only her arms saving her from falling. She dangled there a moment before her half boots found purchase beneath the brown skirts of her dress.

"Not that I blame you," he added, "given the unfinished business between us."

Anna turned.

He sat in the armchair, the grate to his right casting enough of a glow that she could see the burnt-umber reflection of his left cheekbone. She knew this for a fact, for she stared at that cheekbone, and only that cheekbone, not, heaven forbid, his eyes.

"I am not avoiding you. I merely took a meal with Molly and her family this eve."

"Really?" he questioned, and she knew if she'd been looking into his eyes she'd have seen his black brows lift above them signaling the sarcasm she heard in his voice. And his mouth would be tipped up on one side as he smirked.

"Anna, you will not turn to a pillar of salt if you look me in the eyes."

Her gaze snapped to his, her chin lifting, even though, clinging to the ladder as she was, she had to tip her gaze down to keep eye contact.

"If by that you infer that I am afraid to look at you, nothing could be further from the truth."

He stared at her for a moment, his eyes nearly as black as the air around him. "Did you know your vowels even out when you're vexed? Indeed, you sound almost to the manor born."

"Do I?" she said in her mother's voice. Her mother *was* to the manor born, little did he know.

He rose, and as odd as it seemed, even from her perch on the ladder, that made her nervous. She could go up. She could go down. She could run for the door. And yet the sight of him rising from his chair made her feel like a mouse startled from a pantry.

"Don't, Rein," she said, her hands tightening on the rungs they held, her nails digging into the ancient wood.

"Don't what?" he asked, coming toward her, the smell of mint filling the air.

"Don't come near me."

"Are you afraid?"

"Only of myself," she said with a flash of brutal honesty.

"Don't be," he said softly, by now near enough that she could see the details of his face. His chin looked shaven, the smell of the lye soap he'd used crossing the distance between them, the scent seeming to be tinged with mint. He wore no jacket, his white shirt loose from his breeches, his boots oddly on his feet—still—as if he'd slept in them. "You want me, Anna. Want me in a way that leaves you aching for my touch. I know, for 'tis the way I feel about you."

God help her, his words made her hands tighten, made her blood thrust boldly through her veins, leaving heat behind.

"No," she denied.

And then his hand reached out and slipped under the

hem of her dress, finding the bare skin above her petticoat, slipping his fingers up her leg.

*Oh, god.*

"Rein, no."

"Would you rather my tongue replace my hand?"

*What?* "No," she said, ignoring the reaction just the mere image of what he suggested did to her insides.

*Gads, Anna, turn and go back up the ladder, escape through your room.* Only. She. Couldn't. Move. Because it was true. God help her, it was true. She wanted to become his lover. Damn the consequences.

And then his finger found the indent of her woman's lips and she lost her grip on the ladder as she all but fell into his arms.

"There are things we can do, Anna," he said as he clutched her to him, his finger propping between the fold.

*Oh, god.*

His finger found a spot within that fold, a spot that he dragged his finger across, her head falling back as she relaxed her legs and allowed him to touch her there . . . right there. Yes.

"Do you begin to see how wonderful it would be? How marvelous it will feel when we come together? But not right now, Anna," he whispered in her ear. "Not right now. Now I want to kiss you . . . here, where my finger is. Will you let me?"

Kiss her there? No. She couldn't.

He touched her again and she realized she would let him do anything to her, anything he wanted as long as he stirred that feeling inside of her, the one that she knew would only intensify with each masculine touch.

He picked her up, and Anna's whole body went limp.

*No,* her mind cried as he laid her down on the cotton mat before the fire.

*Yeeees,* a voice inside her head hissed as he slowly lifted the hem of her dress.

"You must touch me, too, Anna," he said softly, his body shifting so that he lay alongside of her, and then he undid the front of his breeches, his manhood a solid shape that thrust out, the tip swollen with his desire for her.

Touch him? Yes, she wanted that, too. Indeed, the thought of caressing him excited her all the more.

His hand found the bare part of her thighs again. She reached for him just as he gently turned her so that they faced each other.

"Touch me, Anna, as I shall touch you."

And then, oh, lord, he was kissing her. Anna's thighs fell open.

"Touch me," he ordered again.

She hesitated, and yet the long, hard stalk of him beckoned for her touch. Slowly, tentatively, she reached for him. Soft as kidskin, he was. She gently clasped him, afraid her work-worn fingers might hurt. She needn't have worried, for he groaned in pleasure. They were perfectly on level with each other, so perfectly that she had only to bend forward a bit, to reach out and lightly touch him with her lips, something she'd caught glimpses of before—in dark alleys, in the room across the street. She did it to him now, touched him with her lips . . . and heard him gasp.

Feather-light kisses rewarded him for the pleasure he gave her. He dragged his tongue across her moistness. She gasped this time.

"Take me in your mouth, Anna."

Her mouth? She wasn't sure how to do that. She opened her lips, touched him with her tongue, the coolness of his shaft a startling contrast to her warm tongue.

"Take me," he said.

She grew more bold, taking more of him in her mouth. "Anna," she heard him moan as he began to move his hips, helping her to give him pleasure. And the more he moved, the more of him she took, the forbidden thing they did causing her not shame, not embarrassment, but a pleasure so sensual she wanted more of him, and to give him more of herself. Her hips writhed as she moved beneath his tongue, her own mouth working the tip of his masculinity in an effort to bring him equal gratification.

"Anna," he gasped, stopping for a moment. "I am going to . . ."

Yes, she was going to, too.

"I need to . . . Something will happen." He moved from her thighs just as she felt ready to crest.

"Forgive me, Anna," he said, moving away from her so that he lay on his back. She watched it happen then, watched as he clasped himself, something erupting from his tip as he stroked his hand down his length and, god help her, the sight of his seed spilling made the pulse between her legs beat harder.

And then he was moving, moving between her thighs, his hands parting her all the way. And she held herself open for him, told him wordlessly that it was her turn now. His tongue thrust into her.

She cried out.

He thrust into her again. She bit back the cry this time. She had to contain her cries, her grandfather—

"Rein," she moaned, lifting her hips to his mouth.

Once again he thrust into her, sucking at her this time.

She fragmented apart. *Oh, oh, oh,* how she fragmented, her hips lifting off the ground as she melted into his mouth, his tongue lapping at her as her body pulsed.

The room turned oddly quiet. An ember popped and then shifted in the grate. The clock her grandfather had invented tick-tick-ticked in the background.

Rein moved up her body so they were face-to-face.

"I want to bury myself inside of you, Anna," he said softly, his breath, with her scent tinting it, wafting across her face. "But not here, on a hard mat. I want you in a bed."

She wanted to reach up and touch that face, to memorize every aristocratic feature.

"One day we shall come together," he promised. "One day very soon, my love. And when it happens, I promise you, you shall never look back. I can take care of you. Give you things, things you've only ever dreamed of. You shall want for nothing."

Her hand froze.

"But not now," he said. "Not now."

With those words, he left her.

# Chapter Fourteen

Where he went, Anna didn't know, she only knew she needed to escape, too, to regroup to her attic so she could regain what little sanity she had left.

Dear God, what they'd done . . .

Her body tingled and warmed as she threw herself on her bed, the straw crinkling beneath her weight. She'd known a woman could take a man in her mouth. She'd caught glimpses of enough tarts working their charms on their patrons that she knew most of what occurred between a man and a woman.

But she hadn't known this.

She hadn't known a woman and a man could pleasure each other at the same time.

*You shall want for nothing.*

What had he meant? He'd left her so quickly she hadn't realized what it was he was saying until he'd gone.

Had he truly meant what she thought? Had he asked her to be his mistress? Could he be wealthy enough to set her up in such a way? And if so, what in the bloody blazes was he doing in St. Giles engaged in a bloody wager?

Sleep didn't come easily that night. When she awoke

the next morning, she ended up losing courage and crossing to the rooftop next door to exit.

"You've not been yourself, Annacries," Molly said from her position in the market next to her later that morning.

"Been thinking," Anna said, looking away from the faces in the crowd.

*Looking for Rein.*

She wondered if he would track her down, if he'd want to see her, speak to her . . .

"'Bout Mr. Hemplewilt?"

Yes. "No. I've been thinking about my sails."

Silence. Anna chanced a glance in Molly's direction.

"Ach," her friend said. "Go on with you. I knows you better than that. Quiet all day, you've been. Too quiet. Can't get a word outta you. Driving me batty."

Anna shook her head. "Molly, I don't wish to talk about it. Not now."

"No? Then I suppose you'll be pleased to know Charlie the fish trader is coming this way. Gives you as good an excuse as any to ignore me some more."

Anna looked up, and indeed, here came Charlie, his long face looking more fishlike than normal as he ran between the permanent stalls, baskets of fruits and vegetables and those buying wares. His gray hair looked mussed, the white apron he wore stained with fish guts. With hurried glances at the faces he passed, he navigated his way toward them.

"Charlie. What is it?" Anna asked as came to a stop before her, his brown half boots skidding on an orange rind one of Molly's customers had dropped on the stone that paved the square.

The man swallowed, the knob on his long neck bobbing up and down. Someone jostled him, for the market
was crowded this time of day. "Anna, I've got bad news,
I have."

Anna came around the back of her cart, resisting the
urge to bunch her hands in her white apron as she did so.

"What news?"

He swallowed again, nodded at a black-hatted gentleman who nodded at them as he passed. Anna's heart took
on the winged beat of panicked sparrow's.

"Well, now, Anna lass, I suppose there's nothing for it
but to tell you honest." He paused before speaking, and
when he looked at her again, her heart took flight.

"Me brother's ship set sail for Spain this morn."

She stiffened, not at first understanding his words.

Ship set sail? What ship?

*His brother's ship.*

She stiffened in horror. The ship that she needed to
hoist her sails on the day of the competition. For that matter, the one that she needed to use for testing those sails—
though if the ship couldn't be there the day of the
competition, what point was there in testing?

"No," she said in disbelief, shaking her head because
it just couldn't be true.

"Left port this morn, Anna. I just got his bloody note.
Seems he got an offer from a gent what paid him triple
the rate to carry cargo to Spain. He couldn't pass that up.
He's always short on cash, what with a wife and seven
bairns to feed."

*Then he shouldn't reproduce like a bloody rabbit,*
Anna wanted to yell. No, she wanted to go find that

bloody captain and yell at *him*. Only she couldn't because he was on his way to bloody Spain.

This couldn't be happening, she thought. It just could not have happened, not after everything she'd gone through, not after all that she'd done to earn the coin for more canvas.

She almost sat down. If Molly hadn't been looking on, she just might have.

"Anna, you all right?" Molly asked. "Do you want me to take over your barrow for a bit?"

No, she was not all right. The ship she was supposed to hoist her sails on was gone.

Anna looked up, meeting Charlie's gaze, the horrified look in his eyes prompting her to say, "'Tis all right, Charlie. Ain't your fault. Your brother had to do what was best for his family."

The old fish trader nodded. "I'm glad you understand, Anna. I were truly worried that you'd be upset."

Upset? Upset didn't begin to explain how she felt. Disillusioned. Disappointed. Devastated. That was how she felt, for without a ship to fly her sails, she couldn't enter the competition. The rules were very specific. Competitors must have their inventions present the day of the competition and in working order . . . and for her that meant hoisted.

"I am sorry, Anna," the man said, obviously reading her disappointment. "I truly am."

She nodded, turning away.

"Anna," Molly said when Charlie left. "You can still enter the competition, can you not?"

No. This meant her disqualification.

"Perhaps you can find someone else—"

"Find someone else?" Anna asked, turning on her friend. Though a part of her knew it wasn't Molly's fault, though she knew it was wrong and unfair to raise her voice to her longtime friend, she couldn't seem to stop herself. "I'm tired of this, Molly. Tired of being upended. Tired of working my fingers to a nub only to have all my hard work pulled out from under me at a moment's notice. There are days when I wonder what it is I've done to deserve such a fate. If maybe I should live my life differently. Be mean. Evil. Sell myself for blunt. I coulda become like those cats we've always scoffed at. But I've kept my legs together, kept myself out of trouble, kept my grandfather and me in food even though it's near impossible for a woman to find honest work. I've worked hard, I have, and yet here I am again, knocked out of the water."

"You don't know that for certain."

"Do you think it will be easy to convince a ship's captain to give my sails a try and then be present for the whole morning of the competition? Not only will I have to find a man willing to do that without expecting any favors in return, but I'll have to convince him to trust in my design. Impossible. I know. I tried for weeks afore Charlie agreed to help me."

Molly's expression turned to one of sympathy.

Anna shook her head, instantly contrite. Lord, what was wrong with her? "Molls, I'm sorry for yelling."

Molly's face softened. "Don't give up, Annacries. You can do it."

No, she couldn't. Lord help her, she was bright enough to know she fought a losing battle.

"Where are you going?"

"Leaving," Anna said, beginning to pack her wares.

"But it's not even noon."

Anna shrugged as she threw her instruments into her barrow, the metal clinking in an almost rhythmic way as she did. "'Tis a slow day."

Molly looked horrified.

Anna ignored the look, smiling bravely as she pushed off, even though she knew her smile was a lie.

Rein had hoped Anna might return for a midday meal, but he'd scarcely believed that she might. Thus when he saw her pushing her barrow down St. Giles High Street from his position on the roof, the feeling he got could only be described as euphoric. At last he'd be able to talk to her and resolve the issues between them—*ask her to be his mistress.*

He waited a full ten minutes before going to the trap that led to her attic. He expected she might bolt when she heard him, thus he was shocked when he found her sitting on the edge of her little bed, her hat tossed on the floor, her hands clasped in her lap, her apron and brown work dress still in place.

"Anna?" he called, thinking she might not have heard him.

She didn't say a word, just sat there, her gaze firmly fixed upon the windows opposite her. Sunlight cast large squares of light on the floor, the pattern casting a glow up the walls of the room. A fly buzzed a loud and lazy circle until landing on Anna's work-worn hand. She didn't move, didn't so much as swat it away, just stared un-blinkingly at the windows.

"Anna, what is amiss?" he asked, knowing it could not

be her grandfather. He'd just left the man moments before climbing to the roof. "What has happened?"

He thought she might not answer, thought she might continue staring at that damnable glass. To his surprise she said, "'Tis over," trying to pull her hands away.

"What is over?" he asked.

She was silent a moment, Rein suspecting that she debated with herself whether or not she should tell him. At last their gazes met, the misery and anguish in her eyes doing something to Rein's insides that he scarcely understood.

"I had a ship set to hoist my sails," she said softly. "For the competition. It needed to be present at the competition so the naval board could inspect my sails, only the captain what gave his word to help me left port today."

The mind he despised for being so slow worked hard to understand how this would affect her.

"He had an offer from a trader. Triple his usual fee to run cargo to Spain and back. It'll be weeks before he returns."

And at last he understood.

She would not be able to enter the competition.

Rein would have expected to feel a certain amount of distress over her unhappiness. What he didn't expect was the swell of sympathy he felt, one so great, it robbed him of breath.

"Anna," he said at last, "I am so sorry."

She blinked at him, her beautiful and spirited amber eyes so devoid of their usual spark, he almost pulled her into his arms.

"Do you know I have tried for six years to come up with a way to escape this bloody rookery? That I've spent months—nay, years—devoting myself to the task? And do you know that I realized today that I would have been better served to simply do what all the other pretty girls in the market have done—find myself a protector rather than battle against a society determined to keep me in my place?"

He listened, troubled by her words.

"If I'd been born a man, there'd be no end to the ships' captains lining up to help me. Wealth in exchange for a few hours of their time. What is there to balk at? Because I'm a woman, they won't trust me. They believe me incapable of thinking beyond what to cook for supper. They refuse to admit that I could invent anything so revolutionary as a new staysail. I know. I tried for weeks to find a captain to hoist my sails. In the end, it was only Charlie the fish trader who got it done, and then only because he threatened to quit selling the fish his brother caught if he didn't lend a hand."

"Anna—"

"I'm tired, Rein. Tired of it all."

She stood, the smell of her wafting toward him in a sudden current of air, his nostrils flaring at her scent, the memories that her smell evoked instantly arousing him.

"This morning you told me you'd take care of me."

Rein tensed.

"Were you asking me to be your mistress?"

He had been asking, had intended to ask her yet again. Suddenly he wasn't certain he should. "Anna, I—"

"Were you?"

He had to tell her half-truths about so many things, he wouldn't tell her another one. "I was."

She nodded, and to Rein's absolute shock said, "Very well. If the offer is still open, I should like to accept. Assuming, of course, that you're wealthy enough to take me away from all this." She motioned at the room around her.

Did she jest? Could she be serious? "I am," he replied.

He didn't think she could assume a pose prouder than any he'd seen before, but somehow she did, the angle of her chin not changing, yet her pride seeming to be more pronounced as she squared her shoulders, her eyes darkening, her face firming into a look of determination.

"Then I accept. But only if you promise to provide for my grandfather as well."

"I will."

She seemed to lose some of her bluster then, her eyes darting away from his for a moment, but only a moment. "Will you tell me your real name?"

"No," he answered honestly, surprised that she'd reasoned that Hemplewilt was not his given name. Then again, what should surprise him about it? Her intelligence was one thing he prized above all. "I cannot reveal that now."

"Your wager?"

"My wager."

She was back to looking proud again. "One day you shall have to tell me what's so important that you agreed to come to St. Giles."

"One day I shall," he agreed. "Just not now."

"When do we begin our bargain?"

And God help him, her words delivered such a stab of desire to his groin, he almost flinched from the force of it. "Tonight," he found himself saying. Today. Now.

She nodded, stepping around him as she headed toward her ladder. "Tonight it is, then," he heard her say without a backward glance.

# Chapter Fifteen

A rash decision? Anna asked herself as she waited upon her rooftop hours later, the sky above her the dark, midnight black only ever found beneath mushroom caps, the moon a period that dotted the sky. Or a wise decision? For even now she could feel the slick moisture of her woman's mound as she anticipated.

Desired.

Craved.

Yes, even burned.

For the truth of the matter was, she wanted him. Indeed, when looked upon as a bargain of mutual satisfaction, she might not have done so badly.

And yet still . . . to do such a thing, to agree to become a man's mistress . . .

And so, as she stood near the edge of the roof, she tried to reason out the logistics of how she'd arrived at such a place, but the simple truth was, she was tired. Tired, she thought, as she leaned her head back and closed her eyes, the fall of her hair an unfamiliar tug at the back of her scalp, for she rarely left it down. Tired of the worry that came along with being the sole provider of food and blunt. Tired of the fear that one day something might happen to her, something that would cause them to lose what little they had. Tired of working so hard to get . . . nowhere.

Tonight she would secure her future.

"Anna."

She didn't flinch. Indeed, she'd been waiting for him.

"You may still change your mind."

She slowly turned, her coverlet clasped around her. As an answer, she let it drop. And though there was only the light of the moon by which to see his face, she could tell that the sight of her naked body was such a shock, such an instant arousal, he might have refused to let her change her mind should her answer have been no.

But she wasn't changing her mind. Instead, she crossed to the bed she'd made near the center of the roof, and she felt the quickening already, felt her body warm and heat and moisten in anticipation of their joining. She stopped next to the ruined canvas that she'd covered with blankets, then slowly stepped into the center, the canvas a sigh against her tired feet. When she faced him again, she discovered he hadn't moved.

"I feel I should be remiss if I do not point out that you do not have to do this. We could try, on the morrow, to locate another ship. You might still be able to—"

She moved her hair, which had fallen over her breasts, behind her back. And standing there with her nipples erect, her body quickening, she realized that Rein staring at her was the most erotic feeling she'd had in her life. It was more erotic than spying on the woman and her customers across the street, more so than listening to Molly's tales of erotic adventure, more, even, than the fantasies she'd had in recent years.

He didn't say a word.

She waited, wondered . . .

"Do you have any idea," he said, "how often I've dreamed of seeing you thus?"

The skin along the curve of her breasts tingled.

"I've touched you in my dreams, Anna. Seen your body arch with a woman's pleasure, but all that pales in comparison to the vision you are now."

As if he touched her now, the back of her neck prickled. The heat between her legs liquefied, culminating in a slick wetness that awaited his touch, too.

"Lie down," he ordered.

She shivered in . . . what? Fear? Anticipation? Desire?

She sank to her knees, flicking her long hair over one shoulder as she slowly lie down.

He came to her then, stood over her, stared down at her as she looked up at him with desire claiming her mind. For long seconds, neither of them moved, then he slowly flicked open the catches on his shirt.

And through it all, she lie there. He had hair on his chest. She hadn't known that about him, the sight of that masculine trait making her throb all the more.

*Get to it,* she silently urged, taking in his muscular shoulders and well-shaped arms.

He bent and removed his boots, straightening so that he could undo his breeches. Every muscle in her body froze for an instant as he pulled them off, her eyes following the material's descent until he flung the things away and straightened, naked.

He was hard. She'd known he would be, but at the tip

of that hardness was a glistening drop of moisture that made Anna's thighs begin to burn twice as hot.

"Spread your legs."

This was it, then. She hadn't expected it to be so soon. Or so businesslike. But she shook her head. They'd made a bargain, the two of them. She couldn't blame him for wanting to get to it.

He knelt between her legs, and when he did that they touched, though only in one place—one unexpected and erotic place. His manhood rested in the valley of her womanhood—just there—no place else, though his minty breath warmed the coolness of her cheeks as he said, "I'm going to do things to you tonight, Anna, things you've never dreamed of. And when I've finished, I shall do them again, and again, so that you will never, ever forget this night." He bent his head, drawing his tongue across her nipple, her body arching into him with such speed, she let out a moan.

"And me," he added, green eyes so full of promise, they sent new shivers through her. "I shall never forget it, either."

And then he was gone.

She pushed up on her elbows. His head hovered over her womanhood.

*Oh, lord . . .*

Would he do that to her again? Would he kiss her as she'd dreamt of him kissing her the whole time she'd been at the market today, her mind replaying what they'd done the other night?

He drew his tongue over the center of her.

Her head arched as she let out a moan, her knees falling open farther. He licked her again and she realized that she didn't care if they never joined, as long as he would do this to her, over and over and over— His tongue thrust inside her.

"Rein," she moaned, her eyes opening, blurry stars above her as she moved her hips toward him in offering, moved in the way he'd taught her to move. And then a new sensation filled her, one less soft . . . more hard.

"Show me, Anna," he said, drawing his finger out and up her slick wetness. "Move for me. Let me learn from the way your body writhes how you like to be touched."

His finger. He had his finger inside of her and she wanted—

He entered her once more. She wanted him. She moved, just as he asked her to do. At that point she would have done anything to gain her release. She wanted to feel it again, to experience the bliss, the lovely, wonderful bliss . . . the forgetting.

"That's it," he said. "Yes," he whispered.

She moved, lifting her hips as he held his finger inside of her. And there was no shame in knowing that he watched her like a male cat watched a female cat. She moved until she felt pain, drawing back a bit and then trying again, disappointed when that pain prohibited her from having him touch her deeply. But then he touched the nub of her womanhood and she about came up on her elbows. Her hips lifted, the pain stopping her from hitting that place again, but she didn't care, for now he used the palm of his hand to rub up the length of her and she forgot all about pain as her slick wetness created a new kind of longing, a longing that made her want to join with him. That was truly what she craved. Him. Inside of her. Now. But instead he moved alongside of her, his dark hair falling around his face as he bent his head and gently, lightly kissed her, his breath smelling oddly of mint. That was all he did—kiss her. No pressure to open her mouth, just a brush of his lips that felt like a stray hair and that took her by surprise with its gentleness.

"I'm in awe," she heard him say.

In awe? In awe of what? And then he touched her again and she didn't care.

"You are a virgin."

Did that matter? She had a momentary thought that it might, but then he kissed her again and this time it was as unlike the previous kiss as the earth was from the sky. This time when his tongue entered her mouth, she recognized the rhythm now, the same rhythm they'd shared in the past. She knew herself to be close now, could feel the pressure build, that gloriously wonderful, heavenly building of release. She rode his hand as his tongue flicked and flicked and flicked until she could no longer breathe anymore, until she pulled her lips away, crying out, "Rein."

That was the moment, the moment she'd been waiting for, the pulsing, pounding pleasure that rolled and rolled and rolled like the pressure of a wind, one that took her breath away with its force. He watched, his face now drawn back, his eyes black and intense as he watched her gain her pleasure. A breeze drifted over them, stirring her hair. She knew she should be cold, but she was so very far from cold.

"I don't think I'll ever tire of that."

She saw his teeth flash in the darkness, saw his lips pull into a masculine smile.

"I don't think I'll ever tire of watching you gain your release."

She did something then, something she'd been wanting to do since almost the first day she'd met him. She lifted her hand and swept his hair off his face. He seemed surprised by the gesture, for his eyes widened.

"What of you?" she asked. "If this is to be a partnership, I'm not living up to my end of the bargain."

"No," he said, reaching over her, pulling one of the scraps of material out from under the blanket, then sitting up so suddenly she moved onto her elbows to see what it was he did.

He reached between her legs and dabbed at her womanhood.

"What are you doing?" she asked, closing her knees and swinging them away.

"I'm cleaning you." He held up the rag, and to her shock, there was blood on the surface.

"But, I— That is, we—"

"Didn't couple? No. That we shall do later, when your body has had time to adjust."

He'd broken her maidenhead, she suddenly realized, without using his manhood. "You've done this before."

"I've initiated women before. Aye."

She stared across at him, unblinking.

"Does that disturb you?" he asked.

Her eyes narrowed a bit, her full lips pressing together into something not quite a smile, not quite a smirk, Rein thought.

"No," she said.

Of course it wouldn't, Rein admitted. Why would it matter to her that he'd had other women? Why did it matter to him that she hadn't had other men?

Because he hadn't expected it, damn it. He'd assumed,

living as she did in St. Giles—as willing as she was to engage in the giving and taking of satisfaction—that she'd not been innocent. And yet as incredible as it might seem, she'd been pure.

"How have you done it?" he found himself asking. "How have you kept yourself from men?"

She looked surprised by the question, and as he finished wiping, throwing the rag aside, he lay down next to her, the hardness of his groin making him want to groan when it came into contact with her leg. Bloody hell, if she only knew how much he wanted to part her legs, to push into her, to feel the silky softness of her womanhood as he took his pleasure.

She hadn't answered, he realized. Had she felt his manhood touch her? Did she know how he trembled? Did she feel the slickness of his shaft?

"Anna?" he asked, because he needed her to talk. Needed her to distract him. Needed her to help him turn his thoughts from the two words pounding through his mind. *Take her. Take her. Take her.*

Yet still she didn't answer.

"Most women in your circumstances would have long since sold their bodies.

"I'm not most women."

No, she wasn't. And therein lay the crux of the problem. She wasn't like any woman he'd ever known. She wasn't like any other woman in *all of London*. Brilliant. Beautiful. Beyond amazing, she was a woman to treasure.

"Besides, if I'd given myself to a man for money, my mother would've likely turned over in her grave."

She had a hair that clung to the side of her face as tenuously as a spider's web ripped from its perch, and despite the warning to himself not to touch her, he reached out and gently drew his finger down her face, shocked at how that one touch seemed to terrify him at the same time it softened him.

"She taught me values, ideals that I've kept with me throughout all the years she's been gone."

"You were close?"

"As close as a mother and daughter could be."

"And yet she left you to go off with your father."

"Sailing was the love of her life, aside from my father and me."

"Who stayed with you when she was gone?"

"We had staff."

That made his hand still, a hand he hadn't even known he'd been stroking her cheek with. "Staff?"

"I didn't grow up as poor."

He straightened a bit more, wondering—but, no, that was too far-fetched to be believed. "You come from wealth?"

"I come from brains. My father was clever at investing in things that paid out returns. Sad to say that when he died, the money went, too."

Good heavens, for a moment there . . .

"Were there no other relatives? No matronly aunt with connections and wealth just waiting to take you in?"

"If there were, do you think I'd be here?"

And then her smile faded a bit. "Doing this?" she added. "Selling myself to a man for the coin he'll bring me?"

Her lashes fell over her eyes like a cloud, blighting out the light that had been there a moment before.

"I have not *bought* you."

She touched *his* cheek then, her eyes meeting his with a direct, amber stare. "Yes, you have, gov, but if I'd known how amazing it could be between a mort and a cull, I might have sold myself long ago."

He drew back a bit, not liking her words. "You make yourself sound common when you speak in such a way."

"I am common." She smiled winsomely, sadly. "Selling yourself to a man makes you about as common as they come."

He found himself cupping her face then, moving so that he half covered her, the heat of her body causing his manhood to ache.

"You are *not* common," he said sincerely.

And then he saw it.

He saw the glimmer of light that caught the edge of her left lash, that sparked there for just a moment, glittering as she looked away and blinked and blinked, obviously trying to hide the evidence of her one tear.

"Oh, but I am," she said softly. "As common as they come. My father was a simple seaman, my mother a pastor's daughter afore she wed, and if she's not rolling in her grave over what I've done, you can wager Grandfather Hartnell is."

"You've done nothing to be ashamed of," he said. "Indeed, what you have agreed to do will better your station." But even he knew that didn't sound right and so he added, "You are amazing, Anna. Lovely and intelligent and witty and courageous. If you'd have been born into a different family, you'd have likely netted yourself a besotted fool who possessed a title and a fortune and would love you until the day he died."

*Someone like me.*

But he shooed the voice away, for if he and Anna had moved in the same circles he'd have stayed away, knowing that a woman such as herself wouldn't have cared a whit about his title. She'd have met him and quizzed him and realized he'd the intelligence of an otter. Anna Brooks needed a man who was her match. That man was not him.

He rolled off of her then.

"What is it?" she asked, looking like a mermaid, her golden hair falling over her breasts as she rose with a white sheet around her.

"I am . . ." What? What did he feel? Inferior? Beneath her? "Ashamed," he found himself saying.

*"Ashamed?"*

He nodded his head before answering, trying to gather his thoughts as they floated through his mind. "I took advantage of you," he said at last. "I saw the desperation in your eyes and took advantage of your plight."

She stared him. "What do you mean?"

" 'Tis why I am here, Anna, here in St. Giles—because of the way I've spent my life, engaged in one scandal after another. I thought I had learned something during the week I have been here, and yet the moment I am faced with a situation where I could use my wealth to gain something I want—you, Anna—I accept." He looked out over the rooftop. Looked out over the world, her world, the black smoke that rose from numerous flues noticeable even in the darkened sky. "I should have told you no. Should have insisted you continue your quest to win your competition, not sell yourself to me."

"Rein, if we are being honest, I wanted you to have me."

And that made it all the worse, for he sensed her growing regard for him, sensed that they would end up as far more than mere lovers.

Friends.

He stood.

"Where are you going?" she asked, her amber eyes puzzled as she sat there, the sight of the breasts he longed to touch and suckle causing him to turn away. God's teeth, what was he doing?

*Acting like a bloody fool,* said the old Rein, the one who took his pleasure wherever he wanted. Who commanded the world to do his bidding. Who had never, not once, considered the welfare of another before his own. Who, even now, urged him to turn around and go back to her.

But the new Rein, the one he suspected his uncle had hoped to find, straightened after he'd hurriedly dressed, turned to her and said, "I must think."

"Think?" she asked with a wide-eyed look, her eyes, Rein noted, still moist from her tears.

It made him stiffen his resolve. "Yes, Anna, think—as difficult as that can be for me at times. Good evening," he said with a bow, ludicrous, really, when one considered what had just occurred between them and the state he was still in. There would be nothing good about this evening, he would wager. He turned on his heel to leave.

"Rein—"

But he ignored her because, God help him, if he turned toward her again, he wasn't sure he would leave.

*        *        *

It was a long night complicated by the fact that he knew Anna slept above. And as Rein lie in his chair, thoughts of being with her at the forefront of his mind, he also relived his life, going over his childhood and youth, trying to discover when he'd become the way he was. Certainly there were things in his past that had helped to shape him, but when had this hedonistic pursuit of pleasure become the basis of his life?

In the end he supposed it didn't matter. He was what he was, but he would not drag Anna down because of it. He was many things but not that depraved. At least he hadn't supposed he was until that moment.

It was a sleepless night, which was why when the note came he heard it pass under the door with a swish of sound that immediately caught his attention. The fire he had stoked all night still glowed brightly. When he sat up on the pathetic little mat he slept on he could see the room perfectly, Anna's grandfather's odd inventions and pieces of furniture black shapes in the room. The door lay on the opposite wall, a rectangular shape that he immediately went to, spying the folded note visible beneath its edge, his blood thrust into instant speed as he stared down at it.

His name could clearly be seen on the outside. His *real* name.

Lord, what if Anna had seen it first? He bent and snatched it up, wondering what new game this was. Could it be from the Runner? Or was this a new taunt?

*My Lord Duke—*
*This is your final warning. Leave St. Giles today or*

*the next unfortunate event will happen to your lady friend.*

The note whitened before Rein's eyes, the disbelief the words roused within him making him read the thing over again. Then another time.

*Leave or the next unfortunate event will happen to your lady friend.*

Good God, had whoever wanted him to fail the challenge been behind Anna's ship setting sail?

*Lady friend.*

Someone was threatening Anna.

Without thought, Rein crumpled the note and threw it into the grate. His hands shook as he considered the words.

Someone had threatened Anna.

Fury made him stiffen, made him turn toward the door.

Threaten her? Threaten one of the most brave and noble creatures of his acquaintance? Well, he would just see about that.

Mr. Stills was none too pleased to see Rein burst from Anna's building, cross the already busy street with a few backward and then forward steps (to avoid carriages and, in one instance, a loose pig) and demand his assistance.

"What the blazes are you doing out here?" Stills asked.

"I must speak with you."

"About what?"

"I received another note this morn."

Mr. Stills straightened. "When this morn?"

"Just now."

"Bloody 'ell. I just arrived."

"They threatened Anna."

For a moment they both lapsed into silence as the coal porter walked by singing his rhyme.

"Where's the note?" the runner asked.

"I burned it."

The man looked like he'd announced Rein had set his hair on fire. "You *what?*"

"I wasn't thinking," Rein admitted, feeling rather foolish suddenly.

"Did you keep the first one?" the Runner asked.

Rein shook his head. Bloody hell. Should have thought of that, too. How he hated being bungle-brained!

"Next time you get one, don't throw it out. The writin'. The way of speech. A person can tell a lot about someone by the way they write and phrase things."

Yes, Rein supposed one could. Damn it all to hell. It made him all the more angry. "They threatened Anna," he said again.

"I'll talk to your uncle's man about doublin' up on a watch. Obviously, someone means to frighten you into giving up in the hopes that they will eventually come into your title."

Rein straightened. "Well, they shan't. I will not allow a hair on Anna's head to be harmed."

And the feeling that overcame him was not unlike when he'd finally gotten tired of being beaten as a youth and finally fought back.

"The blood of a warrior runs through my veins," Rein

answered. "I may have forgotten that for a bit, gotten soft, as my uncle ofttimes pointed out, but I will not allow anyone to harm a woman in my protection. This is war. A war someone will lose."

"What do you intend to do about it?"

"As to that, I have an idea."

Mr. Stills rolled his eyes. "God help us."

Molly wasn't certain what to expect of Anna when she saw her that same morning, but it sure as certain wasn't the hangdog face.

"Lord, Anna, you're as pale as the corpse what fell outta that casket on Oxford Street."

"Sleepless night," Anna said by way of greeting.

"Oh?" Molly asked with a suggestive leer, wondering if she and his arrogance might have gone at it bread-and-butter style.

"It's not what you think," Anna said, the gray cloak making the half-moon shadows beneath her eyes more pronounced. She gave a shake of her head, then turned to walk down the alley.

"Is it having to bow out of the competition?"

She shook her head.

Molly stopped her before she'd taken three steps, the two of them ducking out of the way of people passing by.

"It's that man, isn't it? Got your corset in a twist, ain't he?"

"*Isn't* it, Molly. One says *isn't*."

"Ach, now you're startin' to talk like the bloke."

She thought her friend might turn away from her then, but Anna shocked her instead when tears entered her eyes.

Molly had never, not once, seen her friend cry—not since she was sixteen and she'd come back from that god-forsaken little town where she'd grown up, broken-hearted and nearly destroyed over something that had happened there.

"Anna, there are tears in your eyes," she felt the need to point out.

"Of course there's tears in my eyes, you great booby. I learned yesterday that the ship that was supposed to fly my sails has left port, and then when I offer myself up to a man in a fit of desperation, he doesn't want me."

Molly felt her mouth drop open, all the more so when Anna turned away—not to fetch her barrow down the long, dark alley, but instead to stand there, her shoulders stooping as she lifted a hand to wipe tears away.

"Annacries, Annacries, look at little Anna cry."

It was a rhyme Molly had coined years ago when they'd first met near the water pump, Anna sitting nearby and all but spewing more water than the bloody well.

"Anna, don't cry," Molly said softly, gently. The thing of it was, it was one thing to have known a sad and fright-ened little girl who cried—quite another to see the coura-geous young woman she'd become having a fit of the vapors. It frightened Molly half to death. What was the world coming to if the one person Molly was certain would escape the Giles was crying?

"Anna love, you can't be cryin' over that silly cull of a man?" she asked, because she truly couldn't believe Anna, of all people, would do so. "What do you mean, he doesn't want you?"

Anna whirled to face her. "He doesn't want me, Molls. He left me last eve on the rooftop after he'd, he'd—"

"Diddled you?"

Anna shook her head. "No. Not precisely."

"What do you mean, not precisely?"

"We had agreed," and Anna, confident Anna, suddenly looked uncertain. "That is to say, I had agreed to be his"—more uncertainty—"paramour, only when it came time for us to join—"

"His *what*?" Molly cried. "Lord, Anna, are you saying you agreed to become his mistress?"

"I did."

Molly slapped her forehead. "And I thought you bobbish." She shook her head. "I said to lie with the man, not agree to become his mistrees."

"I *am* bright, Molly. 'Tis why I agreed to become his, his . . ."

"Whore," Molly finished for her.

Anna winced. "His mistress," she said in a low voice. "He is wealthy."

"How do you know that?"

"Because I know it." She looked pensive for a moment. "I think he might even be nobly born."

"Think?"

"He has a mark where he wore a ring, it might have been a signet ring."

"You think he might be nobly bred? Ach, Anna, ain't you always the one telling me I have me head in the clouds?"

"I asked him about it. He said it was a family heirloom that he removed before coming to St. Giles."

"But you think that's a clanker?"

"It might be. He speaks so eloquently. Looks so arrogant. But more than that. 'Tis the way he acts, too. The way he was dressed when I first saw him." But then her friend shook her head; her cloak fell farther back as she did so. "But it matters not, for he doesn't belong to this world whatever his name or title, and he doesn't want me."

"Oh, he wants you, all right," Molly said. "No man doesn't want to bed a woman. That, Annacries, is a certainty like the rising of the sun."

"Not this man."

"Did he say why?"

Anna nodded. "He said to take advantage of my situation was wrong."

Which made Molly feel as if she stood upon a rotted board, one that broke beneath her feet and caused her to plunge down a hole.

"He said what?"

"That he refused to take advantage of me."

Lord above. Maybe the bloke *was* a nobleman, for only a nobleman would be so full of himself as to think that.

"And this was before or after he touched you?"

"After, of course."

Which confused Molly all the more. In her experience, a man didn't stop diddling a woman until he'd been diddled himself.

"Mayhap you should tell me exactly what you *do* know."

But what her friend knew was precious little indeed, which was why Molly asked Anna to watch her basket so she could dash off. Anna had looked at her oddly, but truth be told, her friend was not herself this day—not surprising, given all that had happened.

"Who is he?" she asked Mr. Stills after coming up on him from behind.

The man jumped what must have been a foot off the ground, nearly bouncing off the narrow walls of the alley like a ball tossed between them, his foot kicking over a nearby crate of refuse.

"Lord, woman, don't ever sneak up on me like that."

"Who is he?" she asked Mr. Stills again, having guessed that their meeting on the stairs might not have been a coincidence.

"Who is who?" he asked.

"Don't you be playing no games with me, Freddie. You're involved with Mr. Hemplewilt's wager in some way, ain't . . . aren't you?"

"How did you sneak up on me?" he asked, peering around and then back down the alley. "And how the blazes did you know I was here?"

Molly snorted. "At least five people knew of a strange man who's been on watch in this alley since the day Mr. Hemplewilt arrived, a Runner, they're all saying."

His brows rose and Molly felt self-satisfied. "You were asking after Mr. Hemplewilt that first day, not whatever name it is you gave me. You wanted to know if he was staying with Anna, didn't you?"

The surprise followed by immediate hardening of his eyes told her she'd reasoned out the truth.

"Who is Mr. Hemplewilt?" she asked.

Her new beau, a man she'd had over to dinner three times since she'd first met him, wouldn't look her in the eyes.

"Who?" she asked.

"I can't say," he said at last.

She took a step toward him. "Is he wanted for murder?"

His blue eyes lifted from her breasts so quickly and with so much surprise in them that she knew he found her question a shock.

"Whatever gave you that idea?"

"I just want to make certain Anna's not falling in love with a shady cull."

"She's falling in love with him?"

Molly thought about it for a moment, then nodded. "I've never seen her so addled afore. That it's over a man is tellin'. She's falling for him. The question is, does he care about her?"

"He does," Freddie answered.

"You're certain?"

"I'm certain."

"How do you know?"

Freddie shook his head this time. "Because he's out there spreading the word that Anna's life may be in danger—"

"Danger!"

He held up a hand. "We've got things handled, but you should likely keep close watch out for trouble, too."

Molly nodded.

"Plus he's determined to help her."

"Help her?"

"Aye."

"In what way?" Molly asked.

"I can't tell you."

"Ach," Molly said in exasperation. "You'd try the patience of a sitting hen."

"He won't hurt her," Freddie said.

"Who is he?" she repeated.

Freddie shook his head. "I can't say. But," he added when she drew herself up to give him a basting, "I can tell you I believe him to be a good man. A bit high in the instep, but good. What he wants to do for her will likely be an answer to Anna's prayers, but he needs my help to do so."

Molly felt her eyes widen; felt, for a moment just the tiniest bit of envy for her friend. Perhaps Annacries had finally found herself a man. And then the envy faded, for she had, too.

"Then help her, you daft fool."

# Chapter Sixteen

It wasn't like Molly to run errands in the middle of the day. Nor was it like her to return from those errands with a frown. Anna might have asked why she looked so serious, but she was too busy trying to come up with a way to face Rein again. What the blazes did one say to a man who'd done the things to her that Rein had done and then got up and left her in the midst of it all? *Thank you* hardly seemed appropriate. *My apologies* seemed more in line, especially given the state she knew he'd left her in.

So hard did she think on the problem that she barely heard Molly say, "You have a visitor, Anna."

*Perhaps I could sneak to my room over the roof.*

"Anna," Molly said, coming alongside to lean a shoulder into her arm. "Look."

Anna looked.

Rein walked toward her.

Her heart stopped.

It was the only way to describe the way the organ stilled and then popped from the force of catching sight of him. And on the heels of that flush came tingles, great masses of them that radiated to the tip of her fingers and then back to her center—that secret center that seemed to light on fire whenever she spied him from across a room. Or a rooftop. Or a bed of sheets.

And then his gaze caught her own. And though it was another overcast day, Anna felt as if the sun settled around her heart, warming her cheeks and her neck and shoulders. Embarrassment. That must be it. She'd not anticipated seeing him here, in the middle of the busy market, people swarming by and around him as they bargained for vegetables.

She turned to Molly. "I can't face him."

"Ach, Anna, when'd you turn into such a coward?"

A coward.

"Stay. Talk to him."

Anna picked up a knife. She didn't know what she intended to do with it. Likely throw it into her barrow, pick up the handles and make a run for it. But when she glanced toward Rein again, he'd stopped, his eyes going wide as he lifted his hands in a beseeching gesture.

And as unbelievable as it seemed, just that one gesture, just the small smile on his face, just the shared look of camaraderie in his eyes made her forget what had happened up on the rooftop. Made the embarrassment fade, the self-doubt fade, too, the realization that he obviously didn't think less of her for what she'd agreed to do with him making her heart sing for a moment.

She dropped the knife.

His smile spread.

She smiled, too, wondering what was happening to her. She was no coward, had never once since coming to St. Giles been afraid to confront a problem head on. Certainly she'd made a muddle of her life in recent weeks, but that didn't excuse her from facing Rein and her problems.

And so as she watched him approach, she noted to herself how handsome and tall he was compared to the other men in the market. And as she stared, she realized that this was why she thought him more than a simple gentleman, this was why she sensed there was more to him than met the eye. He had a way of walking, indeed, of just simply *looking* that made a person think of the aristocracy.

Closer and closer he came, and Anna's spine straightened with each of his steps.

"Ach," Molly said from alongside her.

"What do you mean?" Anna asked.

"He doesn't walk, he prowls."

Yes. It was a good description.

"Well, I see you'll be needing yourself some privacy. Go on by the church. I'll watch your barrow."

She almost said no, but when Rein finally stood before the two of them, Anna admitted she didn't want Molly to hear whatever it was he'd come to the market to say.

So she slipped out from behind her barrow, leaving her cloak behind, motioning with only a tip of her straw hat that Rein should follow. He did, moving alongside her. Other costermongers watched them pass, male and female alike, some calling a greeting, others—the females— mostly eyeing Rein up and down. Anna ignored their curious stares as she led him away from the market and to the granite steps of St. Paul's.

"I was worried you would tell me to leave," he said as she turned to face him, the busy market behind him, the pillars that lined the church behind her. Anna felt tempted to use one of those pillars for support. Tempted to place her hands against the cool surface, or perhaps press her cheek against the marble.

He'd touched her. Intimately touched her. And then he'd left her.

"Why wouldn't I see you?"

He stared down at her, the look in his eyes one she'd never seen from him before. There was no predatory gleam in the blue depths, no flirtatious smile lifting the edges of his lips. Indeed, if not for the smile he'd shot her earlier she'd have thought him the one who was angry with her, so intensely did he stare down at her.

"Because I bungled things rather badly last eve."

"Did you?"

"I did."

He hadn't, not really. He'd hurt her, though God knew why when he'd only done an honorable thing. But for some reason his walking away had wounded her.

"And so I am here to make it up to you, Anna Brooks."

She blinked, her heart beating at such a rate it almost seemed to hurt. "What do you mean?"

His eyes never wavered as he stared at her, the look in them so intense, so unwavering, she felt like one of her grandfather's insect experiments—her wings pinned to a board.

"I have arranged something for you, Anna. A ship. For your sails," he added when she could do nothing more than stare.

A ship?

What did he mean?

"You shall have access to this ship for as long as you like. It is only a brig, but I am hoping that will do.

A ship? He'd arranged a ship?

And then the full import of what he'd done sank in.

"You know someone who owns a ship?"

"I do. And I have arranged through the help of a friend for you to use it whenever you like, for as long as you like."

She stared up at him. Stared and stared and stared. And then all of what had come before that moment fell away, replaced by a feeling that swelled in her heart to the point that she couldn't breathe.

"Of course, you shall need to sew your canvases."

Thump-thump-thump, so fast did her heart beat she could barely tell where one pulse ended and the other began.

He'd arranged a ship.

He was giving her the chance to prove herself on her own merit, not with her body.

She bowed her head, not wanting him to see the embarrassing way her eyes filled with tears. Again.

"Anna?" he said softly, his hand reaching out to tip her chin. "Have I done well?"

She kept her eyes downcast. Lord, she didn't want him to see her cry, had a feeling if she met his gaze she'd throw herself into his arms and never stop releasing the tears.

"Anna?" he said again.

And then a hot tear fell from her lashes, belying her silence.

"Anna, don't cry," he said gently, his hand dropping to catch her hands.

She fell into his arms as if it were the most natural thing in the world to do. And perhaps it was.

# Part Three

*"My destiny is you,"*
*said the prince to the maiden.*

# Chapter Seventeen

Anna received word that the textile trader had found some canvas for her to use the next day, fate seeming to finally shine down on her. It wasn't premium canvas like the first roll of material she'd bought, but it was canvas and thus it would do. And so during her three-day wait for it to arrive, and then later during the long evenings when she sewed, Rein—much to her dismay—kept close watch on her, though he never, not once, tried to touch her again. In some ways that felt worse than before. He seemed . . . different. Distracted. It drove her mad. It made her burn.

The only thing that seemed to help was working herself into a stupor, exhausting herself as she sewed, falling into bed at night looking forward to the mornings when Rein would break his fast with her. She sewed. And sewed. And sewed. Until finally, at last, the day came when she was done.

"I am finished," she told Rein the moment she descended the ladder. He stood staring out the window, his face in profile as light from outside cast a glare onto the ceiling above. There was a look on his face, one unlike any she'd ever seen before, though he didn't turn to face her fully. Sad, it seemed. Perhaps even pensive. Concerned.

"We'll have to spend some coin on a wagon to transport them to the docks," he said.

"Charlie the fish trader has agreed to let me use his cart. He feels badly."

"He shouldn't," Rein said.

No, he should not. "Did you ever send word to the bastard that destroyed my sails?"

He faced her then, and she could have sworn she saw the look in his eyes change. He seemed to almost shield his gaze from her, to look away for a moment.

"I have tried," Rein said, clasping his hands behind his back.

"Tried?"

"Through a mutual friend."

"And did he respond?"

He shook his head, straightening, and suddenly he looked so autocratic, both like and yet unlike the man she knew. "It means no matter, for I vow nothing like that will happen again."

Could he truly be a lord? Gads, at such moments he looked and acted such.

"Thank you," she said.

He inclined his head, just a brief inclination, but one done so easily, so precisely, she was certain he'd done it a hundred times before.

And likely had. So what did that matter?

She felt a frisson of . . . something. Concern? Worry? A premonition? She looked away from him, trying to

understand what it was. It was then that Anna became
aware that they were alone.

"Where's my grandfather?"

"He insisted on going out."

She felt light-headed as she stood there, aware that her
breaths had quickly grown irregular. But that wasn't the
worst of it. The worst of it was the sensation she had as
she stared across at him, a sensation of falling, falling,
falling.

"Rein—"

"No, Anna," he interrupted. "Do not tempt me by saying what is on your mind. I know what you are thinking.
I see it in the way you look at me. God help me, 'tis the
way I feel for you. Having tasted you once, I find myself
craving that taste again. Sometimes I swear I can smell
your woman's essence in the air. I want you, but I shan't
indulge myself. For once I shall do the right thing. I believe I owe you that."

She didn't want him to do the right thing. She wanted
him to sweep her up in his arms. To place her on her bed
abovestairs, to show her more ways to gain pleasure. She
almost told him that, except she felt absurdly embarrassed to do so. Ridiculous, given all that they'd shared.

"Be ready to leave at first light," he said, turning away
from her.

"Where are you going?" she asked.

"Out."


So they left at dawn, Charlie having brought the cart
for her to use after dropping his wares at his stall on
Dyott Street not many blocks away. Rein drove, many of
her friends in the rookery seeing her off. All of them

knew of the importance of this day, and all of them rooted for her.

Anna thought she might be uncomfortable sitting next to Rein on the narrow perch that passed for a seat during the long ride to London Dock, the smell of the black nag that pulled the cart drifting back to them. But she hadn't taken into account the anxiety she would feel over the coming test. Apprehension stepped in to take the place of desire. Would her sails work? What would she do if they did not? And what was this ship going to be like that he took her to? She had asked Rein, but he would only tell her that it was a two-masted brig he claimed never to have seen before. That filled her with a new worry, for what if the ship wasn't seaworthy? What if the captain resisted hoisting her sails? Rein claimed not to know the crew, so then what was their motivation for complying with his requests?

So many questions, so many fears. When they reached the square-shaped docks, the horse that pulled their cart lifted his head in protest as his iron-shod hooves struck the giant stones that formed the man-made harbor. Anna felt her heart begin to beat in rhythm to the clip-clop-clip-clop. They had arrived. It would finally happen. She would get to test her sails. And what a perfect day it was. The sky was a blue only ever seen near the bottom of a rainbow, so perfectly clean it didn't look real.

And then Rein transferred the reins to one hand and used his other hand to clasp her own. "It will be all right," he said, glancing down at her with a slight smile.

God help her, Anna knew in that moment she was losing her heart.

And was that such a bad thing? she asked herself.

Whoever he truly was, he had proven himself to be an honorable man. Would it be so horrible to fall in love with him? To share a future with him? To be with him?

It would if he were a nobleman, for then she would face new obstacles—loving a man who was far above her reach, who would be unable to wed her because of her low birth, who might one day have to wed another woman.

But she wouldn't think of that now.

She faced forward, so nervous her tongue seemed to swell near the back, making it difficult to swallow.

God help her, it might already be too late, because the thought of him with another woman . . .

"Do you know where you are going?"

"Here," he said, pulling the cart to a stop next to a schooner.

"It has three masts."

"It's not that ship. 'Tis that one." He pointed with his chin. "I undershot the mark a bit, I'm afraid."

She looked, the ship in question obscured by another, but slowly, as they walked along the stone pier, the ship took shape.

She came to a halt. "It is a *yacht*."

"So it is."

She looked up at him. "It's as big as the *Royal George*."

"Is it?" Rein asked, for he truly did not know.

But then he noticed Anna's gaze had sharpened to a point like shaved stone. "Who owns the ship?" she asked softly.

He'd expected the question, but that made it no easier to answer.

"The duke of Wroxly."

"A duke? You know a bleedin' duke?"

He had known she would ask this and so he told her the truth, which she would misinterpret, but the truth nonetheless. "No. Not really. The man was a veritable stranger to me."

"Yet he's letting you use his ship."

"Anna, the man in charge of the duke's estate is letting us use the ship. The duke is dead." Which, for the first time, filled Rein with a touch of sadness. Gone. The one person who'd seen through his jaded and selfish facade to the man beneath.

"Come, Anna," he said. "Let us go and test your sails."

She nodded, though she suddenly looked a bit ill. Thus it was Rein found himself leading the way up the swaying gangplank. Rein, who steadied Anna as he boarded his ship. Yes, *his* ship, for the fifty-foot brig was his, should he complete his time in St. Giles. The ship and several others, income-producing ships—tea clippers, merchant ships and the like—all belonged to the ducal estate, several of them moored near the yacht, though by rights such a fine ship should be moored in the Pool of London, away from the grunge of the dock.

"Mr. Hemplewilt?" cried a man in a tan jacket and gray trousers that Rein assumed must be the captain. He wore no hat, his red-brown hair swept over *à la* Brutus. He had a face so browned by the sun that when he didn't squint, white lines emanated from the corners of his blue eyes. Yet the man was as finely dressed as a nobleman: buff nankeen breeches, dark-blue tailored half coat and tails with brass buttons down the front, starched white shirt beneath his jacket, which made Rein wonder how much he paid the man.

"I am Captain Jones," the man said. "The duke's man told me you're wanting to test some new sails for His Grace. Can't say that I'm not curious, though he said nothing about your bringing a woman."

"She is the inventor of the sails we wish to test," Rein replied with an edge to his voice.

"Beg pardon?"

"She is the inventor."

"*She* invented the sails?" he asked without looking at Anna.

Anna chose that moment to throw back her hood. Captain Jones's gaze moved to her, then away, then back again rapidly. His eyes widened as he got his first glimpse of her, the blond hair Rein found so striking gathered at the top of her head and yet flying about her face when strands came free.

"Indeed I did, sir," she said.

"God help us," the man muttered, looking at Rein again. "Does the new duke know?"

"He does," Rein snapped, wondering if walking the plank was out of vogue.

"He does?" Anna asked with a lift of her brows.

Rein realized he suddenly trod upon vastly unstable ground. "He does," he decided to state simply, because . . . he did.

"He knows about me?"

"He knows *all* about you, Anna. Indeed, once he heard about your plight, nothing would do but that he help you."

"Truly?"

He nodded. "Truly."

He saw Anna's eyes soften then, saw the look of gratefulness she shot him before turning to face the captain again.

"When you hoist my staysails, Captain, tell your crew to use a loose knot; the more play in them, the better."

"I beg your pardon, ma'am, but I'm not so certain this is a good idea."

"Whether or not it is a good idea is not your concern."

"I beg your pardon," he said again, this time to Rein.

"Do as she says," Rein ordered.

"She is a woman."

"And I am the man the duke has ordered you to obey."

Captain Jones stiffened. "Aye, sir," the captain said, though he looked none too pleased about it. "But if she sinks my ship, they'll be hell to pay."

"I believe the ship belongs to the new duke of Wroxly," Rein reminded him. "A man you have never met, which means his opinion of you can yet be swayed."

Rein left the threat hanging, something the captain obviously didn't like, for his eyes narrowed.

Anna stepped in by saying, "Find us a commanding wind, Captain. And when you do, toss out your log line to gauge the speed of your ship."

One last glance between the two of them and then a small bow. "As you wish," the man grumbled before turning away, Rein wanting so very badly at that moment to tell the bloke who he was.

"Shall we go to the front of the ship?"

"Bow," she said softly, smiling at a crew member in a blue half jacket and white trousers. Rein saw the man almost bash into the mast as he caught a glimpse of her. "'Tis called a bow."

"Why?" he asked, because he thought she might need to keep talking. He could tell, in the way her eyes shifted about, never landing on any one thing for longer than a moment, that she was as nervous as a horse at a steeple-chase.

"Why what?" she asked as they made their way along the rail and up a small flight of steps that led to the bow.

"Why is it called a bow?"

She draped her fingers over the smooth surface of the rail, her gaze catching on the gold gilt inlaid into the sur-face. "It's an old word that means *shoulder,* the front of a ship meant to be the 'shoulder' of a boat."

"Indeed?" he asked.

"Indeed," she said, pausing beneath one of the lines that stretched to that bow. "And this is a beautiful bow . . . and ship."

"Is it?"

"As lovely as the royal yacht, I suspect."

"I do not know."

She looked up at him, studied him, but she didn't look like she believed him. "Do you not know?" she asked.

"No, Anna, I do not."

"You've never ridden on the *Royal George?*"

She still suspected he was nobly bred, and for a mo-ment Rein cursed her cleverness, but he could answer this question honestly, too, and so he said, "I'm afraid not," taking her hand and leading her toward the front of the ship in the hopes of distracting her again. Ice-cold, that hand was, and, unless he missed his guess, trembling. And in that moment a very odd thing happened. Rein's heart began to ache for her. Actually ache. Not in pain or fear, but in mutual sympathy.

"Frightened?" he said as they stopped near a rather stunning masthead of a mermaid coming out of a foamy sea, her red hair streaming back in waves.

"Terrified."

"Do not be."

She bit her lip, the gray cloak of hers swinging out behind her as a wind caught the edges, revealing a gray dress beneath.

"What if they don't work?"

"Then you shall have some very unique window coverings."

She looked up at him sharply.

He smiled.

She stared at him a second and then smiled, too, strands of her upswept hair flying free and loose around her face. God, he found himself thinking, there could be no more beautiful woman in all of London. None.

And then he found himself doing something he'd never done in the past, not when the boys at the university had pounded at his face, and certainly not when his father had done the same before.

He prayed.

# Chapter Eighteen

As it was, they didn't catch a good wind until they were far down the Thames, and so by the time they'd tested the old sails, Anna felt ready to toss her accounts all over the pristine deck of the duke's brig. Time to test her sails.

"Triangular," she heard one of the crewmen say as they unrolled them.

"Unusual shape," said another as the sails drooped above their heads, empty of wind now, as were all the sheets, the gray shadows of the canvas shielding Anna's view.

"Are you certain 'tis the way they go?" a yardman asked.

Anna called up to them, "Aye," her hand cupped to her mouth so that her warm breath made her realize how chilled she'd become.

Chilled? Or frightened?

Frightened, she decided. She was too nervous even to glance at Rein. Too nervous to do anything but watch as the crew put everything in place. The captain gave a nod and a call. The anchor was lifted, the bow of the ship pointed downstream. Anna watched, breath held, as the mainsails filled with air, the staysails behind filling, too. She'd worried there'd be too much play, that the main-sails might spoil her air, but she needn't have. The shape fit exactly as it should, the dimensions she'd been given of most mainsails exactly right. Thank the Lord.

"Steer her course," the captain cried.

And all Anna could do was wait, Rein standing by her side as they ran the same path they had three times be-fore, three tedious times, just to be sure they could get a fair average. Only this time they used *her* sails.

"It feels like we are moving faster, does it not?" Anna asked, clutching the rail as if she could push on the thing and make the ship go faster.

"'Tis too soon," Rein said honestly.

And it was.

She waited as they approached a grove of trees that sprouted up from the shoreline. The ship groaned, leaned to the left a bit.

It felt like they were going faster.

"It feels . . . smoother," Rein said.

It did. She closed her eyes. There was no wind when one sailed with it, but there were other things: the near musical melody of water falling away from the hull as they sliced through the water. The vibration beneath her feet as the ship strained. The low murmurings of crew members as they spoke to one another.

Silently, she ticked off seconds in her head, only she must have started late because all too soon the captain called for a stop. She turned to the man, her heart beating so hard she worried it might stop altogether.

"Ach," Captain Jones murmured. "Must have caught us a good wind."

"How much better?" Rein asked.

"Near three full knots faster, but we'll need to do it again. The wind might've picked up."

Three knots? Out on an ocean, those three knots might add up to more.

"Steady, Anna. He might have a point," came Rein's calm and steady voice. "We knew the wind would be a factor in the test. We need to wait for the average."

She nodded, swallowing, though her tongue felt thick near the back of the throat.

And so they keeled the ship to the right and tacked back to the starting point, the whole process so tediously long Anna felt ready to jump overboard again by the time they started at the same point.

"Steer her course," the captain cried out once more.

And they did it again, only this time it felt faster. Anna was certain of it.

"Avast heaving," the captain called.

Anna looked over at him. His hair had come completely free of its style, mussed as it lay around his puzzled face. "Four knots faster," he said.

Her heart began to slap in her chest like the hands of gypsies when they did their dance down at the market for coin. She met Rein's gaze. They shared a look.

It was working.

"Let's do it again, lads," Captain Jones said. And so they did, only this time before they set off the captain threw a bit of string in the air to gauge wind speed.

"Doesn't seem any faster," the first mate said, looking past his captain and giving Anna a slight smile that reached his eyes. A tall man with a long, angular face, that smile seemed to be just for her.

"It doesn't, but it must be," the captain said. But when they flew down the Thames a third time, Anna began to realize that she might—just might—have done it.

She looked at Rein.

He thought she'd done it, too.

She could tell in the way his whole face had relaxed, the look in his eyes one of such pride, of such happiness for her, Anna felt her heart melt.

It took two more tries to convince the captain, and then a run with the old sails, but by then Anna knew. So did everyone else on the ship. Anna could tell, the eyes of the crew smiling at her even if their faces did not.

She had done it.

"My congratulations," the captain said grudgingly.

Anna could afford to be magnanimous. "Thank you for hoisting my sails," she said, her lips and chin and cheeks twitching as she fought back a wide smile.

"Where did you get the idea to change the shape from trapezoid to triangular?"

"Mathematics," Anna replied.

The man's brows lifted. "Mathematics?"

"A triangular shape allows for more mass, more mass allows for more air, more air allows for more speed. By my calculations, I reasoned that the ship *should* pick up three or four knots."

And that was when the captain smiled, as if privately applauding her very unladylike skill.

"Like to take her a bit down the Thames, if you don't mind, just to see what she can do."

Anna smiled. "I would like that, too."

The captain turned away. Anna faced Rein.

He opened his arms. She needed no second urging.

Laughing, she flew into his embrace, Rein picking up and spinning her around as he said, "Anna, my love, you are the most clever woman I know."

He stopped. She leaned back and before either of them knew how it happened, they kissed, but it wasn't a kiss like the other—a vortex of passion that spun out of control. This kiss was one that shared a joy and a happiness unlike any either of them had known.

She drew back, her heart and mind seeming to soar with the gulls that followed their ships. "Thank you," she said, placing her hands against his cheek, a day's growth of hair making his chin a prickly surface of masculinity.

"For what?" he asked with a soft look in his lovely green eyes.

"For believing in me," she said.

He smiled and the warmth of camaraderie changed to desire. A crew member called out to another and brought her back from the brink, but only barely. Goodness, but her body ached beneath the heat of his gaze. It remembered, Anna realized, what it was like to be held in his arms.

"Excuse me, miss, but cap'n thought you might like a tour of the ship afore we set off."

Anna turned to see a cabin boy of no more than twelve looking up at her through wide, light gray eyes, his black hair ruffled by the Thames breeze.

"And might I say that your sails be mighty fine, miss? Mighty fine."

Twelve or so. About the age she'd been when her parents had died.

*I did it,* she silently told them. *I did it.*

"I believe we'll wait until after we sail down the Thames."

The boy nodded. Anna and Rein turned to face the front of the ship.

They sailed for an hour or more and when the ship turned, the lad returned and said, "C'mon, then. 'Tis a beauty of a ship, she is."

Exhilarated by their trip, Anna followed, the joy over the success making her cheeks ache from her smile. She hadn't been calm enough to notice the details earlier, but now she noticed the craftsmanship of the woodwork around her. The end posts of the railing were carved to look like mermaids, two brass rings breaking the other rail posts into thirds. The deck beneath their feet looked smooth enough to use ice blades upon. And everywhere she looked, instruments were made of brass. The clock near where the captain steered, the bell nearby, too. Even the boy before her wore a blue half jacket with brass buttons, his white trousers pristine and new.

That was the word to describe the ship. It all felt new, and luxurious, and likely something she'd never see again.

"Lead the way."

"The officers' quarters are astern, crew sleeps below," the cabin boy said. "Would you like to see the stateroom?"

"I should think that would be private," Rein said.

"Ach, gov, the new duke ain't even been on board yet. There's no privacy to disturb."

Which was why when the young man moved forward to lead the way, Anna decided to follow. She thought for a moment Rein wouldn't. Indeed, he hung back a few paces.

They were led toward a door tucked beneath the poop deck. Here, too, were accents of brass, the door as ornately carved as one that would be found in a fine home, brass hinges to match the knob. Beyond the door lay several other doors, captain's quarters and the like, a big door at the very end. A double door, no less, also carved, but this one painted with a gold leaf pattern.

"Here we are."

Anna felt excitement thrum in her veins. The boy swung the doors wide.

"Oh, my goodness."

"Amazin', ain't it?" he asked. "Go on in," he encouraged when they both hung back. "Ain't no one been in 'ere in a while, the old duke bein' sick, and now gone. Used to love this ship, he did."

"I can see why," Anna said, and it was odd, for while her immediate impression was of gold leaf and dark furniture, it wasn't until she paused in the middle of the room that she began to notice other things, ordinary things—at least ordinary in the duke's world, and once upon a time, hers.

A dark cherry wardrobe closet.

*Mama, what dress should I wear?*

A beautiful writing desk with the fine parchment, quills and ink resting in a special holder so they wouldn't slide in rough seas.

*Mama, may I draw?*

And the bed.

*Sleep tight, my dear.* Her mother's voice, her pretty brown eyes staring down at her with love.

Anna moved forward. A red tapestry coverlet lay over the bed, gold tassels hanging off the corners. A big bed, one that stood beneath a panel of windows that revealed the V of the ship's wake.

A bed. A real bed.

She reached out, the world seeming to drop away as she admired the coverlet, then pressed on it. Soft. Feathered.

A childish giggle. *The feathers tickle my nose, Mama.*

*Then do not breathe them in.* Her mother's smile had been one that teased.

"Anna?"

It was only then that she realized Rein stood next to her. She looked up. "I'd forgotten what a feather mattress felt like."

She saw Rein turn, heard him say to the cabin boy, "Leave us," in an autocratic tone that left no doubt that he was used to giving orders, and that was just as well because suddenly Anna felt a keening sadness that nearly brought her to her knees.

She'd forgotten. Forgotten what it was like to have things, normal things like tables that weren't held together by twine or rusty nails, beds that weren't filled with straw that always poked through and stabbed at a person when one needed one's rest. Closets that held clothes. Lots of clothes, not the three dresses Anna owned: two brown, one gray.

Once upon a time she'd had dresses . . .

"Anna?" he said again as the door closed behind them.

The ship shifted a bit beneath them, but Anna hardly noticed. "I'd forgotten," she said.

"Forgotten what?"

"All the things that come along with wealth."

He'd moved to her side. "You will have them again, one day soon."

She looked up at him. "Will I?"

"Of course you shall. Your sail is a success. You shall win the naval competition, and the money that goes along with it. And let us not forget that I have promised you twenty pounds when all is said and done."

When he left. When her handsome, kind and noble Rein left.

"I don't want you to leave."

"I— What?"

She turned into his arms. "I don't want you to leave. I want things to stay as they are, with you as just you, not . . ."

*A nobleman. Please, god, don't let him be that.* Such a thought filled her with uncontrollable, irrational fear.

"Anna, I shall always be who I am today."

No. He would not. He would be above her. She would have to be his mistress. But even the mistresses of noblemen suffered a public life. It was one thing to be the mistress of plain Mr. Hemplewilt, but quite another to be the mistress of a baron, or a viscount, or, God help her, an earl.

She drew back, her gaze as imploring as she could make it. "Please, Rein, tell me who you are."

"I cannot."

She lurched away from him. "Damn you."

"Anna, please," he said, gently pulling her back around again. "Don't ask this of me. Not now. Not here." He wrapped his arms around her. "As you said, let us remain as we are."

She pulled out of his grasp again, going to the window and placing her hands against the smooth surface, looking out. The panes she stood behind suddenly made her feel like a caged bird, one that looked out on the world through bars, a world she knew she would never join.

"Anna," he said softly, turning her again.

"Your name's truly not Hemplewilt, is it?"

He shook his head.

"I'd thought not," she said, wondering if it mattered what his name was. To her he was Rein, always Rein, and for today that would be enough.

She slid her hands up the front of his coat, then the side of his neck.

"Anna," he said softly. "Do not tempt me."

"But, you see, I want to tempt you. I want you to kiss me. To touch me the way you've touched me before." Her other hand reached from beneath the cloak, finding his manhood, gliding her palm up its already hard surface.

"Anna," he hissed, his eyes closing.

"Touch me again, Rein. Touch me now because when you do, I forget what it is that you're keeping from me. I only want you to touch me, to kiss me in that way you have of kissing me that makes me moan—"

His lips covered hers so swiftly she gasped. His tongue found hers. She answered his thrusting warmth with a heat of her own, her hand still stroking him, going to his waistband, slipping in between the catches and down to the solid length of him.

"Anna," he hissed into her mouth.

"Lock the door," she said, stepping back from him to release her cloak from around her neck. It fell from her shoulders like a lover's hand, making her burn for her real lover. She reached behind her next, beginning to undo the catches.

He didn't move.

She almost told him again to lock the door, but something about his watching her, something about the way his green eyes turned dark, his lids lowered so that he almost looked furious, only it wasn't fury. It was need. Lord, but knowing he needed her as badly as she needed him made her lower her arms, made her turn her back to him and say, "Help me, Rein."

Her eyes closed as she waited for him to come to her, knew that this moment was where it would all end or begin. He didn't move behind her, and for a second, disappointment fell upon her hard. Then she heard him move, heard the snick of the lock, heard him cross back to her. And still she waited, the skin on the back of her neck tingling as she anticipated his touch . . . or his kiss.

She received neither, for instead he must have bent down, lifting her skirts, his hands finding her wool stockings beneath her chemise, the wispy feel of his fingers gliding up her legs making her body spark and tingle in anticipation. The hands he'd used to lift her skirts pushed her back, guided her in such a way that she knew where he wanted her to go, and what he wanted her to do. And so on the edge of the bed she sat, his hands lifting her heavy wool skirts and tucking them around her waist.

"Open your legs."

She did as he asked, exposing herself to him, watching as his head lowered . . . and lowered, until she was arching, leaning back, her hands coming out behind her and digging into the covers as his tongue found her and made her burn at the same time she turned wet. She began to move for him as all too quickly she felt ready to break apart.

He was giving her what she wanted without taking what he needed. Again. Damn him.

She wouldn't let him. Not this time.

Leaning forward, she gently tipped his head back. He looked at her through eyes gone glassy with need.

"Don't," she said.

"Don't what?" he asked.

"Don't bring me there . . . not without you inside of me."

"Anna, I might get you with child."

She reached behind her, undoing the last of the catches.

"What are you doing?"

But he knew. God help him, Rein knew. The taste of her still lingered in his mouth, the need for her such an ache in his manhood that he feared he would bury himself up to the end of his shaft.

"Anna, don't."

In a move that surprised him, she stepped back and up onto the bed as she shrugged out of her dress. God, but the sight of her undressing, of peeling her clothes off one layer at a time, held him immobile. His chest rose and fell in short, shallow breaths.

Her breasts were beautiful, but he'd known that. She lifted her arms, the nipples budding as they were pulled into a graceful curve by her movements, her brown areolas framing the hard tips.

She undid her hair, the golden strands falling around her shoulders, covering a portion of her breasts, the side of her neck. When she'd finished that, she wiggled out of her stockings and lay upon the bed, completely naked before him.

"Touch me," she said, one of her hands moving to her womanhood as she spread her legs. "Touch me, for if you do not, I shall touch myself."

God help him, he should resist. He should do the honorable thing and wait until he could tell her who he really was. But then she began to glide her hands up the wet folds of her womanhood, and the smell of her drifted over to him, flaring his nostrils, making him move toward her without thought. He undid his breeches.

She watched, her hips moving now as she stroked herself.

Rein gave up all hope of resisting then. He nearly ripped the buttons off his jacket, only undid the first two of his shirt, tugging the thing over his head so harshly it popped seams. Did he take his breeches all the way off? God, he didn't know. He just found himself on the bed with her, their bodies entwining as they found each other's lips and kissed, his tongue sinking into her mouth just as his manhood found her valley.

She panted. So did he as she spread her legs wide. Rein knew then that this would be no subtle seduction. This would be a mating. A covering. A joining both craved and shared and that had them kissing and moaning and then sighing as he entered her at last.

"Rein," she cried out, arching beneath him.

He thrust, then thrust again, her body so hot around him he gasped for breath, tossing his head back as he thrust and thrust and thrust. She was his. His. His. His. The words repeated themselves as he looked down, met her gaze, their climax nearing, though Rein knew she would have hers first.

She did, his name cried out as she allowed herself fulfillment. Watching her climax prolonged his own, the feel of her pulsing around him filling him with such a passionate sense of rightness, he could only watch as she gained her release, as she drifted back to shore, her eyes focusing on his own.

"I love you," she whispered.

He climaxed.

And in that moment he knew he loved her, too, loved her with a fierceness and a passion that would never go away.

"I love you," she repeated as this time *she* watched *him* climax.

# Chapter Nineteen

*I love you.*

Anna cradled Rein as his breathing returned to normal, his face in the crook of her neck. His breath whispered over her with the softness of the wingtip of a bird.

*I love you.*

And she did. She knew it, for there could be no mistaking the emotions she felt. No other man knew her like Rein. No other man had done so much for her. She'd shared all of herself with him—her childhood, her longings, her secret desires—and that, she knew, was something she'd never done before.

The question became, What to do about it? Never had she backed down from a challenge. Oh, she'd had her moments of weakness, but in the end she was always a fighter. Should she fight for Rein? Fight for marriage? A position among his set, whatever set that might be? She knew there were ways to keep herself from childbed, but they were not foolproof ways. Lord help her, she might be with child now.

"Anna," he said, pressing his head against her own as his breathing returned to normal. She closed her eyes, the sensation of him inside of her stirring emotions that felt foreign, and yet completely perfect.

"Anna," he said again, slowly lifting his head. When their gazes met, he seemed pleased. "You said you love me."

"Aye, you lucky cull," she said with a brave smile, brave because she truly wondered if she could pull it off, wondered if a gentleman could fall for a woman like herself.

He chuckled a bit, but then his laughter faded, his gaze suddenly so fierce and intense that she found herself holding her breath.

"I shall take care of you, Anna. Always, forever, take care of you."

He hadn't said he loved her back. Only then did she realize that she'd been hoping he would. That he'd pull her into his arms and say, *I love you. I shall marry you.* What a silly sod.

A half hour later they stood near the bow of the ship as they returned to London Dock. How much time did they have? A day? A week? What would she do when the time came for him to resume his old life? What would she do? Go with him? Stay?

"I'd give much to keep your sails and show them to my friends."

Anna and Rein turned, Captain Jones facing them with a small smile on his face.

"I will admit that I was skeptical at first, but you proved me wrong. Now tell me truly, who gave you the design?"

Anna stiffened.

"I assure you, Captain," Rein lashed out like a bosun's mate with a cat-o'-nines. "Miss Brooks came up with the idea for her staysails all on her own."

"Did she, now?"

"Indeed, she did. So if you are looking to undermine the work she has done by claiming she could not possibly come up with such a stellar notion on her own, you are sadly mistaken. She is as brilliant as a man . . . rather, she is *more* bloody brilliant than *most* men. You'd do well to remember that."

And if she hadn't been in love before, Anna would have fallen in love with him then. As she watched his handsome, wonderful, arrogant face harden with his anger, she wished for a moment . . .

*Wished what?*

That she was the type of woman a man like him would marry.

"Rein," she said, touching his arm, smiling up at him with such blinding love he must surely see it. "It is not his fault he is a silly, soddin' fool of a man."

"I *beg* your pardon," Captain Jones said.

"'Tis true," Anna said. "And no fault of your own that you were born with the brains of a monkey. Most men are, you see. I suspect it to be the reason why men don't want women learning from books. If we did, you'd be unmasked in a trice. But never fear, my good captain. Your secret of stupidity is safe with me." She leaned toward him and said in a conspirator's way, "I shan't tell your crew."

"Why, you nasty little bum-trader. You are fortunate the duke has *ordered* me to fly your sails the day of the naval competition, for if not for those orders, I would toss them overboard."

"Do, and you shall be tossed with them," Rein said, stepping between her and the daft man.

"And you, coming in here and acting as if you own the ship. I shall remind you that 'tis I who controls what you see. *I,* not you. So while I am ordered by the duke to aid the . . . lady, it does not mean that you may take that tone with me, sir."

"Why, you—"

Anna watched as Rein's fists clenched at his sides, as he fought for very obvious control of his temper. "You, sir, shall be released without wages. This I vow."

"Hah. As if the likes of you will ever get an audience with the duke of Wroxly."

"You might be surprised at how easily such a thing could be accomplished—"

"Rein," Anna interrupted, knowing a hopeless situation when she saw one. "Let it go. I do not mind his insults. I assure you, I've been called far worse by the fancy toffs that come to market thinking they can buy me along with my wares." She stepped in between them, placing her hand against the side of his face to get his attention. "He's not worth your temper. I assure you."

"Insolent bit of muslin," she heard behind her.

She turned on the man. "Captain, were I you, I'd see to your ship. Or hadn't you noticed that your topgallant is in need of a fresh nip?"

To her surprise the captain looked up, spying the kink in the line that grew more and more noticeable with the tightening of the line.

"You would do well to pay attention to your rigging rather than our social station."

"You there," the captain turned and called to a main-topman. "Freshen that nip."

"I pity the duke if he ever takes his new ship out," Anna said to Rein. "Like as not he wouldn't make it back alive."

Rein didn't react. Rather, he stared down at her, his head starting a slow shake back and forth. "You know how to sail a ship."

She drew back. "Of course. You did not think I happened upon a sail design by chance, did you?" She grabbed his arm, leading him away from the captain, who had turned his temper upon his maintopman. "My father taught my mother, and my mother taught *me,* much to my father's amusement."

"Remarkable."

"Indeed," she said, mimicking his way of speech. "There are a great many things you shall miss about me when we part ways."

She'd hoped for a declaration that he would not be parted from her. What she got was a fierce look of unease. She turned away, looked out upon the horizon, at the bell tower of St. George in the east, the white spire visible from where they sailed. A ship passed between them, its reflection a distorted shape that vibrated atop the Thames's gray-blue surface. Anna hardly noticed while her hands clutched the rail.

*Say it,* she all but screamed at him. *Say it. You care for me. You love me. You must.*

But he didn't. And she was too frightened to come right out and ask him, to ask where this all would lead, to ask what would happen when he became once again a lord of the manor, for she was certain he was.

She reached for his hand, took a step toward him, meant to tell him she knew he was of noble birth, perhaps even possessed a title, but just then he staggered back from her, clutching at his arm at the same time he cried out.

"What the devil?" Captain Jones said as a pistol retort echoed over them.

Rein met her gaze. "I've been shot."

"Shot? What do you mean, shot?" Anna asked as she turned to face him. Then she saw the blood on his jacket, the tiny black hole that sat in the center of it.

Shot.

"I need the ship's surgeon," Anna called just as Rein fell against the rail, sliding down it as if suddenly light-headed.

"Now," she yelled, following him down.

"What? Why?" Captain Jones called as he made his way toward them. "What the devil do you need a surgeon for?"

"He's been shot," Anna said, looking up, having to squint as she did so, for the sun was right behind him.

"Shot?" but the captain must have seen the wound, too, for he straightened, turning toward his crew. "Get Langdon, and some bandages."

"Can you remove the jacket?"

"I am not sure," Rein said, and she noticed then that his face was as pale as the lace around her collar. He had pain brackets around his mouth, too, a groove plowing its way down his brow. "I am not so certain it would be wise to move."

It didn't seem possible that her anxiety could increase, but his words made it so.

"Let me try," she said, bending forward to remove the jacket, slipping it off his good arm first. And as she did so a tin of mints fell to the deck. Smith and Sons Confectioners, a place that sold treats only swells could afford. But there was no time to think of that. As quickly as she could, she pulled the jacket off.

He gasped.

She said, "Lean back."

"I feel rather . . . odd."

Someone handed her a strip of canvas then. Anna moved to wrap it around his arm.

"Please do not touch it," he gasped.

"Rein, I have seen corpses lying on the streets of St. Giles, women beaten to within an inch of their lives, babies being pushed out in alleys. I know how to wrap a wound."

She moved again, gently yet firmly, wrapping the wound, Rein gasping as she tugged it tight.

"We must stop the bleeding," she explained, but the canvas filled instantly with blood.

"I'll have to do it again," she said. "We need more canvas," she said to her audience.

Someone set off to find some canvas. Rein closed his eyes.

"Let's get him to my cabin," the captain said. "Langdon can tend to him there. Help him up, men."

Two men came forward, the one on Rein's right taking care not to jostle his arm.

Anna fell back, fear making it hard to breathe.

Someone had shot at Rein.

Someone had tried to *kill* him.

"Good god," she mumbled as she hurriedly followed behind.

Rein's hand shook as he tossed back another shot of gin, a few drops falling from the edge of the glass to land on his bare chest, not that he cared. No, he was a fair way to not caring about anything, the liquor emptying his mind in direct relation to the emptying of the bottle. They were alone in the well-furnished room (further proof Rein paid the good captain entirely too much), Captain Jones having gotten the ship to port. The moment the ship was secured to the dock, Rein had asked Anna to find Mr. Stills.

"Mr. Stills? Who is Mr. Stills?"

"A friend," Rein had answered. "A Bow Street Runner."

"You have a friend who is a Bow Street Runner that I can find in an alley across from my building?"

"Indeed."

"What is going—"

"Anna, please," Rein asked on a gasp, for the muscles in his forearm spasmed. "Do not ask questions."

She hadn't looked pleased, but she'd backed away from the bed. She'd looked back at him one last time before closing the door.

And so that was why he was near three sheets to the wind when Mr. Stills and Anna returned, the ship's surgeon, one Mr. Langdon, having charged Rein with imbibing as much gin as possible, for the pistol's ball was still in his arm.

"Ah, they return," Rein said, their two bodies turning into four for a moment.

"Rein, what the blazes is going on?" Anna asked. "This man would tell me nothing."

Rein looked over at the Runner. "Am I allowed to tell her, my goosh man?"

The man shrugged. "Up to you, gov. Your money to lose."

And even in his befogged state, Rein understood the words. His time was not up. If he told Anna the truth, he'd forfeit his inheritance.

"Sh-shouldn't keep her in the dark."

"Keep me in the dark about what?" Anna asked, her amber eyes looking between them.

"I'm not at liberty to say, mum," the Runner said.

"He's about ready for me to work on," Mr. Langdon said, probing Rein's arm.

"Oush, damn it," Rein cried. "That hursh."

Anna stepped back, and though the shape of her face looked devilishly odd, Rein saw the concern and worry and fear in it.

"Is someone trying to kill you?" she asked.

Odd, but her mouth moved before the words came out. That perplexed Rein for a moment before he realized she waited for an answer.

"Yes, my dear Anna, I believe it shafe to shay some-one is trying to kill me."

"Why?"

Rein opened his mouth to answer, but Mr. Langdon jabbed what felt like a mallet into his arm. "Gadsh," he cried, having to blink to focus on his tormentor, the fingers of his good arm digging into the padding of the red armchair. "Mush you?"

"I must."

Anna stood, though to Rein's eyes a ghostly outline of her gray cloak seemed to be a few paces behind her actual body. Lord, he hadn't been this boozy since that time his father had decided to use a switch instead of a hand. One of the staff had brought him a bottle, saying it would help . . .

"Would one of you please tell me why the blazes someone would like Rein dead?"

"Can't," he said, shaking his head a bit to dispel the ringing in his ears. "Too mush at shake."

"Too much at stake," Anna repeated. Rein tipped his head back, the liquor having finally diluted in his blood to the point that he felt rather like sleeping.

"Are you telling me someone wants you dead because of this bloody wager?"

"Miss Brooks, please—" Mr. Stills said.

"No, you please. I am not about to stand by and watch the man I love be killed over a bloody wager. Not, I say."

"He doesn't hear you," Mr. Stills said.

"Who doesn't hear me?"

"'Im," he said, pointing with his chin toward Rein.

Anna looked, Rein's face having gone slack, her whole body following suit when she realized the liquor had claimed him. Mr. Langdon went back to work, moving swiftly now that his patient felt nothing.

"Who is he?" she asked, turning to Mr. Stills. "Who is he really and why does someone want him dead?"

"I can't say," the Runner said, his blue eyes glancing

away from Rein for a moment, that gaze as direct as a one-way road. "'E's the only one what can tell you."

"He was just shot." Her gaze caught on Rein, a sudden fear making it hard to breathe for a moment. "Surely things have changed."

Mr. Stills looked at her and it was only then that she realized she fought a losing battle.

"If you care for him, then you'll try and convince him to give up on his challenge."

"Is it truly a challenge?" she asked, her mind experiencing some measure of relief that at least that part was true.

"I've told you more than I should already."

Anna spun away, crossing to the cabin's door before turning back again. "Someone wants him dead, someone who has much to gain if Rein loses his wager."

Mr. Stills remained silent.

"Obviously, the person who wants him dead must be the man he's wagered against."

Still no words.

"Well, then, what *can* you tell me?"

"Nothin'."

Anna came toward him, her face only inches from his as she said, "Do you realize my life might be endangered, too? And my grandfather's?"

"I do."

"Then should I not be told what that danger is?"

Mr. Stills looked away from her; Anna felt hope.

"Obviously what's happened has changed things," he said at last—not the words Anna had hoped for. "I'll need to speak with someone to find out just how much. I can't promise I'll be able to share with you all that I know, but

I'll try. Meanwhile, I'll arrange with the captain to have you and Rein stay here."

"Absolutely not," the captain said to Freddie a short while later. "This is not a passenger ship. This is a yacht. Without the duke of Wroxly's permission I shall not allow those two to stay."

"Then you'll have the duke's permission by sunset. I'll see to it myself."

The captain looked none too pleased, but Freddie held his ground. The way he saw it, Wroxly would be safe here. But now that he knew whoever had sent that threatening note truly meant business, he had to go to the solicitor and explain that the challenge needed to be stopped . . . and whichever cousin who stood in line to inherit the title should be questioned about his involvement.

"Why is the duke involving himself with these people?" Captain Jones asked.

Freddie chose his words carefully. "The new duke has a great interest in the lady's sails. More than that, I'm not at liberty to say."

"And the man she is with?"

"He is a personal friend of the duke's."

The captain let out a scoff-filled laugh. "Him? Why, he looks like an outcast from Little Dublin."

The man was closer to the truth than he might know.

"He dresses so as to look in place, but I assure you, Mr. Hemplewilt is well acquainted with the duke."

Captain Jones looked a bit concerned for a moment, and Freddie wondered just what the man might have done. Whatever it was, it wasn't his problem. He had other problems to contend with.

"I'll be back with your letter of permission."

"No, no. No need for that," the man said, waving his arms. "I'll take you at your word."

Freddie nodded, already turning away.

# Chapter Twenty

Hours later Rein woke in the captain's bed, the immediate pain that gnawed at his arm an instant reminder of all that had transpired. He looked around the small room, eyes squinting as he tried to make out the face belonging to the dark blob in a corner.

"Mr. Stills, is that you?"

The shape rose, the big man like a horse in a too-small stall. The chair he sat in scraped the wood floor until it hit the blue and white rug that lay next to the bed. No window allowed light to filter into the room, but Rein didn't need any to see Freddie Stills move the dark-blue armchair closer to the bed. Rein closed his eyes, moving his uninjured arm so that he could place a hand against his aching head. "I've not felt like this since I was a lad."

"Should drink a bit more, it'll ease the pain," he said as he took a seat, the black wool cap he wore clutched in his big hands.

Rein shook his head, "I need to think," he said, his eyes opening and then peering around the room. "The time?"

"Late afternoon."

"Anna?"

"Up on deck."

"Has she been asking questions?"

"Aye, a passel of them, all of which I've been avoiding or ignoring."

And it was then that a new thought penetrated his brain with the blinding clarity of a light being shone into his eyes. "Someone tried to kill me," Rein said, his rather muddled head clearing.

"Aye."

"If I hadn't have moved when I did . . ."

"You'd be dead."

"Damnation."

"I believe," Mr. Stills said, his hands idly spinning the hat, "that your threatening letters have gone beyond a threat."

"Indeed so," Rein murmured, the notion that someone wanted him dead almost too much to comprehend.

"Went to see Mr. Lassiter," Mr. Stills said.

"And what does my uncle's solicitor have to say?"

Silence. Outside Rein could hear water lapping against the side of the ship, and though the cabin looked sparkling new, Rein could still smell the sour tang of sea salt. It clung to the ship like the smell of vinegar clung to a decade-old vinaigrette.

"He refuses to let you cancel the challenge."

Rein's arm fell back to the bed.

"He says the provisions of the will are clear. You've started the challenge, you finish it twelve days hence. There ain't no provision about canceling, and certainly nothing about what to do if someone should try ta kill you."

"I wonder whyever not," Rein said sarcastically.

But Mr. Stills seemed unamused.

"You should give up, Your Grace. Challenge the will in a court o' law. No magistrate on earth would think ill of you for calling an end to this nonsense."

"No, I would think not. But I cannot be certain." He shook his head slowly, though it'd begun to ache nearly as much as his arm. "And therein lies the crux of the problem. Dare I wager my future upon such logic? Is it reasonable to assume that a court will agree that this challenge is a farce? Would they have not done so already during probate?"

Freddie jumped up from his chair even as he bent his big body so that their heads were near. Rein felt his brows lift. "It's not you I worry 'bout. 'Tis Miss Brooks."

Rein felt the weight of those words as if they'd fallen atop him and pressed against his chest.

Anna. His brave Anna. If she'd taken one more step . . .

"And it's not just her," Mr. Stills continued, "but her grandfather as well. I went to check on the cull and the daft cove let me in. Who's to say someone else might not do the same, enter his rooms, take the man hostage and use him as leverage to get you to leave St. Giles?"

"Bloody hell." Fury at himself for not having thought of such a thing made Rein shake his head—a mistake, for it sent pain shooting around again.

"Who?" Rein found himself asking. "Who the blazes would go to such lengths to frighten me?"

"Frighten you? Whoever it was meant to *kill* you."

Dead. An unknown cousin wanted him dead.

"And does it matter who?" Freddie asked, straightening. "The point being that you and those near to you are in danger."

Rein opened eyes he hadn't even known he closed as an old suspicion returned. "Who's to say you are not involved somehow?" Rein said before he realized that it might have been more wise to wait and hurl such an accusation until other people were present. "You were outside Anna's building the day her sails were destroyed."

Freddie's eyes turned as cold as a winter storm. "I'm not the bastard what shot at you today. Nor the person what tried to ruin Miss Brooks's chances at the competition."

"No?" Rein challenged recklessly. "You might have had someone working with you who might have shot at me today."

The big man leaned toward him again. "If I wanted you dead, Your Grace, I'd no' have missed. And if I had missed, I'd be taking care of the matter now, at this very moment, if you catch me meaning."

Yes, Rein did, his fears somewhat allayed. Or was it a clever ruse to turn his attention? But, no, the man had a point. So if not the Runner, could he truly have a cousin after the wealth? And how did they catch the fiend? And what about Anna? What did he do about her?

"You have to leave the ship."

Rein's gaze swung back to Mr. Stills.

"Mr. Lassiter insists upon it. He was none too happy to allow you the use of this ship in the first place. Frankly, I was surprised he agreed. But he seemed swayed by your argument that you had nothing to gain from the use and that Miss Brooks was the one who needed the help. But now he says you must leave and go back to St. Giles else he'll consider your stay aboard the ship as flagrant use of your resources to keep out of harm's way."

"Leave," Rein repeated, honest enough to admit that such a thought filled him with fear.

"We've the cart waiting. The sails are ready to be transported back to shore, but before you and Miss Brooks leave, I'll ask you to consider her safety. I'm beggin' you once again to give this whole thing up and place your future in the court's hands."

"I shall speak with someone on the morrow about my chances of contesting the will. In the interim Anna and her grandfather must be moved out of harm's way."

Mr. Stills straightened, nodding his head in approval.

"She'll not want to go," Rein admitted.

"You want me to take her?"

"If it comes to that, yes."

"Leave?" Anna repeated, looking at Rein in surprise. His bloody shirt caught her attention so that her stomach rolled yet again. "Rein, someone tried to kill you today. Over money. I've no idea how deep a game you play, but it must be deep indeed if someone is willing to kill you over it. I want to know who you wagered against. I want to know what is at stake. And I want to know *now*."

She had waited all afternoon to hurl the questions at his idiotic head. All afternoon she replayed the morning's events: the blood, the fear, the mad dash back to St. Giles. She was furious at this Mr. Stills for keeping all to himself, unsure of what exactly the Runner's part was in this. Thus she wanted answers and she wanted them now.

"Anna, what you ask is reasonable, especially given the danger you are in."

"Danger? Me?"

Rein nodded, his green eyes serious. "The game has reached a new level, one that might ultimately involve you."

"Game," she hurled back. "'Tis what you consider this? A game? Someone tried to kill you, now you say someone might try and harm me. Over a wager? Do you think me daft? This is no game. There is something much larger at stake."

"I cannot tell you what."

"Can't tell me," Anna all but yelled, closing the distance between her and the bed to wave a finger beneath his nose. "Damn you. Do you have any idea what it was like to see blood on your person? To not know for a moment if you were mortally wounded or just grazed? I thought you might die. . . ."

She turned away, knowing he would see her tears if she did not, so disgusted with him she didn't want him to know how much she cared.

"Anna," he said softly.

"Don't you 'Anna' me," she said, turning on him. "I want answers, Rein, now. How deep do you play? What is at stake? Who would want you dead?"

"They are answers I cannot give you, Anna. Not at present," he said, pushing the covers back to get out of bed.

"Don't you dare come near me," she said, stepping back. "The truth, Rein. Now. Or do you fear I cannot keep a secret?"

"No, Anna, I know you would keep all to yourself," he said after a pause during which Anna could feel her heart beat harder and harder. He'd looked away from her as if weighing his words.

*Tell me.*

"I am trying to win back an inheritance, the size of which is quite large. The person who shot at me today is most likely a cousin, one who stands to gain my wealth should I fail this challenge."

"An inheritance? You wagered your inheritance?"

"Not precisely."

"What do you mean, not precisely?"

He got up out of bed, gasping as the effort jostled his arm.

"Do not," she ordered, moving toward him with the intention of pushing him back down.

But he stood, swaying a bit. She was reminded of the first day they met. Damn him, didn't he know how much she fought the urge to go to him, to wrap her arms around him and tell him she loved him?

"My real name is Reinleigh Drummond," he said when he'd regained himself. "There, does that appease you?" he asked, lifting his good arm to stroke the side of her cheeks.

It did appease her. A bit. Reinleigh. It was why he was called Rein, no doubt. And . . . Drummond. She closed her eyes. Drummond was his surname.

"Why would you be so cork-brained as to wager your inheritance."

"It wasn't *I* who wagered it."

"I don't understand."

"Neither do I at times," he said with a shake of his head, one that ended in a wince. "Suffice it to say that even I would never be so foolish." He held up his hand when she opened her mouth to ask another question. "More than that I cannot say."

But there was one question she wouldn't let rest. "Are you noble born?" she asked.

He looked like he wouldn't answer, but then he gave a slow nod. "I am connected to a noble family, yes."

"Which one?"

"It does not matter, Anna. What matters is that you get to safety."

"It *does* matter," she said.

"Why? Will your feelings change for me once you discover who my family is?"

She pondered the question a moment, then slowly shook her head. "No."

"I did not think they would. Thus I shall explain all to you later. For now I would like Mr. Stills to take you someplace where I know you'll be safe. Stay there, with your grandfather and your sails, until the day of the naval competition. By then I hope to have things resolved."

She shook her head, grappling for words for a moment. "Why?" she asked with tears in her eyes. "Why should I go?"

His face hardened as if he meant to turn away, but then his expression changed, slowly at first, only to quickly change to one of resignation. His mouth softened just before he said, "Because I love you."

She searched his eyes, those wonderful green eyes. What she saw made everything still, and then move forward at a rapid rate, her pulse, her breathing, her mind.

"I love you," he said, bending forward and kissing a spot near the side of her mouth. "I love you," he whispered into her ear.

*He loved her.*

She closed her eyes, losing herself for a moment in the magic of those words.

"The thought of you going out there, in danger . . ." She felt him shake his head, draw back from her. "I love you, Anna, and if anyone were to lay a hand on you, I should die."

"Oh, Rein."

He reached up, placed a hand against the side of her face. "But if you do not go to safety, I will give it all up, the challenge, the money, my future. You're more important to me than anything I might win."

"Oh, Rein," she whispered again.

"So it is your choice, you see. Go to where I will send you. Or stay and I will give it all up."

And in the end, she realized it was no choice at all.

# Part Four

*"How do you know I am your destiny?"*
*the maiden asked the prince.*

# Chapter Twenty-one

The directions Rein had written down were not hard to follow. She and her grandfather had lit a lantern when they'd gotten off the main thoroughfares so they could better see the scrap of paper he'd written his map upon. Fortunately, they'd been less than two hours away from their destination. Fortunately because Anna felt ready to pull her hair out by the time they arrived, her grandfather undoubtedly able to drive King George batty with his constant ramblings about the French and militia and foot soldiers and the like.

So as they passed the final landmark Rein had described on his map, she felt a surge of relief—well, as much relief as she could feel given the circumstances. The cart clattered down an overgrown road with tall trees on either side, their outline more black than the star-studded sky above.

"Where the blazes are you going?" her grandfather asked, obviously realizing they'd left the main road.

"I wish I knew," she murmured. A cottage, he'd said. An abandoned cottage. She'd asked him how he knew it was still abandoned, but his cryptic reply had been no help. He simply knew it was.

"You do not know? Those bloody Frogs are at our heels and you don't know?"

"'Tis a hideaway, Grandfather. We'll be safe there."

At least she hoped so. But in case they'd been followed, Anna had taken every precaution. She'd extinguished the lantern whenever possible, pulled off the road a few times to listen. She'd even changed directions once as if heading back to London, for which her grandfather had called her mad.

"Mad, I say," he'd yelled.

She'd laughed. At this point, there was nothing left to do but laugh.

"A hideaway? Excellent. Excellent," he murmured now.

The trees around them opened up, gray stone barely visible through a river of darkness. A small cottage, judging by the shape of it. Of course, it was hard to see this close to midnight.

She pulled to a stop. The poor horse they'd driven lowered its head. Anna gave it a pat and a scratch in thanks, her hands smelling of horse as she turned to face her new lodgings.

Up close, it appeared to be an abandoned farmhouse of sorts. Cozy, she would call it, but more spacious than the rooms they occupied back in St. Giles.

"Come, Grandfather," she said, as she helped him down, then grabbed the lantern she'd lit. Taking a deep breath, she approached the front door. A name hung above the entrance, final proof that she'd found her way even in the dead of night.

Rosewood Cottage.

The name Rein had given her.

In the end she needn't have worried about the place
having a tenant. She suspected the roof had holes in it, a
suspicion that was confirmed when she woke early the
next morning to see pin-point beams of sunlight dotting
the earthen floor and illuminating broken and abandoned
furniture and a tiny hearth she'd started a fire in last
night. Her grandfather lay next to her, snoring, the sails
she'd unloaded last night acting as both bed and covers.
And though they'd only been hoisted once, the smell of
the Thames clung to them. The sweet scent of cut grass
and open spaces mingled with the river scent, giving her
peace for a moment before she shook her head and reminded herself that her world was far from at peace.

So she kept herself busy. That would be her routine for
the next few days: rise in the morning, prepare a meal, set
the house to rights—well, as much as she could—fix a
midday meal, then a supper, only to repeat the process all
over again. And wait. And worry. Worry a lot. And walk.
Walking helped to soothe the edge of her anxiety for
there could be no communications between her and
Rein—they both feared whoever might be after him
would find her that way.

The week was nearly up when she discovered the
house, although *house* seemed far too ludicrous a word to
use to describe it. Estate. Fortress. Castle, though the last
not in the strictest sense of the word. There were no tur-
rets or parapets, but there didn't need to be, not when the
center portion rose two stories above the left and right
sides, a gilded brass dome sitting square in the middle,

the thing glowing with a green patina nearly the same color as Rein's eyes.

It was an estate, one sitting in the midst of a treeless park that stretched far and wide—like the fields near Dover where they grew hay. Hedges shaped into long, rectangular squares stretched out from the front of the home, one after another, like dominoes that lay on their sides, each one with a fountain in the center that was surrounded by red roses.

Magnificent. Palatial. *Old.*

And as she stared, a suspicion began to take form. She turned back the direction she'd come, for she had a vantage point from where she stood upon a small knoll, one that allowed her to visualize roughly how far away Rosewood Cottage was from the estate. There was a wood in between, and a pasture or two, but still . . .

*I breed roses.*

The words came back to her.

She turned and set off down the hill, eyes squinting beneath the brim of her straw hat as she kept her gaze fixed upon the mansion.

It might be a coincidence, she told herself. The name of the cottage; Rein breeding roses. For surely if Rein were in some way attached to wealth and prestige and a heritage such as this, he would have told her.

*What if he hadn't?*

She narrowed her eyes, unsure what she intended to do, but determined to discover what she could.

"Lookin' for work?" a kitchen maid with a gray apron and black dress asked after opening the door to the servants' entrance. Anna'd had to ask three groundskeepers where to find the thing, the number of staff working at the residence seeming to be infinite, the building towering over her now that she stood next to it. The bloody thing was almost as long as the block she lived on, and Anna felt like a tiny bug swallowed by a large shadow.

"I am," she lied. "But first I should like to know where I am."

The maid looked shocked that Anna didn't know.

"I'm new to the county," Anna lied again. "I was told by someone in town to come to the grand house to look for work." She splayed her arms, gave her a friendly smile. "But I confess to not knowing whose grand house this is."

The suspicious look faded a bit. "'Tis Wroxly Park, mum," the girl said. "And I don't know how you could arrive in Wroxlyshire and not know it."

Wroxly. Why did that name sound so familiar?

And then she stiffened.

*Who owns the ship?* she'd asked Rein.

*The duke of Wroxly.*

"Good lord," Anna said.

"Aye," the maid said proudly, strands of her black hair dancing around her face as she lifted her chin. "'Tis a ducal estate you've come to. Course, the old duke passed on a few weeks back."

The old duke had passed on.

Passed on?

*The new duke ain't even been on board yet . . .*

No. She refused to believe it. But her pounding heart belied the words. "The new duke," Anna asked, her heart beginning to beat so hard her limbs shook, too. "Might you know his name?"

"Only the family name, mum. Montgomery, it is."

Anna felt her shoulders slump. Montgomery. Not Drummond. But still . . .

"I thought the Wroxly dukes were connected to the Drummond family," Anna said.

"Drummond? Ain't never heard that name afore."

And yet Anna's mind refused to let it rest. Might Rein have lied? Might his last name not be Drummond? It was possible.

"Well, now. If you're looking for work, you'd best speak with Mrs. Powell."

"My thanks," Anna said as she was led into the kitchen, past the pantries—dried goods on the left, fresh vegetables on the right—and toward a room that contained what Anna took to be the supper table for the staff.

"I wonder," Anna asked the maid as she turned to leave, "do you happen to know the new duke's first name?"

Anna held her breath as she waited for the woman's response. But all she got was a shrug. "Not my place to know." She bobbed her head, saying, "I'll go fetch Mrs. Powell."

Anna turned away. Like as not she was chasing silk clouds. The cottage's proximity to the estate might be a coincidence. Rein couldn't be connected to this grand family—the Montgomerys. That would be too far-fetched to be believed. Even she'd heard of them before, their name entwined with history.

"Lookin' for work?" a stern voice asked.

Anna spun toward the door. A tall, gaunt-faced woman with eyebrows that arched like a frightened cat and a face nearly as sharp as a feline's stared back at her, her black hair drawn atop her head in a knot that looked so tight Anna thought it might hurt.

"I . . ." she forced her mind to work, forced it to think logically. "I am," she said, though she knew in an instant this woman would not welcome questions about the family she worked for.

"We are in need of a house maid. Pays fourteen shillings a year. Are you interested?"

Anna could only nod, uncertain how she'd ended up not only in the bloody house, but in an interview to work for the duke of Wroxly, by the looks of things.

"Have you references?"

"I . . . do."

The woman held out a hand that looked stark white against the black cuff of her dress.

Anna wasn't quite sure what to do. She patted the pockets sewn into her pelisse in a vague way, and when they came up empty (and of course they would), she made a great show of saying, "My references," in a plaintive voice. "They must have fallen out."

The housekeeper's eyes narrowed. "Have they?" she asked.

Anna forged on. "On the way over, I suppose."

"Well, then, my dear, when you find them, perhaps you might return with them."

She turned toward the door, stopped, then turned back, motioning with her hand that Anna should leave.

Anna didn't move. The brows arched higher, the woman obviously not fooled a whit by her.

"I . . ." Oh, bother, why not? "I'm not really here for work," Anna admitted.

The woman's eyes swept her up and down, taking in her white pelisse, the tan hat—the same hat she wore to market—all of it before meeting her gaze again. One brow dropped, but the other remained up in question.

"I'm a market maid from London trying to discover some truths about a man."

That very same day—indeed, at almost the very same hour—Rein stood before his uncle's solicitor, furious beyond belief that he'd spent his precious last coins to ride in and see him, only to have the man flatly refuse to cancel the challenge.

"Surely you understand the seriousness of the situation."

"I understand nothing but that you wish to be released from the challenge, something the will does not allow you to do."

"My life is in danger, sir. Surely that changes things."

"So you claim," the man said, his spectacles perched on the end of his nose like a bird about to take flight. "But I see no proof of this, sir."

"I have a wound in my arm."

"The injury to your arm might have been self-inflicted—"

"Self-inflicted!" Rein shot up from his chair, pain slicing through his injured arm for his efforts. With his good hand he slapped the desk in front of him with so much force, papers fell off the edge. "Someone is trying to kill me, sir. I may have no evidence, but I have no reason to lie."

"On the contrary, you have every reason to lie. Likely you are at the end of whatever funds you managed to raise from the sale of your clothes and your boots. You might be facing a week of starvation, of begging on the streets without my help."

"I have lodgings," Rein gritted out.

"So I have heard from Mr. Stills, but a roof over your head does not help a burning in your belly."

Rein leaned even closer. To his credit the man didn't move. "You think I have fabricated this tale so that I can escape the last days of my challenge?"

"I do."

"You're mad."

"No. I am in charge of your uncle's will and I mean to see it through to the end. Indeed, I have helped you quite enough. There was no reason to let you use the duke's yacht, but I allowed it."

"*My* yacht," Rein growled.

"Not at present. However, I regretted allowing you to do so almost the moment I agreed. Why, you might have pilfered something from the ship to sell. Perhaps asked someone to take a shot at you so you could pretend to be in fear of your life.

"Pretend—" Rein straightened, words failing him for a moment. "I have a hole in my arm, one I should like you to see."

"I have no interest in seeing your injury, most especially when it could have been gotten at any place and any time."

"Why, you—" His neck muscles hurt he had to work so hard to control his rage. Daft fool. And people called *him* slow.

"Very well. You leave me no choice but to challenge the will in a court of law."

"If that is your choice."

"It is."

"Then I shall see you in court."

# Chapter Twenty-two

Anna knew the homes of the nobility were something to be seen, but she'd had no real notion of exactly what that meant until that day. After all, hearing about the homes noblemen owned was one thing, actually being in one was quite another.

"Of all the times for Mr. Camden to be absent," Mrs. Powell, her new champion, said. "He's been here an age and would likely remember what the young lord looked like, though I must say, the name Reinleigh does strike a chord."

Which filled Anna with . . . what? What would it mean if she discovered Rein was connected to a ducal family? Or if he was the duke himself? Would it truly matter?

"Whoever he is, this man who had . . . who—"

"Seduced me," Anna said. Very well, she'd embellished a bit in order to enlist the woman's aid.

"Took your innocence," Mrs. Powell said. "If he is connected to the family, his portrait is certain to be hanging in the portrait gallery."

If he was connected.

And if he was . . .

She looked around her, at the mirrors that hung opposite each other in the great hall, the reflection of the white marble floor broken for a moment by their own passing. Polished, dark oak side tables with plants as big as those found out-of-doors stood around the perimeter of that hall, thick molding as tall as her foot encircling both the floor and the ceiling, all of it carved with the images of lions. It smelled of lemon and beeswax, smells from her childhood, smells that roused memories.

*Do bees really make wax, Mama?*

*They do, my dear. They do.*

They traveled toward the front of the home, a double-wide oak door at the end of the hall. Anna stared around in awe at the red velvet chairs that stood, empty, along the wall. To think she'd once marveled over the velvet on Rein's jacket when by the looks of things the nobility used it for sitting. Sitting!

Shaking her head, Anna tried to walk softly so as to keep the echo of her feet from becoming too loud. Mrs. Powell stopped, turning to her right and opening a door that revealed a room so stunning, so beautiful, Anna felt the breath leave her.

"This was Her Grace's favorite room. It connects the main hall to the portrait gallery."

Anna stepped through the doorway, her feet feeling almost numb as she did so, her eyes traveling around a room so filled with plants, she felt as if she'd stepped into the middle of a forest. Moisture hit her cheeks, warming them, making the air heavy. To her left rose windows that overlooked the front lawn, the ceiling in this part of the home having been designed so that windows could be placed in them, allowing sunlight to filter in.

"Lord above," she murmured.

"Here we are," Mrs. Powell said, opening yet another door.

Anna found herself entering another room with windows on her left, only this one had portraits hanging on the right. Hundreds of them.

"The old duke's portrait hangs near the middle. We've recently discovered the current duke's portrait in the attic. It's next to the old duke's."

"The attic?" Anna asked, curious.

Mrs. Powell's brows lowered. "He was banished as a youth. Lord, people weren't even allowed to speak his name, though I wasn't around at the time they had their falling out. We thought his portrait destroyed until we discovered it while cleaning."

But Anna was too busy scanning the faces of the paintings in front of her, some very obviously from centuries past. The designs of the women's gowns changed with time, ruffs round the women's necks, hooped skirts, powdered hair. The men, too, looked dressed in such a way as to follow history, many in pantaloons and silk stockings, fur mantles around their shoulders. She worked her way down, searching, searching, eyes alighting briefly on the portrait that belonged to the old duke, and next to that on his right . . .

Rein.

She stopped, something that felt like feathers dusting her face, but that she realized in an instant was actually the blood draining down.

" 'Tis the current duke," said Mrs. Powell.

She put a hand out to the wall. Current duke? Rein?

"Miss? Are you all right?"

Anna shook her head. "No, Mrs. Powell, I am not well at all." She took a breath. "How do you know this is the current duke?" Because Anna was certain, quite certain, that the man's name was Rein.

"Because Mr. Camden said it was him." And when the housekeeper realized Anna thought the portrait belonged to the debauching man who'd gotten her with child (very well, Anna'd embellished *quite* a lot), she straightened. "But if it's a name you be needing, I know of a way to find out. We've a copy of Debrett's in the library."

Rein decided he could get used to the view from Anna's rooftop.

If he hadn't been in fear of his life, and at his wits' end about the situation he found himself in, and if his bloody arm and head didn't ache, he'd be quite content. Alas, he could do nothing but challenge the will in a court of law, according to the magistrate he'd spoken to earlier in the week. He'd spent the whole week trying to circumvent a trial, but it was all to no avail. No one seemed to care that a madman appeared to want to end his life, nor that the challenge itself had been so unfair as to potentially succeed where the murderer had failed.

"Your Grace," a soft, familiar voice called to him.

Rein turned, certain the voice had been a figment of his imagination, for Anna wasn't due back until tomorrow.

"Anna," he said when, indeed, he spied her standing there. "What are you doing here?"

And then what she'd called him penetrated his brain. *"What did you call me?"*

Her amber eyes were as direct as he'd ever seen them

as she said, "Charles Reinleigh Drummond Montgomery. Earl of Sherborne, marquis of Randolph, duke of Wroxly." She curtsied, the gray dress she wore pooling around her feet as she did so.

So she had found out at last? Well, he supposed that was a relief.

But when she spoke next, she didn't look relieved. "Clever of you to send me to your childhood playground." And the look she gave him was one filled with . . . what? "You knew of the abandoned house, knew it would likely still be vacant."

He stepped toward her, reaching for her hands, though it hurt his arm to do so. She left her hands by her side. His own arms fell away. "Anna, I am sorry you had to find out in such a way, but truth be told, I'm rather relieved."

Again, that forthright stare, her eyes searching his as if she were looking for something. "She thought you ruined me as a way of amusing yourself," Anna said with a tip to her chin. "Is that true? Did you tell me you loved me just so you'd have a place to stay? A roof over your head? Food in your belly?"

"Who thought such a thing?" he said with furrowed brows.

"Mrs. Powell, the new housekeeper at Wroxly Park."

The accusation made him reach for her hands again. She ignored them once more. The way she looked at him with rage in her eyes made him shake his head, then say, "Anna, there is no need to look at me thus." He lifted his good arm, touched the side of her face with his hand.

She jerked away. "Isn't there, Rein?"

He shook his head. "I have never once misled you

about anything other than my true identity and my purpose in St. Giles."

He heard something, something that sounded like a catch in her breath as she inhaled.

"I love you, Anna. I want to be with you. I see no reason why that has to change."

Another inhaled breath that caught in her throat.

This time, she let him touch her. Gently, firmly, he tipped her chin up. "Did you think that once you discovered the truth I would cast you off?"

She nodded.

He gave her a small smile. "For an intelligent woman, you have a very foolish imagination."

She shook her head, looking up at him with tears in her eyes. "I thought you might have been using me to win your challenge, that your words of love were all a sham."

"No, Anna. I may be slow in the head, but I am no fool. I love you. I want to be with you."

She held on to his gaze with her own. "Will you marry me, then?" she asked.

The words stunned him to the point that his hand fell back to his side. "Marry you?"

And when she heard his words, he saw something fizzle and die in her eyes, something that had been hovering within the amber depths, something that seemed like fear, but that he realized now had been hope. "Do not say another word, for I see the answer in your eyes."

It took a moment for him to formulate words to say, to understand that he'd upset her. "Anna, I asked you weeks ago to be my mistress. Nothing has changed now that you know who I am. If anything, it should make you understand all the more why it must be so."

The word made her facial muscles flinch. And as he stared into her eyes, he noticed the telltale signs of redness, the moisture which still lingered along her bottom lash: She'd been crying.

"Anna—"

"No," she interrupted. "Do not say more." He saw her paste on a look of bravery, one that made him feel almost ill. "You are correct. You have always been honest as to your plans for me. I understand."

Plans for her?

She looked away, and the devil of it was, Rein knew he'd hurt her, knew it though he didn't fathom how things had come to that point.

Another deep breath, another direct stare. "Have you—" She swallowed. "Have you discovered anything more about who might have fired a pistol at you?"

It was a blatant attempt to change the subject, one that made Rein want to reach for her again, to pull her against him, to look in her eyes and ask her to please not cry, for he could see the longing to do so in her eyes.

"I—" He struggled with what to say, but in the end, he lost his courage. She must understand. Perhaps, given time, she would. "No, actually, I have not."

And as quickly as he could, he told her the truth, though he suspected he did so as a way of turning her attention. A coldness had begun to fill him, a coldness born of the pain he saw in her eyes.

"And now I must wait to be heard before a court," he finished, his fears only multiplying when she failed to move toward him, to express her shock and horror. It was as if she were numb. "I dare say I haven't left your rooms but for a bit of fresh air up here," he said, trying to tease her out of it.

Nothing.

"I see," she said.

Rein suddenly felt miserable. "Anna, I—"

"Who has the most to gain?"

Rein jerked, lifted his head. Anna's grandfather had joined them on the roof.

"Mr. Brooks, if you would give us a moment—"

"Who has the most to gain?" he asked again, gray hair sticking out as if the ride back to London had mussed it.

"Grandfather," Anna said. "Please. Not now."

"Who has the most to gain?" the old man repeated, his brown eyes intense.

"Pay him no heed," Anna said. And then she gave Rein another brave stare. "You were about to say?"

Rein opened his mouth, only to be interrupted again.

"Who has the most to gain?"

Who has the most to gain *what*? Rein wondered. Curse it all, the old man's timing was ill, indeed. He needed to work things out with Anna, for if he did not, he feared she might change her mind, that she would leave him. He couldn't lose her. Not now. Now when he'd—

"Who has the most to gain?" Mr. Brooks repeated, causing Rein to curse.

"Let me take him below."

"Yes, I think that would be wise."

Only, as she turned to leave him, the wrong words played themselves in his mind.

*Who has the most to gain?*

The old man was driving him batty now. He needed to concentrate on what it was he needed to say to Anna, to convince her that life as his mistress would be every bit as good as life as his wife. More so, for she would have freedom, status and a lifestyle few married women enjoyed.

*Who has the most to gain?*

And then Rein stiffened.

A lifestyle . . .

Who had the most to gain?

Rein felt the blood drain from his face. "Good God."

Abraham Lassiter had been expecting the knock on the door. His evening tea usually arrived about this time and so he didn't look up as he said, "Enter."

There was silence, Abraham thinking his servant might not have heard him, and so he turned in his padded armchair, looked right . . .

And gasped.

"Thank you for the invitation," the duke of Wroxly said.

The cheroot he'd been smoking dropped from his fingers, sending lazy spirals of white smoke toward the sitting room's ornate ceiling.

The duke. Here. Why?

There are moments in some people's lives when they realize things have just taken a sudden, dramatic turn for the worse. Such was this moment for Mr. Lassiter.

"Your Grace," he said, coming to his feet, tugging his black jacket down, the simple tie of his cravat suddenly feeling too tight. "Might I ask why it is you have called upon my private residence?"

Rein Montgomery moved into the room, Abraham relieved to note he seemed to be alone. The oak door behind him closed with a squeak of its hinges—something Abraham had been meaning to see to for months.

"Why, Mr. Lassiter, I feel certain you know exactly what it is I am doing here."

Abraham nonchalantly stepped on the cheroot, snuffing it out, though the red and white carpet would have a permanent mark there. He faced the new duke of Wroxly, who came toward him. Though the room was absolutely silent but for the sound of the street outside the paned window at Abraham's back, he had the sudden and unshakable feeling he heard an animal's footfalls, the click-click-click of toenails upon hardwood floor, except a carpet lay there.

Wroxly stopped an arm's length away from him. He looked horrid. Long, unkempt hair. Unshaven jaw. The jacket he'd worn to Lassiter's office earlier that week looked stained with grime, as if he'd gotten in a scuffle or two, black and brown smears upon its surface. The same stains covered his buff breeches, too, the brown boots that encased his legs obviously too big for him, something Abraham hadn't noticed during His Grace's last visit, but now he could plainly see.

"Bastard."

And though he'd told himself to be calm, told himself not to sweat, Abraham jumped.

"I ought to kill you with my bare fists."

Calm. Calm. Calm. "Has your challenge made you unbalanced, Your Grace? What reason would you have for saying such a thing? Indeed, you have no business being here—"

"Silence," the duke said, his arm snaking out to clutch Abraham's cravat by the loose ends. "One twist. Perhaps two, that is all it would take to suffocate the life out of you."

"I say—"

Rein jerked, all but flinging him away. Abraham very nearly fell to his knees. Any hope that the duke did not know faded with each breath.

"If you had harmed her that day on the ship . . . if she had been standing near me, and the ball had gone through her heart . . . if that had happened, right now, Mr. Lassiter, you would be dead. By my own hand."

And as he looked into the duke's eyes, Abraham knew Wroxly spoke the truth. He began to shake, his limbs suddenly as unstable as a three-legged table.

"Why?" he asked. "All the way here I have asked myself why."

Abraham swallowed. He didn't answer, for there was still a chance . . .

"But then, as I arrived at your doorstep, saw what you have managed to afford on a solicitor's salary, it hit me." He lowered his head so that they were all but nose to nose. "My uncle was ill for two years prior to his death, too ill to manage his own money. The estate was put into your hands until his passing, into your care until the day I inherited the title."

Bile began to bubble up his throat. The trembling became visibly noticeable.

He'd been discovered.

"How much did you take over the years?"

"Not a farthing, I swear."

Rein jerked him so that their noses hit. "How much?" he asked in a voice that was low, yet filled with terrible menace.

Abraham found himself saying, "Just a pound here and there."

The duke released him. There was still time to salvage this. Straightening his cravat, said, "I'll pay you back. If you give me some time, I can—"

"Pay me back?" the duke interrupted. "Pay you back for dropping me in the worst of London's slums, a rookery, where you planned to have me killed so that you could go on stealing from the estate?"

"No. I never hired—"

"Silence!" the duke roared, Abraham jumping in his shoes. "You," he said more softly, "lied to me about the existence of a cousin. I broke into your offices this evening. There are no cousins. Indeed, I began to wonder if there even was a codicil to the will requiring my 'test,' though I've no doubt you could have forged the one I saw."

"No," Abraham said truthfully. "There was a test. I assure you."

The duke did not reply. Indeed, Abraham knew he was being studied for the truthfulness of his words. He looked beyond the man, judging the distance between him and the door. The duke was a bumble-brain. It was a well-known fact. Perhaps he could trick him into moving aside—

"How many days was I truly supposed to stay in St. Giles?"

The astuteness of the words had Abraham glancing up at him quickly. How the blazes . . .

"A week? Two?"

Perhaps not as much a fool as the man's uncle had thought.

"No. It wasn't even that long, was it? I would wager it was four *days*. That way it was simple enough for you to change the word days to weeks. Such a small change. My uncle wouldn't even have noticed it when he signed the will."

Abraham decided that from this point forward he should likely remain quiet.

"Indeed, I wonder if I look at my uncle's copy of the will what I would find."

Desperation forced his feet to move. Abraham found himself lunging past the duke. But the man was twenty years his junior and light on his feet. A hand snatched out to stop him, another hand capturing his other arm, though the duke winced with pain as he did so.

"How long?" he said. "How long was the test originally supposed to be?"

Done for. All the duke would have to do was look at his uncle's copy of the will . . .

"Four days."

Wroxly released him, his face looking impassive. No, that wasn't true. One side of his mouth tilted up a bit, his eyes suddenly bright. "Four days?" He threw back his head and laughed—yes, laughed. "Why not three, or five, Uncle?" he asked. "Surely you did not think four days would do me any good?"

Abraham made another dash for the door, this time opening it.

Mr. Stills, the Runner he'd hired just to make things look more legitimate, stood on the other side next to a stunning young woman Lassiter could only assume was Anna Brooks.

Rage, red and hot as bricks, suddenly caused him to

lunge at her. If she hadn't taken the duke in . . . if she hadn't interfered—

The pistol blast hit him in the chest, knocking him off his feet, and at first he didn't feel the pain in his back, at first he wondered what had happened to bring him down. Then he felt the heat, followed by a keening pain that made him gasp, only he had no breath. He couldn't breathe.

"You've . . . shot me," he managed to hiss in Rein's direction.

Darkness began to descend.

"Indeed, I did," he heard from a distance. "Just as you shot me."

The darkness grew even more. And then Mr. Lassiter saw no more.

# Chapter Twenty-three

Anna could scarcely believe that it was all over so quickly—and that her grandfather had been correct. Like the pieces of the wooden puzzles she'd loved to do as a child, it all fell into place.

The authorities were notified, Rein was questioned, a constable arrived. Further investigation revealed a will located at Rein's uncle's home. When the two were compared side by side, the word *days* had been changed to *weeks*, but only in one copy—the copy Abraham Lassiter had shown to Rein when he'd gone to the solicitor for the reading of the will.

"Crafty cull," the barrel-chested constable had said, his basset hound cheeks quivering as he shook his head. "Unless one knew to look for the change, one would never have seen it. Like as not your uncle checked only one copy, judged them both to be correct, then blithely signed the original and the copy."

"We'll never know," Rein said.

They'd only just moved to Rein's town home, and what Anna saw there made her feel afraid to move: the plush light blue carpet in the sitting room she stood in matched by the ice blue settee and chairs placed near the center of the room.

*He wanted her to be his mistress.*

And though he was correct, though he'd never misled her about that fact, Anna understood now that she wanted more. So much more.

"Bloody odd business," the constable said from his position on the armchair, the man spilling out over the edges. "I'll wager you wish now you'd challenged the will from the moment it'd been read."

Rein turned to face them. "No, Constable Caruthers, I do not wish that. Complying with the will's challenge has been the making of me, as I suspect was my uncle's intent." His gaze met Anna's, their eyes catching and holding. And as always happened, she felt the same lurch to her world, the same waves, the same sense of peace, his eyes clearly saying to her, *I would have never met you.*

And he wouldn't have. He was a duke. A peer of the realm. Far, far removed from St. Giles. It was as he'd said. She would need to be his mistress. She'd reasoned out on the long trip back to London that he couldn't wed her, though a part of her had hoped . . .

And what a silly hope that had been. He was part of a different world. The *ton.* Wealth. Privilege.

Her stomach tightened. She looked away, her gaze catching on a vase made of crystal, the thing so shiny and large, she could see her reflection in the cut glass, fragmenting into pieces that looked exactly as she felt—broken, shattered, fallen apart.

"Still, I am pleased to be back home."

"Don't doubt it, Your Grace."

When she managed to tear her gaze away from the

splendid vase, she looked at the walls, at the fancy framed portraits that hung on them, at the sconces between, their covers shaped like the shells she used to collect back at the coast.

If she agreed to be his paramour, she would be no better than those other market maids who'd gone off to earn their living on their backs. And though that had once been all right, suddenly it felt far from right.

"Well, then," the constable said, pushing his large girth out of the chair with a groan. "I'll be off then, Your Grace."

Your Grace. There it was again. The correct form of address for a duke. Not My Lord like the majority of nobility in England, but Your Grace, a title as old and distinguished as the Crown itself.

"Pleasure meeting you, Miss Brooks."

She nodded, wondering if she should curtsy, trying to remember what her mother had taught her about rank and privilege. With an answering nod, the man left the room, Anna starting at the soft sound of the door closing behind him.

*He wanted her to be his mistress.*

She couldn't do it.

"Come here," Rein said, opening his arms.

Suddenly, she couldn't move. So he moved to her, wrapping his arms around her, and as he did, a fear rose within her unlike any she'd felt before.

"You may spend the night here, if you wish."

She didn't wish. Goodness, just being in his house, unchaperoned, wasn't really allowed, not that anyone cared about her reputation. But it was more than that. She was afraid to touch things here. Odd as it sounded, she wanted to go back to St. Giles. Or perhaps the cottage she and her grandfather had occupied until that afternoon.

"I should return to my grandfather."

His gaze turned to one of concern. "Anna, I realize we haven't had time to talk—"

"No," she interrupted. "Not tonight. Let us speak of the future tomorrow."

He didn't look pleased with the idea. His eyes searched her own.

"Please," she added.

And then he straightened, nodded a bit, tucked a strand of her hair back behind her ears. The pad of his finger made her shiver as it touched her cheek.

"Odd, but I'm afraid to let you go."

She smiled bravely. "I've spent almost half my life on my own."

"Indeed you have," he said softly, his finger touching her lips now. And despite her fears, despite the heartache that'd begun to gnaw at her insides, she felt herself soften. This was what she wanted, to be with him, alone, in a room, forever. Instead she would have to share him with society, perhaps in a few years a wife and so many other obligations. Anna felt her anxieties multiply like a mound of ants, ones that crawled over her skin and made her want to run.

"Go," he said, bending down and kissing her with a soft brush of his lips.

She stepped away from him then, though he still held her right hand, her worn and callused hand.

"I shall see you on the morrow."

Would she? She wondered as the pad of his thumb lightly circled the knuckle of her index finger. Would he come back to her? Or would he suddenly realize that poor little Anna Brooks was a passing fancy?

She stepped forward, quickly kissing him on the cheek, holding her head next to his for a moment as she inhaled his scent.

*Don't leave me.*

*Don't let me go.*

She moved back. He released her, their hands falling away from each other.

"I'll have my carriage brought around."

"No, don't—don't disturb your staff."

"Anna, you will not find a hack this time of night."

She felt her shoulders bow a bit. He had a point.

"It will only take a trice."

And, indeed, that was all it took, Anna wondering if Rein's coachman had lain in wait for his summons. And perhaps he had. Lord, Rein likely had a staff of thirty just waiting on his every whim. She swallowed.

"What time does the judging start on the morrow?" Rein asked as he walked her out of the study and into a long hallway as wide as her attic back in St. Giles. A servant materialized from nowhere, making Anna jump, the candelabra he held lighting their way. Had all of his staff been waiting for her to leave?

"Anna?" Rein asked, reminding her that he'd asked a question.

She found herself looking up at him in confusion.

"The competition?" he prompted with a half smile.

Oh, good heavens, the competition. She'd forgotten. "Noon," she said, lying to him for the first time since they'd met. But the thought of having him with her tomorrow, the thought of all those people bowing and curtsying to him, made her ill. She couldn't do it. She wanted Rein back. Plain Mr. Rein Hemplewilt.

"Noon," he said. "Good heavens. That seems a very odd hour."

Because it was. The competitors would display their devices in the morning, and judging should be well over by noon. At least she hoped so. "They need to look over all the entries before awarding the prize."

"Ah," he said. "I see."

From the dark street came the sound of a coach and horses. "Your carriage, my lady," he said with a smile, giving her his arm, gnats flying past them and into the candlelight. Anna looked down the steps to spy a black carriage almost exactly like a coach she and Molly had spied once upon a time, one they'd imagined themselves riding in, the two of them laughing at how silly an idea that seemed.

He gave her his good arm. She took it without conscious thought, trying to control her sudden shaking as he led her toward it. And though it was dark, though it was the middle of the night, the coachman still had on his livery, and two postilions sat the horses on the right.

"A damn sight better than that bloody hack, eh?" he said as a tiger—a young man of no more than five and ten—came forward to open the door for her, the smell of the inside wafting out on a sudden draft stirred by the door. It smelled as rich and as fine as the mantua-makers' shops down on Bond Street.

"Goodbye, my dear."

She refused to meet his eyes, felt suddenly shy in front of his staff.

What a bloody fool. They were just people, people like

him and her. They were employed by Rein, was all. Servants of the nobility, just as she had been when she'd sold her wares in the market. Except she'd been asked to become his mistress.

Dear God. He wanted her to become his mistress.

Odd, how it hit her then. Odd, how she'd been through so much with him, felt so much love for him, yet the thought of becoming his mistress suddenly filled her with such a sickness she could barely breathe.

She didn't remember the door closing behind her. Didn't glance at Rein as they set off. The whole way back to St. Giles—the outside noise so muted by the well-appointed carriage, she felt like she rode in a bubble—Anna fretted. Did he truly love her? He said he did—but did he? Was she a passing fancy? Now that he no longer needed her, would he tire of her? Dear God, what would she do if he did?

And though she didn't know it happened, she found herself suddenly sobbing. Hers weren't the slow tears of a woman holding on to herself by a thread, they were the deep, stomach-wrenching sobs of a woman who felt as if she'd lost a dream.

Something felt amiss, Rein thought, his carriage rolling past various ships moored to the quayside for the naval competition, colorful flags flying from their masts beneath a breezy, sunny sky. Odd ships, to be sure, and perhaps that was what bothered him. Two or three had machinery protruding from the decks, one looked to have had a tilted-back mast and, most strange of all, one ship had holes in the side for what looked to be oars. Oars. But as Rein's coachman pulled his six horses to a stop in front of his yacht, he realized that wasn't it. That wasn't it at all.

There were no spectators.

Indeed, the length of pier sequestered off for the competition looked bloody deserted. Rein looked at the gangplank to his own yacht. No crew appeared ready to set sail, and most of all, there was no sign of Anna.

None.

Pulling the stiff brim of his black hat down low on his brow, he walked toward his ship. Perhaps they were all at the judging. But a glance up and down the quayside revealed a domed white tent, chairs set before it, but no naval personnel.

What the blazes?

He stopped, turned in a full circle, a swarm of leaves suddenly pushed by on an oddly warm breeze dancing around his feet. Next he glanced at his pocket watch, then tapped the face wondering if it might have stopped. But, no, his coachman had checked the time, too.

He turned toward his yacht, striding toward it with the firm steps of a man determined to get to the bottom of things.

The ship, however, was not deserted. Indeed, the moment he stepped on board, a man called out to him.

"Your Grace?"

Rein turned.

Captain Jones came at him, obviously having spied the rather grandiose carriage he now owned, the one with the ducal crest on the door. He could claim his wealth now, thanks to the swift action of the courts.

"Your Grace, might I tell you what a pleasure it is—"

Captain Jones came to a wall-slamming stop. Rein

might have laughed if he hadn't been so determined to find out what the blazes had happened to Anna.

"Why, you're . . . you're . . ."

"Just so," Rein said, his eyes narrowing as he snapped, "Where is Miss Brooks?"

"She's . . ." Jones straightened. "Your Grace, might I venture to say that you really should have told me—"

"No, you may not. Indeed, since you seem unable to tell me where Miss Brooks is, you might as well busy yourself packing your belongings. You, sir, are released from my employ."

"Your Grace?"

Rein turned away.

"She's on the poop deck," the man called out, as if by telling him what he wanted to know it would save his chances of remaining ship's captain. It wouldn't. Rein just turned on his heel and headed to the back of the ship. Around the rear mast he went, between the lines that hung down from the sails, up the steps built into the left side of the ship and that led to the deck above the living quarters.

No wonder he hadn't seen her from the quayside, for she stood alongside the rail that overlooked the bay beyond. A shadow cast down from one of her sails turned her white pelisse gray, her matching cotton hat a dark brown. Bits of her lovely hair escaped from the edges of that bonnet, streaming out behind her as she stood with her back to him.

"Anna," he called.

She didn't turn.

Rein clutched the rail, then abruptly let it go as he hurried toward her, wondering if she was angry with him for missing her competition. Had he misheard her last night? Had the competition been delayed?

"Anna, I must apologize. I must have heard you incorrectly last eve."

She still didn't turn.

"Anna," he said, placing a hand on her shoulder. When she remained stubbornly turned away, he removed his hat and placed a kiss against the back of her neck.

"Forgive me, my love."

She stepped away from him. Rein's hand dropped back to his side. "Anna, what is the matter?"

Slowly, she turned, and when she did, her perfectly shaped face looked pale beneath her dapper hat, her amber eyes nearly the exact color of strands of straw. He'd never seen her dressed so finely, the fancy white pelisse she wore over her dress dotted with flowers that matched the shape and color of the silk ones in her hat. She looked like a lady, and for a brief moment he wondered where she'd gotten the gown.

"Good day, Your Grace," she said with a small curtsy.

"Good day?" He drew back a bit at the formality of her greeting. "Why do you greet me so? And what the blazes is going on? Where are all the people? Did I miss the judging? For if I did, I am truly sorry, I had every intention—"

"You did not err."

"Then what—" But in the next instant he understood. He drew himself up, the toes of the black boots he wore snapping at the deck in disbelief. "You told me the wrong time."

"I wanted to do this on my own."

"Why?"

SCANDAL                287

"Because it is a journey I started on my own and one I wished to finish that way."

And what could he say to that? Nothing, apparently, though he toyed with the notion of telling her how disappointed he felt. He'd had an interest in the outcome, too.

"Did you win?" he asked.

She shook her head.

"What?" he asked in horror. All that they'd gone through, all the work that she'd put into her sails . . .

She looked past him, out at the water and in the same direction where she'd been staring before. He followed her gaze, and it was then that he realized she stared at a ship moored on the next pier.

"She's called the *Victoria,* after the wife of the man who designed and built her."

"Someone built a ship?"

She nodded, still not looking at him. "The rules allowed for people to invent whatever they wished, but I never thought—I never imagined—someone would enter a ship they'd designed."

He lifted a hand to her shoulder again. "Anna, I am terribly sorry."

She seemed to startle beneath his touch. "No, 'tis I who am sorry. You should have been here. You are as much a part of this as Molly and Charlie and all the others. I should have realized that last eve, only as I looked around your study, as I stared at your wealth and then later spied your servants, I became frightened."

Anna? Frightened? He didn't think she knew the meaning of the word.

"You are a duke. A peer of the realm, and while I suspected you to be a gentleman, I never once dreamed, I never imagined—well, perhaps I imagined—but I never really believed you might be . . ."

A duke.

The words were unspoken, but he heard them nonetheless.

"The thought of your being a nobleman," she said, "of being a member of the bloody *ton,* of living a life of balls and parties and impossible wealth . . . well, it seemed so implausible as to be laughable."

"And this frightens you?"

The look in her eyes hit him so hard he almost took a step back.

"It has scared me half to death."

"But why? It means nothing, the life I live. It is simply the way things are, much as you once said to me about your life in the rookery."

She began to shake her head, and that was when Rein has his first inkling of the depth of this trouble. There was something in her gaze—a hint of the same fears he'd seen in her eyes yesterday, a look that had worried him all night.

"You cannot compare the two, Rein. You and I both know that. There are duties and obligations that go along with being who you are. One day you will be expected to take a wife. I tried last eve to glean how that would make me feel . . . goodness knows I tried, to understand, to comprehend what it would be like . . . but in the end the thought was too horrible to contemplate."

"Then I shall never marry."

Anna shook her head, the next words she had to say seeming to be difficult for her to speak. "I love you, Rein. Lord, if you only knew how much. But I'm wise enough to know that someday you will want an heir, and when that time comes, it will kill me to watch it happen."

"Anna—"

"No, Rein. I thought I could be your mistress, told myself that it would be easy to live such a life, but I told myself a lie. I have too much pride for that now. Honor, you might call it. You taught me that, taught me that I have self-worth. And the irony of it is, the lessons you taught me made me realize that becoming your mistress would be beneath me now."

"Anna," he tried again.

"I've made my decision," she cut him off. "I love you, but I can't be with you."

# Chapter Twenty-four

Anna saw Rein's eyes widen, saw emotions spin through them. "What are you saying?"

"I am . . ." She searched for words, knowing—oh, lord—knowing that her next words would be hard. "I'm breaking it off."

"But . . . you can't."

"Yes, Rein, I can."

"But you agreed—"

"That was before."

"Nothing has changed," he insisted.

"Yes, Rein, it has."

He looked so taken aback, so thunderstruck, she found herself attempting to explain. "I told you once that I only ever rode in a carriage three times. Once on my way to London, and once when I traveled to visit my hometown, and that is true, but what I did not tell you was what happened to me when I returned home all those years ago."

"Anna, whatever it is, it cannot be—"

"Rein, please, let me finish," she said, reaching up and clutching his hand.

She thought he might ignore her request, but his green

eyes held her own, the stubbornness in them gentling until at last he nodded.

"When I'd left to come to London, I vowed one day I'd return to Porthollow. The days I spent in St. Giles only made the urge grow. Porthollow became a dream. I'd been happy there before; I knew I would be again. But more than that, I wanted to return to Elliot."

"Elliot?" Rein asked, rocking back on his heels.

"Aye, Elliot. I'd fancied him for years, thought, mayhap, he fancied me, too. Childish, silly dreams," she said to reassure Rein, for he looked suddenly jealous. "I ought to have outgrown such feelings long before I turned sixteen. I didn't. In my mind, Elliot became the boy that would rescue me from St. Giles. I even saved the coin to post him a letter. He posted one back. My heart soared. He talked of Porthollow and it only made my longing to return all the greater.

"So I scrimped and saved and somehow managed to gather the fare to ride post back home. I packed my satchel to the brim with all my most precious belongings. I didn't intend to come back to St. Giles. Elliot would rescue me, and if not him, then I'd beg someone else to take me in. I said goodbye to my grandfather—he was better then, more lucid and self-sustaining—and off I went."

"Obviously," Rein said, "things did not go as planned."

He didn't say it with sarcasm; indeed, when she looked up at him, there was such sympathy in his eyes, for a moment she couldn't go on. Rein. Her handsome and princely Rein, if he only knew how hard he made this for her.

"Aye," she said. "The trip was a disaster from the start.

I was forced to sit next to a woman who took up most of the seat, and who kept falling asleep and leaning on me. One passenger had a penchant for eating onions. Another carried his pig in his lap for a large part of the journey, and if you've never seen what happens when a pig becomes loose in a coach full of people, I assure you, 'tis not amusing. A long, arduous journey it was, and when I arrived, my one good dress, the dress I'd spent hours stitching by hand, had pig dung and onion juice all over it." She smiled bitterly. "I must have looked and smelled a sight."

"Anna, there is no need to continue. I can envision what happened next."

"No, Rein," she said with a snap of her chin and a sudden burning in her eyes. And oddly enough it wasn't shame or horror or humiliation that made her eyes fill with tears, it was rage. "You cannot possibly understand what it was like. The wife of one of my father's closest friends all but ran in the other direction when she realized who I was. People looked at me in horror and dismay and I think even a little bit of fear. *I* was what they could all become if fate dealt them an unkind blow."

"Anna—"

She held up a hand that shook with anger. "But the worst was seeing Elliot. His family owned the mercantile and when I came into the place, likely with the sun and the moon and stars in my eyes, it was clear in an instant that my childish dreams were just that: dreams." She looked down at the sparkling water, her hands clenching so that she could feel her calluses. "When customers came in who didn't know me, he pretended I was a stranger, even tried to sell a cream for my hands." She held her fingers out. "They were so worn and ruined. I had just started to push a barrow back then, you see, and my palms had sores on them."

She met his gaze again, her hand dropping back to her side. "I remember what it was like, the expression on those customers' faces. They looked at me like I was a pauper, one who'd found her way into a store only to escape the cold, or so they thought. They didn't want me there. Not Elliot, not the town's people, not anyone. I shan't forget that moment. I shall never forget what it felt like to be an outsider, to hear the titters of the women my age, to listen to the matrons who insisted Elliot ignore me so that he could assist them instead."

"That was long ago, Anna."

Anna nodded. "Aye. And I know that mistresses are accepted in certain circles, but there will always be those looks—the looks of pity and condemnation, and, from members of society, scorn and derision. I don't want that—not for me and not for our children."

"Children," he said. His eyes lit from within. "But I would take care of you, and our children, if we were so blessed."

The look of love he gave her, the way he reached up and stroked the line of her jaw, brought fresh tears to her eyes. Yes, he would be there for her, for them. She had no doubt. But that didn't erase the fear, nor the worries, nor her conviction that in the end it would prove too much. It would hurt too much, just those looks.

"Rein, please. Try to understand. I love you. Too much to put us through the eventual turmoil that would come."

"Then what do you want to do?"

She almost said, *Marry me,* almost gave in to the riptide of longing that made her heart ache to say the words. "I don't know," she said in genuine anguish. "I just know that I cannot become your mistress."

"Is it me? Is there something I've done to put you off staying with me?"

"No." She shook her head.

He turned on his heel and began to walk away.

"Where are you going?"

He turned back to face her, his face so full of anger, she found herself stepping back.

"I am leaving. Obviously there is something more, something you do not wish to tell me."

"No, Rein, there is not."

"The least you could do is be honest with me."

"I *am* being honest."

"You mean to tell me that you, a woman who has lived her life in one of London's worst slums, are afraid to believe in me, in our love?"

God help her, that was exactly the problem.

He waited for her to answer, green eyes nearly as stabbing as a sharp-tipped leaf. She nodded.

"Poppycock," he said, turning.

"Rein, no. Do not leave."

He turned back to face her again, his hands clenched at his sides. "Then be honest with me," he said again. "If you do not find my intelligence on par with yours, you should have told me so directly."

Intelligence? What the blazes . . . ?

But then she knew, knew with a lurch in her heart. "No, Rein. That has nothing to do with it—"

He turned away again, she moved to follow him. "You are not a dunderhead—"

He reached the steps to the main deck; she followed him down.

"Your Grace," Captain Jones cried, whether in a greeting or a plea, Anna didn't know.

"Rein," she called again, but by now he'd reached the gangplank, stepping upon the swaying board without a backward glance. Anna stopped as she reached the opening, looked down onto the dock.

And spied the most elegant, elaborate carriage she'd ever seen. For a moment the sight of that carriage held her rooted to the spot. Glossy brown in color, it held such a shine it looked almost black. Six dappled gray horses pulled it, two postilions riding the horses, just as they had last night. Only this was not the carriage she'd ridden home in, this was the ducal carriage, more grand, more elaborate, more . . . foreign.

Her feet suddenly wouldn't move.

*Let him go,* a voice urged.

*I can't,* her heart cried out.

But she must. Her mind, the part of it that was always so careful to reason things out, told her that to embark upon such a journey would be madness. Society would not welcome her into its fold. Indeed, such a scandal would fuel a storm of gossip that would see them both hurt. Nor did she want to immerse herself in the lifestyle of a mistress, most especially not a ducal mistress. It would be a public life, despite the lack of a ring, one reported on by periodicals, characterized in satirical drawings, drawings that would likely portray her as a sultry vixen and Rein the stupidly smitten lord. But most of all, the thing she feared absolutely was taking the step he asked, only to see their children suffer.

Rein reached the carriage. The tiger stepped down and opened the door. Rein paused, his back to her, as if waiting for her to call to him.

*Don't leave me.*

She shook her head as if someone had said the words aloud.

He lurched into the carriage. Anna found herself taking a small step. The door snapped closed. Her shoulders slumped as a ball of emotion entwined itself around her heart—hopelessness, fear, longing—it swelled within her, making her eyes fill with tears as she watched his dappled gray horses pull away with tosses of their heads and a jangle of their traces.

It was either the most daft thing she'd ever done, or the wisest.

# Chapter Twenty-five

It was not easy living with the repercussions of a decision made out of fear, especially when she knew that decision had hurt Rein.

She loved him. Like as not, she'd never love another.

"So you let him go."

Anna turned on her bench, surprised to see Molly behind her. Her friend never came to her rooftop, preferring to keep her feet firmly rooted on the ground.

"Freddie told me you bade him goodbye."

"Freddie?" Anna asked.

"Mr. Stills. The Runner what was keeping an eye on your man."

*Her man.* No, society's man. The Crown's man. Never *her* man.

"I had no choice," Anna said. "You of all people should understand why. He wanted me to be his mistress. How many times have we made fun of the fancy pieces what come to market? How many times have we sworn not to become like them?"

"What in the blazes makes you think you'd be like

them?" Molly asked, striding forward. "Lord, Anna, you're nothing like those women."

Anna shook her head, looking out over the horizon. "No, Molly, I'm not, not at first I wouldn't be," she said.

Her friend knelt by her, clutching her hands as she stared into her eyes. "Don't think like that, Anna. Don't be afraid to grasp what he offers. A life of luxury, of love, for no matter what you might think, that man loves you."

"I know."

"Then seize what he's offering. Lord, Anna, you'll be a mistress of a duke. As near to a lady as you'll ever be."

"But don't you see?" Anna asked. "I won't be a lady. Our children will never be lords. One day that will come between us, whether through my resentment or his disappointment in not having a legitimate heir, it will happen."

Molly didn't say anything. When Anna met her friend's gaze, there was disillusionment in her green eyes.

"I can't believe you, of all people, are too afeared to do this."

"No?" Anna asked.

"If you loved him, you wouldn't be afraid."

"Easy for you to say, since you're in love with a Bow Street Runner."

"I wouldn't care if he was the bleedin' prince of Wales. If I loved him enough, I'd do whatever it took to be with him."

"Even if it meant stepping into a world that scared you half to death? Because it does, Molly. I can't imagine socializing with his lordly friends. Even if it meant losing that bit of yourself that was yours? That part of you that could say, do, *be* anything you like? I won't be a lady, but I'll still be judged, branded a tart, a whore. At least this way I retain my dignity."

"Does it matter what people call you?"

"What society thinks would matter to Rein."

Molly snorted. "You're wrong." She shook her head, her mouth tipping down. "But what disappoints me the most, what makes me wonder if I ever really knew you, is that you've always claimed you were better than the tarts what tittered behind their fancy fans at us maids. Here's your opportunity to prove that a woman like that can behave like a lady, and yet you're too blinded by fear to take on the task."

"Molly—"

"No, Anna, I understand. You're a coward."

"Molly, you're being too harsh."

"No, I'm trying to be your friend."

Anna closed her eyes, knowing in her heart of hearts that Molly spoke the truth.

*Coward, coward, coward.*

But she could see no way around that fear.

Molly stood, letting go of her hands. "See you at market on the morrow?"

Anna opened her eyes, nodded.

"Perhaps you'll be less afraid then."


The glass made a satisfying tinkle as it broke apart in the grate, a few crystals landing before the fire, glittering like the embers whose reflection they mimicked.

She'd left him.

Damn her. Damn all women. He had guarded himself

against caring for women in the past, only to realize now that he did so out of fear of them not loving him back.

*Imbecile.*

*Fool.*

His father's voice ran through his mind with the cadence of a raging river. He'd fought such insecurities before, had told himself he was being an even bigger fool for letting such thoughts enter his head, only he couldn't seem to shake them. Not now. Not ever.

*Useless young pup.*

His fears played with him, taunting him to the point that he poured himself another glass of brandy, only to stop himself at the last moment. He would not do it. He would not drink himself into oblivion as he had so many times in his past—his drunken stupor having resulted in pranks no sober man would engage in. When his cousin had died, he had stopped. He would not let Anna's loss start the cycle again. What he needed to do was think . . . think of ways to convince Anna that he was worth the risk, that as much as he wanted to, marriage would be an even bigger mistake than taking her on as his mistress.

*Ought to have thrown you to the bloody dogs when you were born.*

*No,* Rein thought, shaking off the words like a fox shook off droplets off water. He would not let his father win this battle. He would not let Anna reduce him to the man he was before. No one would have that kind of control over him again, that much he'd learned during his time in St. Giles.

He just wished he knew what the blazes to do.

\*     \*     \*

The next day, she'd lost none of her fear. And when Rein sent her a note at market, the other maids looking at her strangely when a liveried servant delivered the letter on a sparkling silver tray, she returned it unopened. What was the daft man thinking, to keep after her like he was? Didn't he understand she'd made up her mind?

Apparently not, for when she arrived home a few days later, it was to spy his fancy brown carriage out in front of her building, every chimney sweep, costermonger and coal porter huddled around it as Rein spoke to the crowd, laughed with them, smiled. She watched from a distance, darted back around the corner she'd rounded so that she could peek around the edge and watch.

A duke.

She shook her head, marveling. He didn't act like a duke. Indeed, he joked and jested with the crowd as he waited for her to return.

Anna backed her cart in the other direction and entered her building from behind, then used the rooftop route to gain access to her rooms. When he knocked on the door an hour later, she refused to see him. He went away eventually, Anna's heart breaking all the more at the note he'd left behind. She hadn't opened it. Molly had.

*I love you. Don't be afraid.*
*Rein.*

She'd tipped her head back when Molly had read her the words, had felt tears fill her eyes.

*I love you. Don't be afraid.*

But she was. Desperately. After Molly's little speech, she could admit that now. Her mind had chewed over her friend's words, tumbled them, assimilated them, and in the end, judged them to be true.

Afraid. Their future children had nothing to do with it.

"What are you going to do?"

"Go to market," Anna had said, even though included in the note was a draft for twenty pounds, the money he owed her for living with them, though he hadn't stayed for the full month.

"You could try living with him for a time," Molly offered.

Anna nodded, going to the window in her attic and peering out. She could. The idea held more and more appeal with each day that passed.

"Anna?"

"I'm thinking on it," Anna answered.

A week went by, a week that left her in such misery Anna knew she had no choice. With a shaking hand she wrote:

*Dear Sir,*
*If the offer is still open, I should like to accept your*
*offer of protection.*
*Yours, Anna.*

It meant the end of her ideals. It meant living a life she truly didn't want to lead, but it would be better than not having Rein at all. She knew that now, too.

Rein read the note, his relief so great that he found himself running to his writing table.

Only as he lifted a quill to begin writing his reply, something stopped him.

It felt as if the floor dropped out from beneath Anna's feet when she heard Rein's voice from belowstairs.

"Mr. Brooks, it is I . . . Wroxly."

"Don't know no Wroxly," her grandfather said in an angry voice.

"Mr. Hemplewilt," Rein corrected.

"Don't know no Hemplewilt, either."

"But I've lived with you . . . helped you bathe—"

"Bathe. I will not bathe with you, you bloody bugger."

"Grandfather," she interrupted as she climbed down her ladder. "Do not fret. I know this gentleman."

"You do?" her grandfather asked. And it was hard to say what pained her more, Grandfather's increasingly broken mind, or seeing Rein standing before her.

*You should be happy to see him, Anna,* she told herself. *Obviously, he's pleased you agreed to become his mistress, at least judging by the look of happiness on his face.*

She swallowed. "Grandfather, if you please, I should like a word with Mr.—" The words died. "A word with Wroxly," she finished.

Her grandfather looked ready to protest, but something in her expression must have nudged into his foggy mind. "Of course, my dear. Of course," he said rather vaguely, turning toward his partitioned-off room. And as he turned his back on them, Anna's breathing quickened. She turned toward Rein. This was it, then, the moment she'd been dreading—yes, dreading, for this was a moment that would seal her fate.

"Rein, I—"

"No, Anna," he said softly. "Do not say a word." He came before her, reached out and gently took her hand, then slowly bent down on one knee.

Bent down on one knee?

"What are you doing?"

"Anna Brooks," he began softly, reaching into his pocket for something . . . a ring, she saw—

And she knew.

Her breath caught. She knew what he was about to do.

"Would you do me the honor, the very great honor, of becoming my wife?"

It sounded as if she heard the words from underwater, as if they came at her through a cold and dense filter. The waves hit her again, though in a way wholly different than before. These waves made her stomach clench, made her feel ill.

*Becoming my wife.*

The three words hit her.

"Are you daft?"

His expression slowly changed.

"I cannot marry you." She pulled her hand from his grasp, stepping back from him. "Only think what society would say should you wed someone as common as I."

Slowly, he came to his feet, his tall form dwarfing her. "I assure you, having watched my cousin marry beneath him, I have thought long and hard of exactly what marriage to you would entail."

And the formality of his words, the clipped way in which he spoke them, twisted at Anna's heart like two fists were clenched around it.

"Rein, you cannot be thinking straight. I explained to

you what happened to me all those years ago when I went back home. If I were to wed you, it would be just like that all over again. People would shun me, only I've a feeling it'd be much, much worse."

She waited for a look of understanding to enter his eyes, for an expression of relief that she refused his suit.

All she saw was a bitter pain.

"You are refusing me."

She nodded. "At least people will not accuse me of overstepping myself should I become your mistress. That, at least, would be expected."

"Overstepping yourself," he said, his words spoken in a monotone.

"Yes, overstepping myself." As she stared up at him, her heart began to beat even harder than before, her chest heaving to keep up with her racing pulse.

"Overstepping yourself," he said, straightening, his hand flicking up the pocket of his black jacket and tucking the ring inside.

A diamond. A large, oval diamond that sparkled like the purest of water split by sunlight.

Oh, lord.

But it was that ring, that precious, rare gem that made her straighten her own spine, made her hold firm as she said, "Rein, you do me a great honor—"

"But you find you must refuse my suit," he finished for her.

He was angry. And hurt. And so very disappointed.

"Yes, I must," she said. "You are not thinking clearly—"

"Oh, I beg to differ," he said. "I am thinking more clearly than I ever have in my life. Indeed, for the first time, I find myself knowing something intuitively, and that something tells me that if you refuse to wed me, it is over between us."

"Over?"

He nodded. "You yourself said it, Anna. You deserve far more than to be my mistress. Thus, if you refuse my hand, I refuse the offer of your company, as charming as it may be."

He stepped away from her.

Anna felt as if her world tilted all over again. What was he saying?

But as he bowed to her, just a short bow, one that conveyed a polite disregard for all that had happened between them in the smart, almost sarcastic tip of his head, she knew.

"I wish you well, my dear." And for a moment, just after he straightened, something flashed through his eyes, a look of such emotion, Anna would be hard-pressed to name just which emotions she had seen.

He turned away.

"Rein—"

He ignored her. She followed him for a step, only to stop just shy of the door. He closed that door in her face.

What had just happened? He couldn't be breaking things off simply because she'd refused his hand in marriage.

She went to the window.

Marriage.

Dear God, he'd asked her to marry him.

And as Anna stared out at his elegant carriage—as she observed the livery on the baby-faced footman who opened the door just before Rein flung himself inside—

she admitted that Molly had been right. Indeed, she'd been spectacularly right, because while becoming Rein's mistress had filled Anna with fear, the thought of becoming his duchess filled her with downright terror.

# Chapter Twenty-six

Anna waited for Rein to change his mind, waited for him to see the wisdom of her decision not to marry him, and to accept her decision to become his mistress.

He didn't.

And when two days had passed with still no word from him, she'd begun to fear that it was over. Well and truly over.

And while they'd had words before, this time she knew it to be different. This time there would be no going back. He had told her goodbye. Apparently, he had meant it. The realization filled her with a sadness so severe, she found herself on the brink of tears at least twenty times a day.

Over.

Why? Why, when they could have so easily worked it out?

Such were her thoughts when she heard a stir at the market. She turned, dashing away tears as she so often had in past days with Molly looking sadly on. A lady made her way through the market, a lady who turned so many heads, Anna stared at her in awe. Beautiful. Poised.

Well dressed, her red hair covered by an off-white silk confection that almost perfectly matched the pale perfection of her skin, and her dress. The sight of her made Anna's misery increase tenfold. She was everything Anna knew she could never be, everything she suddenly wished she could be with every fiber of her heart.

"Coo, would you look at her. Nobility for sure," Molly commented.

The woman walked toward them, her eyes scanning left and right.

And Anna knew.

She knew by the way the woman's shoulders tipped back, even as her hands were stuffed into a white muff that Anna couldn't help but envy. Knew by the way she scanned her surroundings and, when the lady saw her barrow, in the way her green eyes narrowed.

Anna knew she had come looking for her.

"Anna Brooks?" the lady asked, coming to a stop at the end of her barrow, the off-white skirts of her dress rocking back and forth like a bull with its head down.

Anna's own eyes narrowed. "I am she," she answered.

The lady's eyes darted over her worn hat, over the gray dress, the dirt-stained apron. "Lord above, I expected you to be a bugaroach, but you're more of a prime article than even I expected. Curse my bloody husband. I owe him ten pounds."

Ten pounds?

And she spoke cant.

"Who the devil are you?"

With a lift of her chin the lady said, "I am Mary Drummond the marchioness of Warrick. Cousin by marriage to the duke of Wroxly."

Hell's bells.

The lady moved around the edge of the cart, linking her arm through Anna's, a fur muff dangling on a string by her side. Anna didn't move. Truth be told, she couldn't have if she wanted to. The lady's smell took hold of her nose in such a way that Anna wanted to close her eyes and inhale. She smelled perfectly—for a moment Anna marveled at how she smelled like the nosegays the flower girls sold, the ones made of roses and orange blossoms. And then she caught a glimpse of the lady's elegant hands.

They were scarred.

Anna could see the way the skin puckered near the palm. She met the marchioness's eyes.

"I rode horses at the Royal Circus afore being leg-shackled to his lordship."

"You *what*?"

"So you *can* speak. Excellent. Thought you might be crackbrained."

"You rode horses?"

"Indeed," she said, straightening. "Best performer they had. Course, I had to give it up when I wed my husband four years past."

Anna could only stare.

"You'll have to give things up, too, should you stop being so cow-hearted."

*Cow-hearted?* Why, of all the rude . . .

*You* are *being cow-hearted, Anna.*

The redhead nodded as if realizing her words had hit their mark. "Now. We haven't much time. There's a ball Saturday evening and I want you to be in attendance."

"Me?"

The marchioness began to pull her away from her barrow. "Aye."

Anna resisted.

"Unless there's some truth to the fear that's been plaguing Rein." And here her ladyship's eyes narrowed. "That you find him inferior to yourself."

"Inferior?"

"Not a match intellectually," said Lady Warrick, her eyes darting over Anna's face as if looking for answers. "Too much of a slow-top. Dull. A dunce," she added.

"Gads, whatever gave him that idea?"

"Too many years of being told that very thing by those around him. But I can see you don't believe that for a moment."

"Of course not—"

"Excellent," she said, tugging Anna forward again. "You need to be fitted for a gown. And then you'll need some lessons. Rein tells me your mother was gently reared, thank the lord above. You'll have a far easier time of it than me."

Anna stopped once again. "Wait," she said. "You're taking me away?"

"I am," the lady answered. Anna suddenly realized every orange, strawberry and cherry monger had stopped what they were doing to watch, including Molly, who looked from Anna to the marchioness with amusement in her eyes.

"Unless," Lady Warrick said. "You're too afraid to come with me?"

Anna drew back, her ladyship's forthright question rocking her on her heels.

"It won't be easy, I shan't lie," Lady Warrick continued, slipping back into her cultured tones. And for a second, just a brief moment, a cloud passed over her green eyes. But then she blinked, a soft smile coming to her face. "But should you choose to come with me, I promise you shall not regret it. You take the good with the bad, my dear. Granted, 'tis not an easy thing to do—learning to conform to someone else's rules—but there are ways around those rules, starting with a house in the country, somewhere far away from society's probing eyes."

And for the first time, Anna felt hope.

"But it'll involve hard work. We have five days to get you tidied up in time for the ball, a ball I plan to introduce you at as my husband's cousin—something he's fond of doing with outsiders," she said with a secret smile.

Lord above, Anna thought, she couldn't do it.

The marchioness's eyes narrowed. "You're looking afeared again, my dear, and it won't fadge. I have stood where you stand and I can tell you quite honestly that learning to waltz is the easy part. Getting your feet used to slippers is the bloody hard part."

# Part Five

*"I have only to look into your eyes
to know I am your destiny,"
the prince said to the maiden.*

# Chapter Twenty-seven

Rein stared at his reflection, his hands shaking as he waited for the last of his guests to arrive at the ducal town home tucked into a corner of Mayfair.

Would she come?

Lord, he'd wanted to kiss his cousin-in-law on the lips when she'd hatched her plan, a plan to bring Anna back to his side in five days' time. Those had been the longest five days of his life, for he'd missed her. And now the question was, would Anna come? He slapped the gloves he held into the palm of his other hand, anxious, tense and out of sorts. If she didn't come tonight he would kidnap the wench and get her with child. Then, perhaps, she would finally wed him.

"Rein?"

Mary's voice called him from his musings, and Rein turned toward her with hope bouncing through his heart.

"Is she here?"

But he could tell by the look in Mary's eyes, by the way she looked away for a moment. It wasn't like her not to hold a man's eyes.

"She balked at the last moment."

"Damn her," he cursed, striding toward the door.

Mary caught his arm as he passed by.

"Give her time, Rein. Perhaps with more of that she'll lose her fear of becoming a duchess."

Rein pulled his arm away, but only to turn back to his room. Both Mary and Anna's friend Molly thought Anna lacked the courage to become his duchess. At first he'd scoffed at such a notion—she was the bravest woman of his acquaintance—but after speaking with her friend Molly, he'd told himself to have faith. But that faith had begun to slowly desert him.

"Perhaps I should give it up," he said, the hopelessness he felt making him want to punch or throw something.

"I . . . don't know," Mary answered honestly. "I thought she would go along with our scheme, thought I had her right up until the moment she began to dress for the ball tonight." Mary frowned, shaking her head, Rein realizing that his cousin-in-law felt as disappointed as he felt.

"Thank you, Mary. Thank you for trying."

"Rein," she said, her hand going to his arm again. "Please. Do not give up hope."

He turned away. Hope was all he had, until that moment. Hope was what had kept him going. Hope was what had made him say no to Anna becoming his mistress, unable and unwilling to see her reduce herself to such a life. Hope was all he'd had until tonight.

But as he turned and faced the window, he wondered if his hope was gone.

Eventually, he went belowstairs, but as he did so all he could think of was Anna.

He'd had his main hall filled with roses. Damask roses, in honor of their first meeting. He'd done that for her.

He'd had his staff keep the lighting low in the event she had to remove her gloves for some unforeseen reason, to better shield that which she most despised from probing eyes: her hands. He'd done that for her.

And in the pocket of his black evening coat was a ring, one he'd forgotten to remove, but one he'd intended to give her as a promise ring until the time came to give her an engagement ring.

He would have done that for her, too.

Instead he stood at the head of his receiving line with Mary by his side, acting as hostess. Mary wouldn't look him in the eyes, and in some ways that was worse than if she'd given him a brave smile.

"Go in and dance," she said as the music started, greeting the last few stragglers with a smile. She'd pulled her hair up in to a design made of braids that looped around her coronet. "You have a room full of young ladies who would give their dowries—literally—to become your affianced wife."

Rein didn't smile, didn't laugh at her sally, didn't feel capable of doing anything more than going to his study and drinking himself into oblivion.

She didn't want him.

"Go," Mary said.

Rein went, though he and Mary both knew his heart wasn't in it, and likely never would be.

So he made an effort to smile at the ladies he was introduced to, asked a few of them to dance, none of them for a second dance. Through it all he thought of her, thought of what it would be like to hold her, to be with her right then, close his eyes and simply inhale her scent. That was what he missed the most. Holding her. And talking to her. He missed their rooftop conversations.

The dance he'd been engaged in ended, and Rein decided he couldn't take another moment. He looked around the room for Mary or Alex to tell them he was leaving.

The crowd fell silent.

It was one of those odd pauses that sometimes falls over a crowd, that momentary suspension of noise that seems even more noticeable in the wake of such a cacophony. Perhaps it was Rein's imagination, for as he looked toward the entrance to the ballroom, mirrors giving him a glimpse of all four sides, he thought he must be dreaming.

Anna had come.

His breath left him, his heart swelling with so much emotion that he couldn't breathe. Relief. Gratitude. Love. His guests stared at her, too, and Rein heard someone nearby say, "Who the devil is that?"

Anna. It was Anna Brooks, the woman he loved.

Anna had never felt so much fear in her life. Not even when she'd been in that bloody ship she'd invented as a child, water covering her head. Not even when she'd been driven away from Porthollow, her parents gone, on her way to live a new life. Not even during the past five days as she'd been drilled and primped and educated in the ways of the nobility. Never. Not ever.

"Anna," a feminine voice said.

Anna turned. Mary Drummond stood there. She'd become simply Mary, rather than Lady Warrick, to Anna sometime between teaching Anna how to curtsy to a viscount, an earl, a marquis or a duke, and helping her to garb her legs in petticoats.

"You came," Mary said.

"I came," Anna said back, careful to keep her voice low, the syllables flat.

"Thank God," Mary said, sudden tears in her eyes.

Anna swallowed, her gloved hands clenching the silk of her gold gown until she remembered she shouldn't do that.

Where was he?

Did he see her? Had her latest bout with fear made him too angry to forgive her? She wouldn't blame him. As she'd fled the marchioness's fancy home where she'd spent the last five days learning how to become a lady, she'd left nothing more than a note:

*Mary,*
*I can't do it.*
*A*

And she'd meant the words, too, meant them until the moment she'd hailed a hack, her eyes filled with tears as she rode home. The only time she stopped staring ahead of her was during a magical moment when she'd tipped back her head and looked up at the sky.

The words came back to her again.

*What are those, Mama?*

*Those are stars, my love.*

*What are stars?*

*The souls of angels staring down upon us.*

*Angels?* she had asked.

*The souls of loved ones who've died, my dear. They look down upon you, watch you from afar, give you hope when things seem to have failed you, give you courage when you need it most.*

She'd forgotten the words until that moment, had banished them from her mind like she had so many happy memories of her life before . . . before St. Giles.

*Give you courage when you need it most.*

She needed courage. And so, sitting in that hack, she'd closed her eyes, tipping her head back as she asked, "Give me courage, Mama. Please."

And then a voice answered back, *I always have.*

And so now she stood in a ballroom, her knees shaking so badly she thought she might fall, hoping, praying, she hadn't muddled things too badly.

"Mary?" a masculine voice asked. "Will you do me the honor . . . the very *great* honor of an introduction?"

Anna's eyes almost closed. Rein. His voice came from her right. But she couldn't turn to look at him, was afraid if she did the whole room would see the tears that she was helpless to conceal.

"Certainly, Your Grace. Miss Anna Brooks, His Grace, the duke of Wroxly. Wroxly, this is the friend of the family I spoke of last eve."

And still Anna couldn't look at him.

"Anna Brooks," came Rein's beloved baritone. "It is my very great pleasure—" His words halted abruptly as if he couldn't go on. "My very great *honor* to make your acquaintance."

At last she looked at him.

He smiled down at her, looking so handsome and regal Anna couldn't breathe.

*Rein,* her heart cried out.

*Anna,* his eyes softly answered back.

He held out his hand.

She took it.

The marchioness made a gesture which Anna saw out of the corner of her eyes. As if waiting for just such a cue—and likely they had been—the orchestra tucked into a corner of the ballroom struck up a waltz.

A waltz. It would have to be a waltz, the one dance she'd been taught, its steps something she'd learned with ease.

He led her forward. She placed her hand on top of his arm just as she'd been taught, afraid to look at him again, afraid to admit that this wonderful, handsome man would be her husband, if she so desired.

"Miss Brooks," he said, though it wasn't just her name, it was a sigh, a caress, a whispered murmuring that conveyed perfectly the love in his heart.

Other couples took to the floor, too, but Anna hardly noticed as he pulled her nearer. She looked into Rein's eyes, and she very greatly feared . . . no, she was quite certain every person in that room could see the love in her eyes as she tipped her head back, held on to his hand, squeezed it for courage.

"You came," he said, looking down at her.

"I came," she answered back, her eyes darting over his face. There was the scar she'd noticed on their first meeting. There were the faint vestiges of the smile wrinkles she loved. There were his green, green eyes.

"Mary told me you'd run away." She darted a glance

at the marchioness, who stood talking to a tall, handsome man Anna knew to be her husband. She'd met the cull— no, *his lordship*—when she'd arrived one morning for her lessons.

"I did," she said as he turned her in a circle so that her view was blocked.

"But you came."

"I came," she echoed back, meeting Rein's gaze again, her heart once again leaping as she took in his black coat, white cravat and fancy gray breeches. He looked so handsome, so debonair. *So out of her reach.*

*Steady on course, Anna.*

He didn't look away as he twirled her around, just stared and stared and stared as if he never wanted to look away, and perhaps he didn't.

"Rein, I—"

"Don't," he interrupted. "Don't say you are sorry."

Did he know her so well? Had he been able to tell so easily what was in her heart?

"You are here. That is all that matters. And that you marry me as soon as can be arranged."

She almost stumbled, and though she'd told herself she would not let her tears spill over, she felt her eyes do exactly that.

Deep breaths. Deep breaths.

"Will you?" he asked as he swept her around, and God help her, she could see tears in his own eyes. And there was no need to ask what it was she would do, for she could read the question in his eyes.

*Will you be my duchess?*

"Aye, I will," she said, slipping back into her St. Giles accent, but little caring that she did, for suddenly it all fell into place. She didn't care what anyone thought of her then, didn't care if she never set foot in a ballroom again. She loved this man more than life itself—and that, *that* was what was important, not what others might think. What a fool she'd been to think otherwise.

And so later that night, Anna slipped out of the ballroom with Rein. No one noticed, Mary having done a bang-up job (as the marchioness would later tell her) of convincing society that Anna had been raised as a lady. And as they held each other's hands and then embraced, no one was the wiser. Only the stars saw what happened next, watched as the duke of Wroxly placed a promise ring upon her finger, and as that ring fell into place, one of the stars flicked and then flared as the couple kissed.

And if Rein and Anna had been looking, they might have seen that star begin to move, might have seen it sail across the sky and then flare into brightness. But they didn't notice, for they were too busy creating their own brightness in the world.

# Part Six

*"You're a bit of a fool, ain't you?"*
*the maiden asked the prince.*
*"Only a fool for love," he answered,*
*taking her hand and leading her away.*
*"One who believes in happily ever afters."*

# Epilogue

Three years later the duke of Wroxly paced the length of his study like a stallion in a stall, at least that's what Anna thought, having recently seen one of her cousin-in-law's horses do that very thing.

"Rein, settle down."

"I cannot help myself," he said, turning on the yellow and off-white carpet to head back in the other direction.

"He will be done when he is done," she said.

"Yes, but what is taking so long?"

"These things take time."

"Too much time," she thought she heard him mumble.

Anna bit back a smile. Since the moment she'd suggested summoning their visitor, Rein had been like this—floating between fear and fits as he waited for the man to arrive, and then to do his interview.

A knock sounded at the door.

"Come," Rein answered.

Anna turned from her position on a settee to see James, their butler, bow in their direction. After all these years she still found it odd that she had a butler. Lord above, when Molly Stills and her husband came for visits, they laughed themselves silly over it all.

"Mr. Dench," James announced.

Anna reclined back in the chair, certain what the renowned Mr. Dench would say. She'd always been certain. It was why she'd summoned him—for Rein's sake she'd wanted the man to confirm what she already knew.

"Well?" Rein asked the bald-headed man.

There came to the man's face a wide smile. "I've no idea what made you think your child might lack intelligence, Your Grace. He is easily months ahead of those his age."

Anna looked at Rein just in time to see his shoulders relax, to see him turn away. Only those who knew him well would know what it was he tried to conceal—relief, and, when he looked at her, gratitude.

"I have always said Connor was bright," she said with a small smile.

"Very bright, Your Grace," the man said. "Were I you, I would start him early at his studies." The man launched into lesson plans, work schedules and the like. Rein kept his back turned the whole time. Anna knew it wasn't disinterest that made him do so. He didn't want the professor to see the tears in his eyes as one of his worst fears—that his child would be slow to learn and thus persecuted as Rein had been as a child—began to fade away at last. Only when Mr. Dench left did he turn toward her, Anna's lips tilting into a wide smile as she spied the relief in his eyes.

"Do you feel better now?" she asked, walking toward him.

He didn't move.

"Rein?"

He turned. There were, indeed, tears in his eyes.

"Oh, Rein."

He opened his arms. She went into them, resting her head against his chest. Those arms had sheltered her through so many storms: her first, frightening year of living among the *ton,* her grandfather's illness, though that was easier to bear now that she had help.

"You know I'd love Connor no matter what his intelligence," Rein said.

And he did love Connor. Rein was so wonderful with his son that Anna blessed her good fortune in finding such a man every day of her life.

"But this has made me realize how blessed we are," he continued. "Truly blessed."

"Aye," she said, using the word from her past with ease. She did that at the drop of a hat, and Rein marveled at her ability to keep her two halves straight. Society had never learned the secret of her past, and they had taken great pains to ensure that Anna's life as a market maid was well concealed. No one would ever know the truth.

He squeezed her one last time, then pulled back, staring into her beautiful eyes. He'd been called by more than one of his fellow noblemen a lucky bastard for winning Anna's heart, no one the wiser that they'd been secretly engaged since the very first night she'd burst upon the London *ton* like a rare and dazzling gem, untouchable by all but one.

He was that one. He would always be her one.

"I love you," she said.

"As do I," he answered back, tipping his head down to kiss her lightly on the lips, and as he did, he marveled at how the way each time felt the same as the first time. Perfect. Amazing. Special.

She pulled back, resting her head against his heart. "We must depart soon," she said on a disappointed sigh.

"What? Does not the thought of seeing a ship launched that is based upon a design *you* drew, hoisting sails you invented, fill you with anticipation?"

She tipped her head back, the expression on her face one of absolute seriousness. "Not as much anticipation as the thought of taking my pleasure with you."

He lifted his brows, murmuring, "Indeed?"

"Right here, in this drawing room." And now her lips lifted in a sultry smile. "Unless, of course, you worry about scandalizing our staff."

"My dear duchess, have you not learned I live for a good scandal?"

"Ach, now, gov," she teased in her St. Giles accent. "I'm thinkin' I might know a thing or two that may still scandalize the likes o' you."

"Indeed?" he asked again.

Anna nodded, loving the way his eyes began to slant down in that heavy-lidded look she knew meant her words aroused him. "I believe I should like to see you try," he said softly.

And so she did, and Anna was to think a long while later that she had likely succeeded. And then later that day, as she watched the launching of a ship that she had designed, she was to think life could not get much better. And then later that year, as she held their second child in her arms, she was to think that, incredibly, life *could* get better.

*There was nothing to fear, was there, my darling daughter?*

Anna tipped her head back and looked into a starry sky, her newborn daughter held in her own arms, a daughter she'd named in honor of her mother.

*No, Mama, there wasn't.*

# Author's Note

Three-sided sails first came into use in 1824. Unfortunately, they never caught on with the Navy. They did, however, find favor with merchant service. And while I never did discover who first came up with the idea, I'd like to think it might well have been a woman.

For those of you interested in ships and their rigging, *Seamanship in the Age of Sail* by John Harland has been invaluable to me while writing two of my books, *My Fallen Angel* and now *Scandal*. And while the idea of a naval competition was strictly my own, its roots are based in having watched and enjoyed *Longitude* on PBS.

# About the Author

**Pamela Britton** was born to tell stories as evidenced by her ability to convince her three-year-old daughter that she is the singing voice of Ariel from *The Little Mermaid,* and that King Triton is her very best friend.

When she's not tormenting her family with her voice, Pamela creates caffeine-induced stories that have won her numerous accolades over the years, including a nomination from *Romance Writers of America* for their Golden Heart and the title of Best Paranormal romance of 2000 from *Affaire de Coeur* magazine. Recently, Pamela's first book for Warner, *Seduced,* was voted as one of the top ten best romances of 2003 by the staff of BarnesandNoble.com and The Oakland Press. *Seduced* also won a Reviewer's Choice award from *Romantic Times Bookclub Magazine.*

Pamela feels privileged to write full-time from her ranch in Northern California. She enjoys riding, hiking and singing along to Disney tunes (very big grin). Alas, one day her daughter will reason out that she is *not* the voice of Ariel. Until then she plans on milking it for all it's worth.

You may contact Pamela c/o P.O. Box 1281, Anderson, CA 96007, or on her web site at *www.pamelabritton.com*